# Sucker

ALSO BY DANIEL HORNSBY

*Via Negativa*

# SUCKER

Daniel Hornsby

ANCHOR BOOKS
A Division of Penguin Random House LLC
New York

AN ANCHOR BOOKS ORIGINAL 2023

Library of Congress Cataloging-in-Publication Data
Names: Hornsby, Daniel, author.
Title: Sucker / by Daniel Hornsby.
Description: New York : Anchor Books, 2023.
Identifiers: LCCN 2022017735 (print) | LCCN 2022017736 (ebook) |
ISBN 9780593469675 (hardcover) | ISBN 9780593469705 (ebook)
Subjects: LCGFT: Novels.
Classification: LCC PS3608.O7673 S83 2023 (print) | LCC PS3608.O7673 (ebook) |
DDC 813/.6—dc23/eng/20220414
LC record available at https://lccn.loc.gov/2022017735
LC ebook record available at https://lccn.loc.gov/2022017736

**Anchor Books Hardcover ISBN: 978-0-593-46967-5**
**eBook ISBN: 978-0-593-46970-5**

*Book design by Steve Walker*

anchorbooks.com

Printed in the United States of America
10  9  8  7  6  5  4  3  2  1

*For John and Kristin*
*and for Alice*

# Sucker

# 1

I'm an American, so I always assumed I'd be famous. When it was clear I was no Thurston Moore or David Byrne, I figured I could at least be a crusty hybrid between Malcolm McLaren and David Geffen. And so, in an unlikely move for this black sheep in a family of twenty-four-karat fleeces, I became an entrepreneur and started my own small record label.

I ran Obnoxious Records with my girlfriend, whose album had come out as our third official release. Louise, and the rest of Obnoxious, had no clue about my devious parentage. When I moved to San Narciso, I lopped the *heart* off my infamous surname, synonymous as it is with money and evil, and went from Charles Grossheart to Chuck Gross. With the help of this punk pseudonym, I was able to keep things pretty separate, and figured my notorious bloodline would easily remain discrete from my true passion, my real life.

But it turned out I lacked my dad's capitalist knack and had to subsidize the label with the money his money made. I'll admit, I lied to Louise a little about our finances. She was under the impression that we had the support of an eccentric tech millionaire (not a sinister libertarian billionaire / chairman and CEO of a vast multinational private corporation), but that we also more or less lived in the black. In fact, we'd lived out our entire run plunged deeply into the red, kept afloat only by paternal subsidy.

Obnoxious was my baby, but it was a bastard my parents wouldn't recognize. For me to keep receiving his funds, my father annoyingly required some conventional employment, and my noisy vanity project didn't count. For about three years I managed to fake him out, but eventually he called my bluff. With a single phone call from his wealth manager, Renata, I was cut off.

You have to understand, I had the Buddha's boyhood, spared any hint of suffering (save for the psychic cuts and scrapes inflicted by a self-obsessed father and a Teutonic nanny, along with the mild realization of my scarcity of talent), so I had no immune system with which to fight the little particles of woe that would inevitably find their way inside me. I hung up with Renata, packed a bowl, and prepared myself for a dark fortnight of the soul. I bought one of those seasonal affective disorder lamps, and it was May.

I was determined to keep Obnoxious alive, but I was in desperate need of cash. I owed several audio engineers and one producer a lot of money, and a band was due an installment of their advance. Thanks to a handful of well-received releases, we were just about to rise from boutique status, slowly gaining a national reputation among people who care about these kinds of things. But now that Renata had sniffed out my employment status, all my plans would implode: I'd be penniless until I could find a job that met Dad's criteria. Cutting me off was a codependent ploy. For a year or so I'd been laying the groundwork to someday really and truly break away from my famously evil family, and I think he or Renata might've caught wind of my vague plan. This way he could snip the cords of the puny safety net I was fashioning for myself before it was strong enough to catch me.

Three days after Renata's devastating call, I was baking my face with antidepressant rays and stress-buying old 45s on eBay when Olivia called me out of the blue and asked if I'd be free to meet for lunch. It was the first I'd heard from her in years. We'd been close in college, and the two of us had planned to move from Boston to San Narciso together after graduation—she to get her PhD in biosomething, me to start my label in the city's flourishing punk and garage scene. She wound up moving here sooner than expected, taking a cue from Bill Gates's playbook and dropping out to birth her company, and it was understood that I'd follow her once I finished school. Instead, I backed out at the last minute and moved to Brooklyn. I came to San Narciso three years later, once the boom was really going and all my bridges in that borough were crispy, but I was too ashamed to reach out and spent four years avoiding her as my embarrassment racked up compound interest.

Why had I flaked? At the time, my excuse both to Olivia and myself was my then girlfriend, a bassist in a second-rate Flatbush dream pop band. But deep down I knew that relationship wasn't going anywhere. I think it was Olivia's purpose, her righteous mission, that ultimately kept me from making the move. Sure, I had my own aspirations, but these were daydreams next to Olivia's saintly visions. I'll set my automatic cynicism aside for a moment and say that I considered her a friend, one of the closest I've had. While I was accustomed to depressing my parents, I couldn't stand the idea of disappointing Olivia. When I moved West, I told myself I'd get back in touch at some point, but couldn't bring myself to compose an email or dial her number. Rather than let it grow into something knotted and tangled, I preferred to clip our friendship into a tidy, stunted bonsai.

Minutes after we booked it, I thought about weaseling out of our reunion. I didn't think I'd be able to sit through a report of her successes while my life dissolved. But even I could see the opportunity here: she had a company, and I needed a job.

So a few days later I found myself in the back of an Uber, riding off to one of the popular basement bar/restaurants that had popped up in recent months.

I had some sense of Olivia's achievements and growing fame, but no clue about the particulars. She'd founded a start-up, it was successful. That, and her place at the top of a *Wired* list of up-and-coming women in tech, were all I'd allowed to trickle into my consciousness. Every now and then one of those determined alumni emails would find its way into my inbox, and I'd glimpse Olivia's noble, fuzzy dome, but I couldn't bring myself to read it before deleting. A couple months back I caught her face staring at me from the cover of one of the big tech rags at the newsstand near Obnoxious. I smothered her with a copy of a *National Geographic* featuring a satellite photo of the Pacific's Texas-size mass of plastic waste on its cover—an image more comforting than the sight of a friend whose accomplishments had so greatly outstripped mine. Despite my scant knowledge, I did occasionally brag about her to my dad and my brother, wielding the same two or three facts to give them the sense our friendship lived in the present tense.

Now that we were reuniting, I needed to give the impression that I'd kept tabs on her triumphs, and even with my fluent bullshit, I knew I'd have to do some homework. I put this off until I was on the way to lunch. While my Uber driver delivered a long, unfunny monologue about his struggle to break into the San Narciso comedy scene, I shoved all the Oliviana I could find into my brain, skimming the major articles and profiles, scrubbing my way through a TED Talk and videos of women-in-tech panels. They all hit the same two or three biographical notes in Olivia Watts's epic life: her struggle with cancer as a teen, her venerable dropout status, and her relationship with mentor / early investor / popular capitalist pig Ralph Langenburger. There were a lot of near-identical photos of her holding something resembling a black hummingbird egg up to her eye. From what I gathered, her company, Kenosis, had something to do with a kind of implant that could tell you when you were sick. One profile expanded on the usual, obvious cliché used to describe my old friend, calling her "Steve Jobs, but with a heart," and more than a few sites had her listed among America's most promising young technocrats. By the time I arrived, I wasn't sure I knew much more about what her company actually did, but walking down the stairs to the bar, I knew I'd be able to at least cite the publications that had featured her and sidestep any obvious traps she might set for me, should she want to litigate my shittiness as a friend.

The bar was a perfect re-creation of some bachelor uncle's basement in the 1970s, milking the latest SN trends in decor. As the last ten years went by, the eighties and nineties had relented somewhat in their chokehold on nostalgia, making room for the corduroy, leather, punk seventies. I crossed the shag carpet to the red-vinyl booth where Olivia sat waiting.

"Charles! Holy shit!" She got up and gave me a bony hug. She looked a lot like she had in college, or more like an actor playing her younger self, with a budget for makeup and wardrobe. She wore what I came to learn was her signature as Kenosis CEO: an old, oversize denim jacket, Doc Martens, and a concert tee (Was it the Slits? Did I get her that one?), all giving her the look of a Berlin DJ on vacation in Tennessee. And of course there was her famous head, shorn in solidarity with her fellow cancer survivors. Both in college and, as my hasty research revealed, now, Olivia always cantilevered her geeky ambition with occasional outdated references both visual and verbal to hip-hop and punk. This scuzzy layer to her aesthetic had been dialed up some since we parted, and I would have attributed this to my influence, had we not lost touch for so long.

We exchanged the usual pleasantries. I lightly bragged on my label, which she already seemed to know a lot about, and she told me about her work. I did a decent job, I think, conveying the sense that I'd kept up on Olivia trivia and stored a box of Kenosis press clippings under my bed.

"I feel like an asshole, but I'm still full from breakfast," she said when the waitress came by. "I did this panel thing and pigged out on their spread. Please, eat something, but I think I'm going to make it a liquid lunch, if that's okay?"

As we caught up, I wolfed down a Cuban sandwich and made my way through the major drink taxa: a gin cocktail, piss beer, white wine, whiskey, lapping Olivia once or twice. All the meaningful eye contact made me thirsty, and I needed to wash down my pride if I was going to ask her for a job. She kept ordering bourbons on the rocks she hardly sipped from, asking for another when the melted ice turned the glass pale. She'd never been much of a drinker, and my guess is she picked up this move to show she could hold her own in a land of bros.

"It must be hard, being born into a family like yours," she said when our conversation began to lose steam. "No one really knows what that's like, on that level, except for the kids of presidents or kings. You should be very proud of yourself, for making something all on your own."

"Thanks, Olivia. That means a lot." Despite the emotional armor I'd spent years forging in cynical fire, I was touched by this nod.

"Look, I really did want to chop it up with you, but there's something else I want to discuss." I braced myself for admonishment, but it never came. "Things at the company are going really, really well. We're about to make a big announcement that will mark an inflection point in our life cycle—I'll tell you more about that later. Money is pouring in, and R and D is solving problems that don't even exist yet. I'm not saying we don't have the best team, we absolutely do, but as I face some new challenges, I've been rethinking my staffing strategy. We've had a couple people, a creative consultant and our adviser on ethics, who just couldn't cut it. They were too soft for this industry, I hate to say, and had to go. But the two of them made some good points on the way out. To be perfectly honest, I don't want it to start some exodus or have it look like rats fleeing the ship. More than any of this, I want to get back to the ethos I had when I dreamed this whole thing up." She put her hand on mine. Having been touched infrequently as a child, I'm a sucker for that kind of thing. "I was never more creative than during the halcyon days of our friendship. You were the perfect sounding board, pretty much biologically incapable of sugarcoating. I'm sure that's still true. And with all the cool fucking shit you're doing at Obnoxious, you've proven my hunch about you."

She was blowing enough smoke up my ass to give me rectal cancer—not to make light of what she'd been through. You know what I'm getting at.

"I want to offer you a job, as creative consultant. I need someone to keep me level. Don't worry, the workload won't be too daunting. You'll still be able to run your label, I promise. I mostly just want you there to help me replicate the vibe we had when I got the idea years ago. It would technically be creative consultant and special adviser on ethics." She tore off pieces of her napkin and set them in a pile by the ketchup. Were these swings between geeky tics and self-possession intentional? Part of the pressure of running a company? Was she nervous to see me? "I know I'm asking a lot. I already owe you so much. I wouldn't be here without you. I still believe that."

She was referring to some advice I'd given her in college. More on that later.

"You give me too much credit there. You were going to do what you were going to do. No one was ever able to change your mind." I was overjoyed I didn't have to humble myself before her.

"See, there, this pushback. That's exactly what I'm talking about. I need that. I know you won't be just another yes-man."

I wouldn't. I never said yes, if I could help it. Unless it was to free mind-altering substances, or sex, though even in those areas I could still be picky. And of course I wouldn't say no to her now.

"I feel like I'm a little out of my depth here, but if you think I can do it, I'll do it. Count me in."

A pterodactyloid belch came from an old man seated at the booth

behind Olivia. I peeked over and saw our gassy neighbor was playing chess with himself. Two of the bishops had been replaced with
a pepper shaker and a key chain Statue of Liberty. He studied the
chessboard while hand-rolling cigarettes, and about a dozen of these
sat in a tidy row next to the dead pieces. The back of his head looked
like the cover of *Unknown Pleasures*.

Olivia didn't seem to hear the screechy burp and ignored my
snooping. "There's one other thing. We're about to announce a pilot
partnership with—I shouldn't even tell you this but I will—Rome and
Wieger. The pharmaceutical company."

I was familiar. I'd popped many of their fine products and walked
away a happy, viscoelastic customer.

"I'm going to use that to make a big fundraising push. This is
gauche as hell, but I feel I can be frank with you. If your family were
to invest, I think it might signal something and help us paint the most
robust picture possible. And we can offer them a discounted valuation,
which I think will make it more than worth their while." She went on
like this for a few more minutes—now that she'd moved on from the
subject of me, my interest slipped away—but that was the gist of it.

I looked around the bar. With its velvet Elvis and stack of vintage
TV consoles along the back wall, the place looked like the set of a
popular new prestige drama set here in San Narciso, the latest critique
of greed, excess, and toxic masculinity everyone had been imitating.
*Bad Company* (guess the theme song) followed the moral decline of a
San Narciso–based arms dealer and con artist. It was easy to imagine
the main character in this place, snorting a line off the barrel of an
AMT Hardballer, his signature gun and cocaine accessory.

"Do you think they would be amenable?"

"I'm sure we could make something happen."

I may not have been paying much attention, but I'm not so naive
that I couldn't figure it out. My parents were going to buy me a job.
Or, to be more precise, I would be given a job to sweeten the deal of

my parents' initial investment. The more I thought about it, the more it made sense. Olivia was skillful—she probably didn't even see this as transactional—but I'd been solicited since Mom and Dad first allowed me unescorted excursions out into the real world, which is to say, since I was nineteen. Still, I had the feeling Olivia actually did want me around, and even if the position was complete bullshit, it was just what I needed to get out of my latest snafu.

We hugged goodbye and chatted about next steps. On my way out, I glimpsed a vintage poster from a Paranoids concert hanging in the back. A collapsing ziggurat of boxes stood next to it, and after admiring the artifact of my favorite band, I started rooting through them. It looked like I'd discovered the contents of a pirate's storage unit. A mismatched flock of dusty parrots, framed photos of what appeared to be at least two different pirate-themed weddings, and a tube of eye patches stacked like Pringles. Shit like this overflowed from the bins of San Narciso's flea markets and thrift stores. The (many times disproven) legend was that the city was founded by California's only pirate, Hippolyte Bouchard, a pyromaniac Frenchman with helipad-size epaulets. A popular movie about him in the fifties had started a tiki-like sensation of pirate bars and restaurants that had been local icons until recent years. In all likelihood, this crap was a haul from one of these kitschy joints' liquidation sales. Just for the kleptomaniac buzz, I put one of the eye patches in my pocket.

Walking back to the stairs, I saw Olivia was still seated at the booth. The old guy who'd been playing solo chess had now installed himself across from her, probably lobbing creepy flirtations. She was a modern woman, and I figured she didn't need my flaccid chivalry.

As I climbed the stairs and stepped into the sunlight, I felt as if I was towing my soul, dragging it out of the gloomy den where it'd been hiding since I was cut off. I got ahold of my dad (well, Dad's assistant, Charlotte, who put me in contact with Renata, his thorough harridan), and to my surprise, a week later, I was told everything had been

arranged. Apparently some of Olivia's investors occasionally social-
ized with my folks, which made the proposition much more appealing
and legitimized my new position in my father's beady eyes.

And so, the check dropped like gentle rain from heaven twice-
blessed, blessing him that gives (Grandpa, by way of Dad) and her
that takes (Olivia), but mostly me, as I now had a position as creative
consultant / special adviser on ethics at an up-and-coming biotech
company, and my monthly cash could resume its flow from its hereditary font. By the time of the party—Olivia's announcement of the
pharmaceutical partnership—I'd managed to settle most of Obnoxious's debts. When my money came through, I was able to pay everyone off except the band, who would, I figured, be much more lenient
and, more important, less litigious. They could wait another couple
weeks.

I was finally in the clear. My baby was safe, and I knew I'd easily
be able to compartmentalize my budding tech career, to dump it in
the same junk drawer of my life where I stored my terrible family and
most of my past.

## 2

I'd start at Kenosis a few days after Olivia made her big announcement. For this, she'd booked an old, deconsecrated cloister in Lake Jazmín, a vaguely Benedictine setup with pinched arches and skinny windows. As I stood in the transept, admiring a mural of some demon dominatrix of a saint, someone tapped me on the shoulder.

It was the singer from the band I hadn't paid, a four-piece called Pro Laps. They were about a decade too late to the party of that particular variety of fuzzed-out, Californian garage rock. Still, Thane, whose face was now only a few smelly inches from mine, had played guitar in a couple well-known bands, some of which now commanded the middle third of the festival posters, and their first record had done well for a self-release. Its follow-up, *Sucker*, was my best bet for something remotely profitable. But it was becoming a hassle. Thane had been burning money trying to get it to sound perfect, spending days tuning snares, weeks overdubbing guitar and vocals, and I heard they were even sampling the wind. All this just to scrap these versions in favor of a Steve Albini, live-in-studio approach, fucking with the album rollout. He and the drummer—Sydney, his girlfriend—had been fighting, and he'd even thrown a tantrum at Louise, a woman as universally adored as I was despised. This obsessiveness and instability, extreme even for a musician, had led a lot of us to believe he'd relapsed—a problem I'd decided to solve later, once we could put the album out.

My guess was that he needed money for whatever he was on this time, though his natural obsessiveness alone could have explained his stalking me. If I'd really wanted to, I could've paid him weeks ago, but he'd been such an asshole I thought I'd fuck with him a little and make him sweat, to recoup my own agitated perspiration.

Withholding cash as a power play, I was acting more like my dad than I'd like to admit. I'd done a good job getting as far from my father as I could, but wholly escaping him was impossible. I was like a person who'd lost a lot of weight. You couldn't see it, but I carried it with me anyhow, always trying to jog my way out from under it, counting every calorie of his influence. Really, Dad was more present when he wasn't there.

Thane smelled like a lot of the artists I signed, something like rotting bananas with a dash of sour milk. He was one of those Cobain / young-DiCaprio types, with long, stringy blond hair and the face of a pretty girl. Much to my frustration, the wear and tear of years of heavy partying had only made him hotter. He wore a black Hawaiian shirt covered in flip-flops, which, I have to admit, looked pretty cool.

"How'd you find me here?" I asked him.

"Patty said she saw you drinking on the patio at the Scope as she was leaving work." Patty, my fremesis, played bass in one of our lesser, Louise-picked bands. She *would* be the one to narc on me. I'd long suspected her of planning a coup that would make Obnoxious a girls-only operation. "You were leaving, so I followed you here. I walked in right behind you. It wasn't hard."

This was unfortunate. I didn't want Thane mixing these parts of my life, especially so soon.

"I need that money. We have to pay rent. We're going to get evicted. This is seriously uncool."

Everyone I worked with at the label had a tendency to look a gift horse in the sphincter. "I'll get it to you tomorrow morning, I promise."

"We needed it months ago. Man, I'm this close to just calling it quits and just driving up to Falda Linda and, I don't know, start making, like, pottery. Mugs and shit. We *need* that money. You have the mixes."

"Cash has been tight. I haven't paid myself in two months."

"What are you doing here?" he asked, suddenly aware of his surroundings. It was like talking to a bong. "What is this?"

"It's a fundraiser. For charity."

We walked past a security guard. I sent him a *Help me* look, but he didn't get it.

"Look, I have to talk to some people. Get yourself a drink and go home. I'll have the check for you in the morning, I swear."

He nodded and made his way to the bar. Fortunately for me, there was another bar across the cloister. As I waited for my drink (a cocktail called a Marconi; I'd soon learn that everything Olivia did now was genius themed), I looked around to see if I could spot Olivia. People were packing in pretty tight. It was like a Davos fire drill. Sartorially, this was a mixed crowd. You had your aggressively underdressed, like me in my cutoff shorts and black tee, power-moving their way through the throng. Then a set of corporate types in well-tailored jackets, mostly somewhere in the Theory neck of the woods. And, of course, the nerdy tech people in their Patagonia vest uniforms or hoodies emblazoned with their company logo, younger ones trying to keep their edge in Supreme. Olivia was not among them. Thane was still at the opposite bar, hopefully finishing his drink and preparing to leave.

The music went quiet, and a light appeared on the altar. Olivia stepped forward.

She wore an extralarge black T-shirt that hung down to her knees. She looked like Joan of Arc if the martyr had traded her saintly steed for a private-capital-fed unicorn.

"I won't keep you long. I just want to thank you all for being here to celebrate our big milestone. My life's work in building Kenosis has been to redefine the paradigm of medicine, away from one in which people have to present with a symptom in order to get access to care, toward a future in which every person, no matter how much money they have, where they live, or who they love, already has access to the most sophisticated treatment the very *moment* something goes wrong." Her voice caught. She stopped her speech and tilted her head up into the light, showing off the wetness of her eyes. The crowd rewarded this burst of authenticity, rooting for her like she was a basketball star getting up from an injury. "The work we are doing is going to save countless lives. But before I make my big announcement, I want to welcome Charles Grossheart to our team. Charles, where are you?"

The light found me right away. It seemed like a grand way to intro-duce someone whose primary title was creative consultant. I think she wanted to say my last name in front of a bunch of people for whom it might inspire awe or terror. I wanted to crawl away like a roach.

"Welcome, Charles."

I raised my empty glass and, out of gratitude and panic, gave her the cheesiest smile my face has produced since I received my first blow job sometime during the Bush administration. I prayed Thane was well on his way home to his dilapidated apartment in Moscadera, in the back of a car obsessively checking his empty bank account.

But my bad luck would never allow that. As the light moved off me, I could see he'd snuck up through the crowd and was now standing right beside me, recording everything on his phone. A big yellow slug decal on the back of it tidily captured what I felt like.

Some Kenosis suck-up stepped in front of Thane and congratu-lated me. By the time I shook him off, Thane had disappeared into the crowd.

"And now for the big news. I am so pleased and proud to announce that Kenosis will be partnering with Rome and Wieger for a ground-breaking pilot project. I'll be able to say more about it soon, but just know, when this drops, it's going to be a game changer. Our proprietary technology combined with their resources as *the* leader in pharmaceutical development and innovation means that we are this much closer to making good on the fundamental truth we've built this company around, the radical idea that every person, no matter where they're born or who they're born to, has a right to a healthy life. There's a lot of work to be done, but tonight let's celebrate."

Biggie's "Juicy" started playing. The lights on the altar went out, and Olivia stepped down to mingle. I immediately set to hunting down Thane.

The Obnoxious family, unlike the Grossheart one, had only a reluctant relationship with late capitalism, and this was no coincidence. Given my upbringing, it should be no surprise that I'd be drawn to a lefty scene, much in the same way preachers' children are drawn to underage drinking and clandestine sexual acts. Most of the artists on my label were socialists, or of the socialist aesthetic anyway, and our roster contained two or three admirable community organizers, several noble ecofeminists, and a vocal graduate student in Marxist philosophy who'd radicalized most of our spare, dim nihilists. (Their film club was perpetually flirting with becoming a direct action group.) While I'd started the label as an outgrowth of my firm cynical belief system, fostering these anti-capitalist minds had a strong appeal as penance for my family's sins. In a way I was Robin Hood, except Prince John was my dad.

My musicians would never understand any of this, and now was the absolute worst time for my Grossheartedness to be found out. Thane might not be sharp enough to put it all together himself, but he might show his photos or video to Louise, his band, or the other acts on the label, and it wouldn't be long until they learned who my dad was, left Obnoxious, and outed me. I could already see the screen captures of their Notes apps and long, somber blog posts detailing my deception, all circulated by Patty. It would sink the label, and then any chance

I'd have of breaking away from my folks would be gone. I'd be back, suckling away at the golden teat, a capitalist piglet again. Or at least more of one.

I needed Thane to delete that shit off his phone. I had the leverage, at least, while I still owed him money.

Before I could find him, Olivia found me.

"Charles! Isn't this fucking wild?" She kissed me on the cheek. Her mouth was surprisingly cool, as if she'd just made out with a snowman. "I just can't believe we've done it. All the dreams we talked about in college—your label, my company—it's all happening." She took in the crowd. "Go crazy tonight. Most of us will be taking tomorrow off to celebrate. Or recover."

A large man walked up to her and whispered something in her ear. She nodded.

"Chuck, this is Clif Geggus. Officially he's executive vice president and chief financial officer. Really he's a human Swiss Army knife. A true polymath."

Clif looked more like a refrigerator than a pocketknife. His shirt was unbuttoned down to the xiphoid, and he wore acid-washed jeans and a pair of red Gucci loafers. I'll spare you the two to four servings of low-hanging fruit. He gave me an overfirm handshake and walked off.

"*Clif,*" Olivia told me in a confidential tone. "With one *F.*"

"Like the bar?"

"He's my bad cop. I'm really using his midlife crisis to my advantage. Plus, he speaks fluent Republican."

It felt good to be in her orbit again, sharing gossip.

Guests and employees came over in heats to congratulate her. It felt like being next to a musician after a set, until Olivia started reciting a list of boring numbers and pointing out some people in the crowd I was supposed to care about. As I scanned the crowd for Thane, I nodded along to her name-dropping with an expression of attention I've spent thirty years perfecting on my parents, namely the Charles who sired me, a man whose wealth is, at least to him, qualification enough for a self-endowed chair as full professor in Everything Studies.

As she went on and on about the creative team I'd be joining, my eyes locked on to one of the most beautiful women I have ever beheld. She looked a lot like Rachel Weisz, but with a mass of curly, Dylan-esque hair. Next to the raggedy mortals in the crowd, she looked like she'd been edited in from heaven in postproduction.

"Who the fuck is that?" I asked Olivia.

"Oh. That's Neve Olmert, from the SNIT CoLaboratory."

She explained that Dr. Olmert was currently dating an Academy Award–winning actor (a redhead known for his rotation of prosthetic noses) as part of his ongoing campaign to convince the world he's smart.

"Do you want to meet her?"

"No. Her hotness is making me feel insectoid. Ask me in a year, once I've hired a personal trainer and given up bread."

"That's a relief. I don't want to talk to her right now anyway. I honestly can't stand her. It's hard out here, dealing with haters. 'Jealous cowards try to control. . . . They distort what we say . . . try and stop what we do.' Black Flag wasn't wrong. It's corny as hell, and I know I'm in a sentimental mood, but you really do have to rise above that shit."

Neve vanished into the crowd. As another wave of sycophants greeted Olivia, Thane bounded over to me.

"Dude, *Rome and Wieger*? Even I know who they are."

He hadn't put together who my family was. I could handle this.

"I mean, I think we both have plenty of experience with their products." He ignored this. "I'm just working at a start-up that will be working with them. I have to do a little moonlighting to keep the label going. So I can pay you, and everyone else."

"So it's either some fucked-up Big Pharma shit or fucked-up tech shit. Does Louise even know about this? Look, I don't want to be a fucking asshole, but you've left me no choice. I've got video of them announcing your corporate thing and the Big Pharma stuff. If we don't get our money tomorrow, I'm going to send this to everyone on the label." Thane was drunk. He held a red drinking straw and pointed it threateningly at me as he spoke, like a wizard trying to fling the last drop of magic out of his wand. I was done feeling guilty about the cruelty I'd allowed to trickle down from my father to Thane.

"You'll be paid first thing tomorrow."

Olivia came back over now that the latest group of fans were gone. "Everything all right?"

"Your new lackey owes me and my band twelve grand," Thane told Olivia.

"He's from my label."

Olivia nodded, then turned to me. "Do you need money?"

"No. He's getting paid tomorrow. He's just being a dick."

"He's going to fuck you over, too," Thane told her. "Watch out."

He went on like this for a while, getting louder and louder. I started looking around for a security guard, but Olivia was set on hearing him out.

"I'm sorry," I told Olivia as Thane rambled on, flourishing his straw. "I'd do anything to get rid of this guy."

Olivia looked him in the eyes and pulled a joint out of her jacket. "Charles is good for it. Don't worry. Smoke this with me. I like that shirt. It's cool as hell."

This calmed him down some. He took the joint and she lit it for him.

"Have you seen the murals?" She put her hand on his back to guide him. "I'll take care of this," my Olivius ex machina whispered to me, and whisked him away.

With Thane gone, I gamed things out. The truth was, with his record on the way, we'd both go down together if he tried to besmirch my good pseudonym. If he shared the video with anyone, even his girlfriend, I'd fuck him over on the album release. And he still didn't understand what it meant that I was a Grossheart, so if no one else saw the footage, it seemed unlikely anyone would find out. I could get him to sign an NDA if it came to that. Still, I knew this could be the end of my second, better life. Just to be safe, I got on my phone and sent Thane the money right away.

I needed to relax. I took the edible I'd stashed in my pocket, grabbed another drink from the bar, and wandered through the crowd for a while. As the edible turned my stomach into a lava lamp, I looked around at the angels in the architecture, frozen in their solemn ecstasy. The Thane shit would turn out fine. Everything in my life had finally harmonized. I'd never wanted a job other than to run a label (aside from maybe to collect art or open a gallery), and now, shielded by my sinecure, I was finally free to do so. I felt a great sense of peace wobble through my arms and legs. I could ride down the lazy river of time or life or whatever and tan in the sun. The DJ played a dance remix of "Sexual Healing," and not only did I feel healed at last, but I had an ambient, aimless erection. I needed to piss.

There was a narrow ambulatory past the bar. I saw a set of doors that might lead to the bathrooms and followed the escalating agony of Christ's passion to where I might relieve myself.

The first room was full of stacked chairs and folded tables. A man and a woman had slipped back there to make out. I watched them grab at each other like two TSA agents in mutual frisk.

The woman saw me. "Sorry," I said, and backed away. Only then did I recognize them as Thane and Olivia. Thane mumbled something and rolled his head around.

"He got a little too high. I'm going to call him a car."

He plopped his head onto her shoulder and muttered something else. He looked sick and pale—I could see that much, even in the dim light.

He was her type, I guess. And now that he was cheating on his drummer girlfriend, I had something to hold over him, should he think about showing anyone the video. I considered taking his phone and deleting it right there, but now that I had more leverage, I'd play it cool and let Olivia have some fun. As I walked away, I took a sneaky picture of the two of them on my phone, but when I checked it later, it was just a gray blur. I slipped out and found somewhere else to pee.

I went much farther down the hall of tiny saints and serious lambs and found a room crowded with statues of the Virgin Mary. And a sink. I couldn't hold it any longer. I'd already unzipped my fly to empty myself into it when I heard voices at the door behind me. Literally caught with my dick out, I instinctively hid myself among the statues and put it back in place.

Over the shoulder of God's mom, I watched two men enter the room. It was pretty dark. All I could see was that one had a beard.

"I'm sorry to kill the vibe," the bearded one said. "I'm just so fucking stressed-out."

The other: "You've been working hard. We all have. It's easy to lose perspective when you're busting your ass like that."

"I have plenty of perspective. That's the fucking problem. My perspective is giving me anxiety attacks. If this were a dating app, it'd be one thing, but this is medicine. There are, like, ethics!"

I was impressed by Olivia's ability to wear down her employees like that. Were my father to have witnessed this exchange, he might've adopted her that night.

"The company is *about* ethics. Olivia is incapable of moral compromise. Leave all that to her. Just go out there and enjoy yourself," the other one said. "Get wasted, sleep until two or three in the afternoon, and start worrying then."

"Not a bad idea."

They left after that. I finished what I'd started in the sink and went back to the party.

I got back to my place in La Tristeza—the warehouse where I lived and ran the label—around four. Louise, who had her own setup on the same floor, had crashed in my more comfortable bed, and not wanting to wake her, I slipped into the recording booth, peeled off some of the soundproofing foam, and passed out on that. I briefly woke in the afternoon with one of the pulsating, radioactive hang-overs that mark the end of your third decade and discovered a wave of missed calls and texts from the various members of Pro Laps, which I ignored. They had their money, and if Thane had outed me anyway, I wasn't ready to face that.

The next morning I got a text from the drummer girlfriend, which my eyes now had the aperture to read without making my brain sous vide. Thane was missing.

That was the beginning of the end for me, my first step down a path soggy with blood (not to mention the other human juices: vomit, liquefied organs, incidental semen, some of those symbolic medieval humors, nervous sweat, and piss—my own, excreted as I ran for my life), one that would eventually lead me here, to this dark little box in the Land of the Dead.

## 3

It was the first semester of my sophomore year at that Cambridge institution with an endowment the size of Latvia's GDP, that cradle of illiterate urbanity that gave us napalm and made eugenics mainstream. I didn't remotely want to be there. My dream had been to go to Wesleyan, the Juilliard of indie rock bands and South Asian rappers of the Adult Swim era, but making my case to Dad had proved impossible. As soon as I'd say "liberal," he'd shut down before I could get to the word *arts*. In the end, there were too many rehearsal spaces at Loeb and tiny rooms in Baker Library bearing the Grossheart name for me to go anywhere else.

I was beginning to learn there was no beating him. Sometimes it felt like he was playing interdimensional chess, and my older brother, Peter, and I would stay up late studying tactics and gaming things out for the next few moves only to find he'd changed the game to marbles or rugby. The truth was, he owned the board, the pieces, the table, and the room we played in. He owned us, too.

I still had ways to rebel, though. That year, I declared a concentration not in finance or political science, but art history. It was a deft move on my part. With her collection of impressionist paintings and pet MFA program, Mom was a true matron of the arts, so she granted me some special protection from Dad's wrath. Not that it was purely a rebellious move. The history of art is a history of pettiness, and I loved it. You have your classic Michelangelo / Julius II beef, of course, Gauguin and van Gogh's volatile bromance, and my all-time favorite,

Cellini's psychopathic murders of his rival goldsmiths. In my mind, I'd essentially majored in gossip.

It was in one of the drab art history classrooms where I first saw Olivia, though for a while I knew her only as the back of a mostly bald head, a raised hand, and an assured voice, as she got to class before me, sat in the front, and always left after. It took me a while to figure out that I'd heard of her before. Insulated though I was, I still couldn't escape word of her and her cancer shit.

Precocious cancer research, that golden ticket in the admissions office. Not quite as golden as legacy status, but it was still something. Harvard desperately wants dibs on whoever racks up the Nobel for the cure. Since her diagnosis in high school, Olivia had been working long-distance under the wing of a professor and grad student at the San Narciso Institute of Technology—MIT's hippie California cousin—and they'd apparently done some groundbreaking work with nanoparticles. Thanks to a profile in the *Crimson* that went viral, Olivia Watts was something of a celebrity and walked around campus with the oncological equivalent of heroin chic. She was Patti Smith thin and draped in layers of sweaters with her bald head on proud display, the beginning of her striking signature look. She'd even spawned a squad of imitators, women who'd shaved their heads in solidarity with her and her cause, though I think it was her aesthetic and cachet that compelled them more than her mission. When the Sick Lit boom happened a couple years later and every director was shoving tubes in their gaunt young actors' noses, it didn't surprise me at all. You don't need to read Sontag to understand the attraction and repulsion that give our culture its sick-teen fetish.

Here's the scenario you probably have in mind. I, the scion fuckboy, sought out Olivia, the cancerous wunderkind, to help me squeak by with a B. You won't believe me when I tell you this, but it was Olivia who came to me. While I was a joke in my other courses, I was a strong presence in the art history classroom, due partly to my sad tendency toward connoisseurship, but also thanks to my parents' possession of more than a few works by the artists we discussed. As the semester of PowerPoints plodded on, she closed the distance between us, sliding from the front row back to my slacker latitude.

"You were right about Lancret," she told me one afternoon, speaking to me for the first time since she'd reestablished herself in the back row.

She was referring to my latest spat with our instructor. Ours was a contentious relationship. The two of us argued about once a century as we made our way from the caves of Lascaux up to the Salon des Refusés. In our brisk survey of the Rococo, we'd skipped over the French painter Nicolas Lancret, and I wanted to make sure he got his due. But the professor (whose specialty was Renaissance frescoes) didn't think he was important enough, even though we'd spent a good *giornata* on Masaccio. Looking back, I was definitely being a prick about it, boogie-boarding on the campus's signature flows of unearned confidence, but my mother had inherited one of Lancret's preparatory sketches, so I felt that I had some skin in the game.

She continued, "I googled him and I don't get why we're not taking a serious look at his work. It's a shame." She looked down at my chest. I thought she was checking me out, but then she said, "You have something on your shirt."

A single pepperoni had plastered itself to my breast pocket, a medal awarded for bravery in the field of pizza. I was still getting used to the basics of unassisted hygiene.

I removed the meat disk and ate it, which got a laugh. At the next class she asked me for help studying for the midterm, and soon we were friends.

Had Olivia known who I was when we first met? I didn't think so. Yes, there were those from Dewey Willson who might spell my last name with a pair of dollar signs, but I took a note from my brother Peter's playbook and kept a fairly low profile by channeling my appetite for rumors into my field of interest. (The Dewey Willson Academy, that proud institution named after the ruthless Confederate general. The bottom dog of the top-tier boarding schools had been founded for the moral edification of overprivileged kids who would dissolve under military-school fascism but nevertheless need a firm hand to tug the precious metal spoons out of their mouths; aka Phillips for fuckups.) While Olivia was something of a campus celebrity at Harvard, her single-minded pursuit of her research meant that, at least at that time, she was confined to her own lonely world.

No surprise, I was short on good friends during my college years. Thanks to my less than Christlike personality traits you've no doubt already discerned, my friend group had been distilled down to a bitter trio. At the time I was deeply under the sway of one princeling in particular, a young man of ultrafine breeding. James's family wasn't as rich as mine, but his blood was twice as blue. His veins were pure lapis lazuli. His middle name was Increase, after a prominent Puritan ancestor, and he was, at least for most of our time at Dewey Willson, the human equivalent of a rowing machine. But somewhere along the line James discovered Circle Jerks, Minor Threat, and Descendents and traded in his polo shirts for a Misfits tee and a pair of combat boots. With my desire to be a couple hundred miles east, paying $100,000 to take part in radical politics, I was drawn to the reinvented James, who seemed closest to the aesthetic I felt I was missing out on. Together we were binary stars with strong gravity, pulling poorer rich kids toward us (at least initially) and locking each other in place. James made me feel that I belonged, but never as much as he did, and this toxic dynamic was, for me, a true taste of home. I'd found in him a mini-dad, someone whose company lent me a sense of superiority to everyone else except (crucially) him. Because, silly as it sounds, the truth is, while my inheritance stood to be a dozen times his, and while my mother is technically a Hapsburg, his pedigree made me look like the noble-blood/new-money mutt that I am.

The other member of our toxic tripartite gang was a Muscovite named Eugen. With his fashionably shabby black coats, his shaved head, and mustache (before they were hip that first time), Eugen gave our group aesthetic a shot of Soviet glamour. The general understanding was that Eugen's dad was an oligarch, and so I didn't press him too much about his roots. I could relate to his wanting to be private about his family. If anything, it made me like him more. Eugen was something of a fixer for us, and what he lacked in status he made up for with an array of skills that proved especially useful in a clique whose other members could barely floss without the aid of a minimum-wage employee. He carried around an Austrian hunting knife (with a handle carved from a tiny antler), which he put to use opening bottles of wine, chopping our lines of coke, and, once, repairing James's Vespa when it broke down in some remote corner of Somerville. Eugen could climb like a marmoset. His favorite trick was to scale your building, slip through your window while you used the bathroom, and wait until you came back to find him smoking, as if it were completely normal. And he was a beautiful smoker, able to blow geometrically stunning rings, execute perfect French inhales, and, with just the slightest effort, produce perfect hearts of smoke that, when you were high, were better than TV.

Which brings me to his most important contribution to the group, his bottomless hoard of drugs. Right away I suspected he was engaging in some recreational dorm-room drug dealing, but I couldn't blame him for wanting a true American University Experience.

I kept Olivia separate from Eugen and James that first semester. I feared their devastating negs and asides might ruin her for me. While James sustained my feelings of superiority and Eugen provided me with weed and coke, Olivia gave me something much more valuable, a sense of depth and pathos. I owe a few lays to the air of sensitivity she lent me, and for those early deposits in my spank bank I am truly grateful.

I helped her quite a bit in return. For a genius, she knew surprisingly little about history, probably owing to her monomaniacal obsession with curing cancer. I tutored her as best I could, mostly about art, music, and the despots my dad was obsessed with.

To bolster her spotty education, I took her on field trips to see films at the Brattle and check out some of the medieval shit at the Fogg. After class, we'd wander down to the river and she'd talk about her dream of getting a PhD at SNIT. Around that time, after I'd abandoned my hopeless aspirations toward musicianship and literary fame, I first envisioned Obnoxious. Of course, I couldn't mention my fantasies to Eugen or James. Eugen thought of punk music solely as a discrete set of finished movements, and nothing past 1990 counted for him. James, on principle, thought all dreams were pathetic. As can easily be inferred, I wasn't exactly the supportive type, so I hadn't built up much currency among my second-tier drinking buddies to garner their encouragement.

But Olivia and I had built up an embarrassingly sincere rapport, and while my mind tended to wander whenever she mentioned her future, I did my best to simulate as genuine an interest as my emotionally stunted soul could manage. After I endured a long rehashing of Olivia's lofty postgraduation plans, I told her about mine.

"Oh, dude, you can totally pull that off. It'll absolutely happen. I know it."

It wasn't lip service. Olivia believed in me. She sent me links to interviews with Greg Ginn, Black Flag guitarist / founder of SST, and bought me a signed copy of Mucho Maas's deranged memoir about his years at Indolent. She talked about my future label like it was already shipping units. For my birthday she presented me with a business plan she'd put together based on our conversations, along with an Obnoxious decal designed by one of her arty friends. Together we imagined the magazine articles that would someday be written about our unlikely friendship.

Though Olivia's persona now is dead serious, back then she was funny. She had a talent for voices. During that first session, she did a pitch-perfect impression of our instructor ("the Bar-rock period") and a strangely accurate Jeff Goldblum. If she weren't so smart, she could've been an improv comic.

She had her flaws, so why not enumerate them? I couldn't get her to listen to a record unless I could prove it was critically acclaimed or historically significant. It was the same with paintings, too. Aside from siding with me about Lancret, she had no patience for lesser-known artists or minor works—I could get her to consider a painting only if it had the aura of the famous, the world-class. Like a lot of people at that institution, she wasn't interested in anything that didn't bring her closer to her goals. Which always made me wonder why she wasted her time with me.

Her family, she told me one night as we sat by the rhinoceroses outside the BioLabs, had once been mildly wealthy, but thanks to her father's embezzlement and a series of lawsuits, they'd fallen to the penniless ranks of the upper middle classes. She received her diagnosis a couple years after the scandal, just when she was starting high school, and confessed that she still blamed herself for her parents' divorce, even though the obvious culprit was her dad's white-collar crime. Other than alluding to the fact that my father was an asshole, too, I still hadn't told her anything about my family. It wasn't as big a deal then as it would be later, once I started the label. The Grossheart name had only just begun its climb toward fame in dark money and climate-science denialism and hadn't become shorthand for evil just yet. Remember, ours was an institution with no shortage of sons of war criminals or daughters of dictators, so the bar was set pretty high for bad daddies. For a brief window, circumstances conspired to allow me to have a friend who was completely unaware of the crushing weight of my inherited wealth, and I wanted to make that last as long as I could.

As winter break approached, Olivia and I decided we'd take a road trip to San Narciso, the city we hoped to someday conquer.

It was a formidable drive, and we dedicated most of our vacation to the cross-country journey. My single-minded friend was able to drive long stretches without stopping, and I was able to hold down my shifts behind the wheel with the help of Adderall left over from finals. We stopped in Pittsburgh and Louisville. We breezed through my home state, stopping by a roadside attraction, a sagging mauve "World's Largest Ball of Paint," but speeding past the exit to my parents' house. When we'd both exhausted ourselves, we spent a night in the parking lot of a Nevada Walmart, which, owing to the recession, had become a popular spot to crash.

Finally we reached San Narciso. We stayed at a pleasantly unsanitary hostel in Wormwood, no longer extant, for $50 a night. We bought skunk weed in Morcillo from a street dealer wearing a Santa hat. We drove by the Yoyodyne compound and GetTogether headquarters (this was before they went public and tripled the cost of living in the city). Olivia took my picture outside the Echo Courts hotel— also gone now—where my hero Miles Paranoid used to work, writing his crude lyrics behind the desk on their stationery (I stole a pad or two). We saw the cockatiels in Inverarity Heights, where we smoked our shitty weed as the birds bickered in their famous tree.

Our last day there it was Christmas. We drove along the coast and found a spot that looked like it might grant us access to the Pacific.

There was a mansion, on the cliffs above the water, but it seemed vacant. We found a rope that let us shimmy down the incline to the beach.

It was a foggy day. You could only see out a hundred yards or so until it was all gray, like the limit of a continental video game. We ran out into the freezing water, splashed around, then retreated to the sand to admire the atmosphere.

Olivia spoke up. "The Pacific makes time feel so huge. How can we be expected to get anything fucking done with so little time? Isn't it a shame that we all just die and none of that wisdom goes anywhere? And everyone has to start completely new? Imagine what you could do with the wisdom of several lifetimes, accruing like rings in a tree or whatever. We're all so fucking dumb. We never learn anything."

She kicked the sand hard, sending up a beige spray, then crumpled to the ground and began to sob. I sat down next to her and started scratching her back. With her buzz, she looked like a lonely little boy, lost at a theme park.

"I'm so fucking tired. Every time I need to sleep, I can just feel all the time running away, flowing past me. I fight it every night. I drink a cup of coffee and read. I go on walks. I watch shitty action movies on my laptop to stay awake. But I'm so fucking tired."

She shivered there for a while, and I kept scratching her back until she was ready to go. Eventually we found the rope and began the climb back up. Olivia went first, and however tired she was, she scaled the rocks like a monkey. From below, I could see all the muscles in her arms, and some on the back of her head. It took me a long time to catch up to her.

## 4

Three days after Olivia's party, I crawled out of the studio booth. With the exception of a few obligatory appearances, I'd spent the past seventy-two hours in there, avoiding Louise and the rest of my Obnoxious employees as much as I could, hoping that Thane would show so everyone would stop bothering me.

The site of the building that housed the label's store, my office, my girlfriend, my employees, and me had a colorful parade of past lives. Long ago it had been home to an Indian boarding school before a brief stint as a hotel. In the thirties, the original structure was all but razed, leaving only traces of the past two lives (every now and then we'd still find the odd desk or mysterious suitcase), and the site began its long tenure as a munitions factory. It was this incarnation, more than the utility of the space, that had drawn me to this chunk of real estate. We only used a fraction of the square footage, even once you took into account the handful of employees I let squat there. Aside from their makeshift dormitory, the store, the office behind it, and the quaint studio, the factory was more or less untouched. Go up past the second floor and you'd find yourself in a graveyard of vast, brutal machines, no doubt responsible for the bullets that perforated thousands of young men on the coast of France or the islands of the Pacific or wherever. The machinery was beautiful, perfect for promotional photos or the odd DIY music video. The artists fucking loved it.

I came downstairs around three and found my underlings huddled behind the register. This was unusual. They were typically cold and lethargic as a tank of crocodiles, and I was accustomed to walking in on them lying stoned on the floor surveying the ceiling tiles' endearing mold, or sitting on the counter drawing curly tattoos on their arms with Wite-Out. It was my fault. I'd hired them more for their aesthetic value than their work ethic. Perfectionist that I am, I prided myself on the skeletal beauty of my employees. They were terrible workers, and people, probably, who knows.

"Any word about Thane?" the store manager, a sullen nonbinary punk named Frankie, asked. They'd recently been responsible for the plague of crude shag mullets spreading among my clerks.

"Nothing yet." I sighed and shook my head. "I'll be sure to let you know."

Frankie and the others, a pair of emaciated aspiring models named Deedee and Lindsey (aka the twinterns), gave me the curt nods of cops or security guards, and I relished the sweet indifference they managed to summon for their boss.

Frankie picked something off the floor. "Hey, whose pill is this?"

"I'll eat it," I told them, and snatched the white pellet out of their hand.

It had been a while since I'd proven to them that I didn't give a shit. I popped it into my mouth without much review. It dissolved faster than melatonin and tasted like chalk. My guess is that it was a hunk of plaster, rubbed smooth in the months since I had some guys do electrical work on the store. I'd been hoping for a stray SSRI from one of my sadder employees, but no luck.

My tongue freshly frescoed, I passed our crates of records, which, along with my collection scattered throughout the warehouse, sampled nearly every branch of punk's piss-soaked tree: proto and post, LA and DC, art, anarcho, hardcore, post-hardcore, horror, skate, surfadelic, crust, crossover, cowpunk. We had Dicks, Spotted Dick, the Dictators, Discharge, Death, Dead Moon, Dead Boys, Zero Boys, Big Black, Big Clown, Germs, Jay Reatard, Lydia Lunch (and many more!). I took a look at some of the new releases, then made my way to the office, where Louise, first mate in the hierarchies of both my label and sex life, was waiting for me.

Louise was slightly more tattooed than your average art-adjacent woman of our generation (skulls, a scorpion, some geometric shapes decorating the fingers) and liked to wear giant Iris Apfel glasses that took up most of her face. She possessed both a scrappy capability and an impossibly Zen disposition, and as someone with the maturity and practical skills of a three-year-old, these features struck me as nearly superhuman. She'd worked for a couple small labels and had even moved to Bloomington, *Indiana*, to toil for a year or two at the hub of indies there. A lot of what we accomplished at Obnoxious was her doing, and I have a hunch that, were decisions in her hands alone, we would have already leveled up into another league.

She was a true believer in our cause, which allowed her to extract every last drop of labor from our timid Gen Z interns. I'd earned her eternal love and devotion by putting out her record just before we started dating. It scored some good reviews in minor blogs (the last of their kind) and scratched her arty itch for a while, allowing her to focus more on the business side of things, where I could really use her. But now she was trying to record again. She'd disappear for a while with her laptop and guitar, laying down scratch tracks in some dark corner of the warehouse and popping out hours later to subject me to the demos. She'd done so much work for the label that we'd arranged for me to take on part of her workload until she'd mixed the album. My hope was that she'd shelve the record for a while once she saw I couldn't handle things on my own.

We'd been dating for about a year, so we were now well past the natural point when she would've met my parents. I'd met hers, a witty English-teacher mother and chipper anesthesiologist dad (before he died), and had leveraged her good relationship with them against her, hiding my flesh and blood behind a curtain of painful silence. Had my family not been my family, she would have met them already, and I came up with a suitable excuse that conveyed the degree of their toxicity, if not its global scale. This compartmentalization was their fault and no comment on her long-term aptitude. As you know, I never received proper love training. The chambers of my gross heart were mostly vaults and dungeons, and letting someone in wasn't easy. But with Louise I tried hard to make up for my lack of schooling. I bought her an overpriced Rickenbacker for her twenty-ninth birthday. When we hit the six-month mark, I rented us a cabin near Oregon's most photogenic waterfall. Not long after that, I took her to see Stephen Malkmus, her Gen X crush, a gift that preemptively covered any fucking up I might do, the fucking up I was about to do. We had a good dynamic. I assured and legitimized her, and in return she was my feminist shield, proving that, despite my shittiness, I was probably a good guy. I've done a lot with my performative allyship, but nothing can top that.

Louise's only flaw—and it was a big one—was whatever tragic combo of nature and nurture that made her at all interested in me. I owe something to her previous boyfriend. Before I came into her life, Louise had been with someone much worse, if you can imagine. They'd been in a band together, until his narcissism and neediness drove her away. (A quick example of his terribleness: on their sole release, he replaced all the tracks of her guitar parts with his own takes and didn't tell her until after the album had dropped.) She had stipulated a certain amount of space when we started dating, which is why she officially crashed on the dormitory floor with the rest of the Obnoxious posse, and why we spent so much time apart when we weren't in the office or deliberately hanging out. As someone who traditionally rushed intimacy and then shoved my partners away, this mature arrangement was ideal for me, and it let the two of us date and manage Obnoxious without furtively scanning the dark web for affordable hit men.

"Have you heard anything?" Her eyes watered up behind her 45-size lenses. "I can't think about anything else."

"I've been texting constantly," I said in a serious, cable-drama tone. "It's all I did all yesterday. I got nothing."

In truth, I'd only texted Olivia, a couple hours after Thane's girl-friend told me he was missing. Olivia informed me she'd passed him off to one of her employees not long after they'd made out, and that was the last she'd seen of him. She didn't, of course, refer to her time with Thane in those terms, but I could tell it was from sexual embarrassment. Olivia had always been private about her love life.

"I just hope he's okay," Louise said.

"I'm worried, too. But you know how you artists are. With the record coming out, he probably just has a lot on his mind and needs some time off the grid. Soul-seeking shit."

"God I hope so." I could tell this helped. "I could totally see that. You'd just think he'd tell Sydney. But he's been such a fucking dick lately I wouldn't put it past him. I just hope he isn't using again."

We worked in anxious silence for a while. Louise sent me some forms, which I forwarded to my accountant. I'd hired him on my own. He did all the work Louise thought I was doing.

The door swung open. It was the drummer, Sydney, herself. Her eyes were red and the skin around them puffy. She wore a dirty yellow jumpsuit covered in even dirtier embroidered patches—she resembled a spotted, rotting banana, a look that complemented the uncanny notes of banana wafting around my punks that I've already described. Today she smelled even worse than usual, as if her fear and sadness had its own vinegary stench.

Sydney was the other half of Pro Laps' core duo. After Thane's last band broke up and he and Sydney got together, the two of them sweated it out as a White Stripes knockoff until they answered a post from a bassist on a throwback message board. They joined up with him and his buddies, and Pro Laps 1.0 was born. After that, the two of them convinced the bassist to kick everyone else out until they were whittled down to a trio. Then they kicked him out. Now the two of them helmed the band, acquiring keyboard players, bassists, and rhythm guitar players, then discarding them whenever they reached the limits of their usefulness or ruined the band's ever-shifting aesthetic. I admired their picky vision.

Louise: "Still no word?"

Sydney geysered into a fit of hard sobs and crumpled onto the couch. We'd glimpsed just a short hiatus of tears that had now resumed, making up for lost, clogged time. Snot spilled down her nose and chin. It was disgusting.

Louise sat down next to her and hugged her. Sydney calmed down some, and my girlfriend poured her a cup of coffee as she tried to wipe off the mucus that now frosted her face.

"He said he was going to find you and left our place. Patty said she told Thane she saw you at the Scope, and then he texted me that he'd tracked you down to some corporate fundraiser thing?"

Louise looked at me.

"It was for one of our patrons," I said. "Thane wanted to talk to me about the money. I sent it right away, right there." I poured myself a cup of coffee.

"Yeah, I know. We have a joint bank account. What's weird is that all the money's there. He hasn't made any withdrawals or anything. Not even like for a burrito or a bar tab. That's what worries me."

"This coffee tastes like a brown crayon in hot water." I dumped my mug into the sink.

"I like it," Sydney said, sucking up to my girlfriend. "Do you have a cigarette?"

Louise stuck one in Sydney's mouth and lit it for her. Louise was too sweet to Sydney. It had something to do with her shitty ex / former bandmate, her own terrible Thane.

"Maybe he had some cash," I said. "I still think he's just clearing his head. It was something he said when I saw him. Something vague about needing open air, room to think. He talked about going up to the mountains."

"Falda Linda, I bet," Sydney said. "He went to school there, at the arts high school. God, I hope that's all it is."

"I mean, and I hate to even say this," I said unhatefully, "but do you think he might be fucked-up?"

Louise shot me a worried look.

"I'll fucking kill him if he is."

"Maybe we should send someone down to Morcillo," I said, "just to look around."

In recent years, Morcillo had become home to a tent city. Even the pigeons there were an extra degree of desperate, not above bathing their spotty plumage in spilled Fanta. Despite its proximity to the headquarters of corporations making billions on the nonconsensual tracking and surveillance of mankind, there had been dozens of disappearances there over the past couple years. If Thane had relapsed, it seemed likely that he might have gone there to score. But my stronger hunch was that his flight was a cry for attention and that he'd show up in the next week or so with a five-o'clock shadow and a legal pad full of new, mediocre songs.

Sydney: "If he's using, I almost don't want to find him."

She hadn't mentioned the video. He must not've sent it. I reassured myself that his erratic behavior would eclipse any drama he could stir up with that, and I could leverage the fugue against him if it came down to his word against mine. Besides, now he'd been paid. I was sure I'd be able to come up with some plausible lie about the night by the time he returned from his moody getaway.

I know I've lobbed quite a few insults at Thane so far. I didn't hold all my artists in such low esteem. I related to them fundamentally. I possessed an artistic soul, and I knew that, had I been born to someone else, had the Muses not been so stingy when their togas brushed my crib, I, too, might have turned out like them.

Like a fetish that stamps you in a collision of hormones and circumstance, my calling made itself known when, at the age of twelve, my brother's girlfriend gave me the first Paranoids record. The music seemed universal, at the time. I made my parents buy me a hefty Les Paul—I didn't yet know to request a Jazzmaster or Jaguar—and began a daily regimen of accidentally experimental noise. The trajectory of my musical taste is typical of my demographic, a gradual migration from teenybopper to indie rocker to neoliberal poptimist before settling back into a jazz-infused, Afro-funk-seasoned version of my college tastes. This was squarely in the second phase, an era spent on LimeWire and the MP3 blogs, at the record stores in masochistic submission to the scoffs and lectures of bleach-haired clerks now reincarnated in my store, trapped in samsara's broken record.

Sure, the class-struggle shit and mockery of the more fortunate are time-honored tropes of punk, but the genre's fundamental nihilism meant that not even those jabs mattered. That was key for me. From the moment I heard my first Paranoids record, I was liberated from my double bind: I could say fuck it to Charles Sr., and also to anyone who took issue with my scionhood.

When my musical dreams starved to death by a shortage of talent, I thought I might aim lower and become a writer, my generation's Kathy Acker or Gary Indiana. A passable Tao Lin knockoff. But when the form rejections from the literary journals rolled in, when I didn't manage to snag even an honorable mention in the undergraduate writing contests, I decided to channel my energies toward helping real artists, as a kind of midwife to support and guide, to yank the work out into the world and help wipe off the goo. (And if a glob of glory bounced my way as a result, I wouldn't mind it.) With my generational wealth and exquisite taste, my true calling was finally clear. I was to be a Peggy Guggenheim of independent, difficult music. Another Pannonica de Koenigswarter, the bebop baroness of a dying but necessary art form. I could redeem myself by looking after all these dumb, insolvent artists, waiting in the tall grass and catching them when they started running off some crazy cliff or whatever. I cut my teeth on a few feeble efforts—a tape imprint with career sales generously estimated in the dozens, my disastrous management of my ex's band—before I moved out here and started Obnoxious.

My discoveries as an A&R man erred on the side of difficult. My favorite artists on our roster included a No Wave dronester who scraped his Ibanez with a bow saw and a modular synth quartet whose hour-long atonal singles made the former sound like Shaun Cassidy (the only band of mine that's been permitted to play at the Scope, that legendary nursery of American electronic music, where Patty had spotted me before I went to Olivia's party). Frankly, Pro Laps was the Obnoxious group I cared about least, but I knew they'd bring in a bigger audience and hopefully reverse the flow of the cash suck I'd painstakingly engineered.

Sydney: "I'm filing a missing person's report."

I hoped she wouldn't do it. I didn't need the law prying my life open, especially now that everything was coming together. Thane could show up any minute, and I didn't want him to best me with his emotional manipulation—I'd learned to dodge those traps in the nursery.

Still, I said, "We'll do whatever we can to help you. Just name it. But I'm positive he'll show up soon. If we just focus on the record, I'd bet money he'd pop out of wherever he's hiding once he sees people love it."

Sydney stayed quiet and started cleaning under her fingernails with a paper clip, leaving the tiny slivers of dirt and skin on the arm of the couch. I recalled the image of Olivia and Thane making out and felt a twinge of nausea. This must have simply come from empathy for Sydney, I figured. A new, unfamiliar feeling when it came to her.

"That's fucking bullshit," Sydney said to me. "You're a useless piece of shit. Just absolute human garbage. I wish it was you who'd disappeared."

"What?" I was happy to have the ugly fond-feeling exorcised so quickly.

"I'm sorry. It was a Freudian slip." She leaned over and put her cigarette out on a stray tortilla chip on my desk.

I was about to pursue this further, but Louise gave me a muzzling look.

Sydney: "I'm going up to Falda Linda first thing tomorrow. Do you think I could borrow a car? Our van really can't handle the mountain roads."

"My car would probably break down in the desert," I said. "But I can chip in for gas."

"You can use mine," Louise said. "It's a little janky, but it's yours if you need it. I can drive you."

"That's really nice. But I don't want to hijack you. I'll get out of here soon. I just feel stuck. I'm afraid that I'll get up there and he won't be there and then what will I do?" The blood was refilling her face. I braced myself for the next fit. "What am I going to do?"

Sydney started sobbing again. Louise gave her another hug and dabbed her tears with a spare band tee we had lying around. "Obviously you can sit here with us as long as you need to. If you just want to be around some people."

Sydney lay on our couch for a while. I went over some of the logistics of the coming weeks, including the next month's release party, an event that Thane would surely return for. The drummer nodded along zombielike, looking at her phone as I spoke. I was thinking of disappearing into the mountains of Falda Linda myself.

Louise put a finger to her lips to shush me and then got to work on her laptop. I tried to do the same, but Sydney was keeping me from concentrating. I wanted to kick her out, but Louise wouldn't like that.

"Oh, shit, I have to go talk to some geek about our website," I lied. "I'm already late. Fuck." I walked out, snuck back in, and slept on my soundproofing foam until 8:00 p.m. I had a meeting with Olivia at nine.

I took the scenic route to Kenosis headquarters, through my favorite seedy San Narciso neighborhoods. Out my windows sat the vibrator stores of Morcillo, the pawnshops and mirthless burger franchises of Fangoso Lagoons, Wormwood's strip malls in sour decline. Before the Paranoids injected me with their useful nihilism, my image of San Narciso came from another, even more barbaric source, an incredibly popular video game set in the city's criminal nineties. Another drug-dealer narrative like *Bad Company*, a game of carjacking, ramming pedestrians with the stolen vehicles, then mowing down the surviving pedestrians with exotic weapons from a library of obscure firearms. The game's signature nectarine skies were lifted from an airbrushed T-shirt, and the interiors were a twelve-RGB homage, with pimply stoners serving slices of pizza nearly indistinguishable from their slimy faces. Moving here, I wasn't so dumb as to expect it would match its musical or virtual depictions, but lucky for me, the city—like an aging comedian—had, at least in some sectors, fallen into a caricature of itself. You could get caught up in grieving the death of authentic San Narciso, whatever that was, but I for one was happy to live in the beautiful feedback loop. I ate a lot of pizza.

Kenosis lay in the tech hub near the Rancho Hueco Caverns. On the drive out I passed the corporate headquarters for VoltAire, Manticor, and GetTogether—gargantuan silver compounds that, in their shiny geometry, resembled samples of rare crystals or micro-scopic algae grown billions of times their natural size. These were the strapping grandsons of the first wave of tech out here, starting when the defense contractor Yoyodyne built their first microchip a couple gold rushes ago. Between them I spotted the many statues of saber-toothed tigers with their walrus tusks that had become the hub's mascots in the boom (most start-ups splashed their tigers with their corporate colors, so much of this pride was painted the same calming blue, that default branding hue). In the dark, illuminated in flashes by my headlights, they looked like they might be alive, stalking their prey in the shadows.

Kenosis was only about half a mile from the famous caverns. I'd only ever checked out these underground caves once, and my experience was psychedelically skewed. Louise and I were high on mushrooms, and even then, in my psilocybin-induced awe, it seemed like little more than a hole in the ground, despite how deep it was rumored to go. Olivia embraced the cavern itself, rather than the tigers, as a theme for her compound's design. A tasteful call, as the apex-predator shit was a bit too on the nose for me.

I pulled right into the lot, my first time as an employee, filled with admiration for her architectural vision. The building's forward-facing side was an enormous slab of stone tapered at the top, forming a jagged teardrop. The rest of the structure submitted to the rock's geological grandeur in its corporate neutrality, with the exception of an archway lifted from some church in Bavaria. This last motif betrayed her purpose: to inspire cathedral levels of wonder in all who beheld her domain. I myself was ready to throw on a codpiece and pantyhose and repeat whatever creed she fed me.

I swiped my new access card at the door, approached the clean-cut woman at the front desk, and told her what I was there for.

She punched something into her computer. Behind her hung a photo of Olivia administering a shot to a beaming African child. With both of them smiling hard, I'd say the picture was about 40 percent teeth.

"I'll take you to Miss Watts. Follow me."

She got up from her seat and, out of nowhere, another woman appeared to man the desk. Without a word to her replacement, the original receptionist whisked me off.

On our journey to the elevator, I saw Clif, the bulky lieutenant I'd met at the cloister party, step out of the bathroom. He wore what I'd learn was his acid-washed-jeans, unbuttoned-shirt uniform. I said hi, and he walked right by. I hadn't even subtly dissed his outfit yet! I noted the slight and tried not to let it spoil my first time at the new workplace.

Here and there—along the hallway, above a water fountain—were painted a number of unhealthy maxims I'd come to know simply as the Precepts. Here are the highlights, compiled from my early weeks at the company:

"Insist on perfection."

"Speed matters. Most decisions are reversible."

"Who needs sleep?" (The largest iteration of this one took up an entire wall between ground-floor conference rooms. A smaller version was plastered above the mirrors in the bathroom and had me wondering what issue it had been put there to correct.)

"Obsess."

"Don't just think outside of the box. Live outside of it."

This was a world created and ruled entirely by a single ego. I felt right at home.

The elevator gave me the feeling we were zigging and zagging up a lightning-bolt-shaped chute. Eventually the doors opened and the receptionist led me out.

We stood in a small vestibule with no door. I smelled pine needles— I thought maybe this fragrance was pumped in through the vents to create a soothing atmosphere, something I heard they did at these places. But then the receptionist pressed her pass against a blank patch of wall, which slid to the side, revealing the source of the scent.

We were outside, or at least it looked that way. There were trees all around and, to either side of the path before us, a thick carpet of pine needles dotted here and there with the odd cone. It was like stepping into a screen saver.

Then I registered the ceiling. High above I could see a squirrel backlit by the moon, seemingly levitating on the glass that protected this hunk of domesticated nature from its free-range cousins.

"The sylvarium," the receptionist told me, noticing my awe. "Olivia likes to come here to brainstorm, especially at night."

At the other end of the path I spotted the Titania of this lush indoor wood, along with three men standing in rapt attention.

"Charles!" she shouted over to me. "I have a couple people I want you to meet."

I caught up with her, awkwardly crossing the driving-range-size expanse of her pet forest while they waited. My stride is shamefully short, so I had plenty of time to study her companions. One of the men was very old. His skin appeared to be made of potato salad. I thought I recognized him from a stamp. The man to his right was much younger, wearing (I noticed as I finally completed my hike) a gaudy Cartier watch my brother also owned. The third man, somewhere between them in age, looked familiar. I might have seen him at the cloister party, though the event was packed with people of his exact demographic, so I couldn't be sure.

"Mr. Secretary, this is Charles Grossheart. He's just joined us as creative consultant and special adviser on ethics."

"Oh! A Grossheart? Now that is impressive."

His potato-salad face momentarily roused itself from its limp and soggy state. He and his two younger associates appraised me as if I were an expensive horse.

"Secretary Slobodkin just joined our board, as you know," Olivia explained. "Charles, have you met Sam Paca?"

"I don't know him, but I know of him, of course." I had no idea who he was. I shook his hand like it was attached to the pope.

"And Ralph Langenburger. My mentor. And friend. This particular introduction is long overdue."

Now I knew where I recognized him from: my pre-reunion cram session weeks ago. In the pictures accompanying the profiles, Langenburger's hair tickled his collar in groomed, almost feathered waves, the kind of cut that might result from a treaty between a rebellious son and his straitlaced mother (been there). But now his hair hung in uncompromising locks well past his shoulders. He still had his signature hippie circle frames, but looked oddly younger than the man in the photographs, something I attributed to the salubrious effects of immeasurable wealth.

"I'm no mentor," he said. "I've got no wisdom to offer. We're friends. I'm just a little older."

Olivia: "We were just about to take Mr. Paca on a tour of the facilities. Charles, why don't you come along?"

"I'd love to."

"I'm sorry," Langenburger said, "but I've got to go. It was great seeing the two of you again. Olivia, we'll chat soon. And, Charles, we'll have to jam sometime. We have a space in San Guijuela. You should come by."

"Sure!"

Langenburger gave me a nod, waved to Olivia, and left the way I came.

"The space is truly amazing," Paca said, looking a pine up and down like he was about to buy it a drink.

"I have to interface with nature. This keeps me from running off to the woods or the beach every time I need to think. There are zero invasive species in here. So, in a way, it's almost more pristine than nature." Olivia picked up a handful of pine needles and sifted them through her fingers, sprinkling them back down to the ground. "This was GetTogether's old headquarters, before they went public. And it was the first Yoyodyne plant before that. It's fitting, I think. It sounds silly, but I have a very old-school attitude about places. I really do think they contain power." She scrutinized some bark. "It's magical thinking, I know. But there are hubs that pop up through history—Athens, Rome, Paris, New York, Tenochtitlan—and San Narciso is one of them, undeniably. So we were lucky to get our hands on this special spot, in this city, at this moment. Of course, we've made some serious renovations, but you'll find the same buzz of possibility that defined GetTogether's early years, too."

The path dead-ended into a silver patch of wall—we'd reached the end of our journey's arboreal phase. Olivia pressed her hand against a seemingly random spot, conjuring another doorway, and herded the diplomat and capitalist through.

"Perfect timing," she said to me in a way that, rather than commenting on the coincidence, seemed instead to compliment herself on the choreography.

As I followed her through the doorway, I heard a rustling in the woods to my back. I turned and glimpsed a dark blob roving through the trees. A deer, I thought, until I remembered that we weren't, in fact, outside. It was probably just some employee. Maybe a janitor.

In one of my many soporific art-history courses during my stint at our nation's oldest, costliest academy, I learned of a certain steward of the gardens of Versailles assigned an absurdly difficult task. Thanks to the palace's limited water supply, this poor minion's job was to scramble in advance of his king as he wandered among the fountains of his domain, activating whatever waterworks the monarch might happen to set his bleary royal gaze upon. If the king veered left, the poor servant had to book it over to the lithe sculptural youths so the water would cascade from their orifices in time. If the king moseyed to the right, our man had to race to the arrangement of brawny horses and get them going, pronto. I like to imagine he'd be killed if the king were to behold a dry spout, just to add some stakes, but I don't think this was the case. Still, it was a pleasant enough slapstick to entertain myself with while my adjunct rambled on about the guillotine (a device that, given my background, invited terrifying mental images I preferred not to entertain).

I mention this because, during my first tour of Kenosis headquarters, I had a hunch that a similar steward might be at work, making sure each stop was perfect. Though instead of pumping water through the mouths of slutty nymphs and lascivious frogs, he now managed a network of shining laboratories, filling them with blood.

Olivia's tour followed the life cycle of her high-tech brainchildren, from their formative years among a nursery of nanomedical specialists to the laboratories where they lived out their clinical adolescence among white-coated technicians. The former—the domain of the specialists—was made to look like a block in Park Slope, or maybe Clinton Hill, complete with a coffee shop and a brick wall spray-painted with faux graffiti (another of her Precepts: "In order to build big, we have to think small").

Olivia stopped by a fake storefront, which displayed a buffet of revolutionary technological artifacts: a light bulb, an antique telephone, a dusty radio, and a classic iPod. In the front was a row of chrome cashews laid out like earrings.

"These are the early prototypes. I've always found that we learn more from failure than we do from success. And it's important to remember where you come from. I look at this and I see an evolution in our thinking, a yearslong dance between materials and ideas, taking our time to perfect the beat, so to speak."

She smiled at the little prototypes through the glass like a happy dad in an old maternity ward and began a speech she'd repeat nearly word for word on the many subsequent tours I'd accompany her on.

"This is probably a good time for me to explain just what led us here. I've mentioned my struggle with cancer to the two of you before, but, Sam, I'll go into it just so you can get the bigger picture. When I was fifteen, I was diagnosed with rhabdomyosarcoma, a kind of cancer that develops in skeletal muscle. I was an ambitious, embarrassingly precocious child, as I'm sure you both were, too. My best friends were books. I filed my first patent when I was sixteen. When I had to miss school because of my illness, I started cold-calling labs until I came across a then-graduate student at SNIT—she's at MIT now, tenured, still doing amazing work, consults for us occasionally—and for some reason she let me join her team researching the cancer-fighting potential of certain nanoparticles. You can probably figure out why I was drawn to this work. I went into remission just before I got into Harvard, where I studied biomedical engineering."

Her voice started catching, just like it had during her announcement.

"Halfway through college it came back. Cancer. Thanks to some very cutting-edge and rather risky treatment, we were able to beat it back again. It was like . . ." She gave herself a moment to collect herself, or to look like she was collecting herself. "My body hadn't just betrayed me once, but two times. You can imagine how hard that would be on a twenty-year-old. It was like getting mugged by a member of your family, twice. I was recovering that second time, recovering physically but also emotionally, when I first came up with the idea for Kenosis, and soon I found I had other challenges, almost as difficult as my fight to survive. You see, my course of treatment was incredibly painful and disruptive, and I thought, if we could have detected it earlier, when it was just a microscopic clump of cells, it would never have come to that. That's what led me to the idea for the nanotome."

She pulled what looked like a licorice jelly bean out of her pocket.

"This is the Book of Life. Your life. Page by page, day by day, until your story is clear and legible. Swiss scientist Andreas Manz's work has shown that microfabrication technologies used to manufacture computer chips can be repurposed to create channels that direct very tiny volumes of fluids. At Kenosis, we've taken a big leap from Manz's premise. The nanotome—we call these the Gutenberg I's—uses this principle to conduct microfluidic protein assays, but not in a lab. In the body itself. The tome is powered by your body heat, and unlike doctors or those clanking Siemens machines, it's always on, always vigilant. Sure, the tome is small, but the impact will be huge. These will redefine the paradigm of medicine, away from one in which people have to present with a symptom in order to get access to care, toward a future in which every person, no matter how much money they have or where they live, already has access to the most sophisticated preventive treatment the very *instant* something goes wrong."

A perfect keynote pause. I recognized the rhythm of her patter from her cloister party.

"We're thinking it'll only have to be replaced every three to five years, and with a nonsurgical procedure so clean and simple you'll barely feel it, really not much different than the technique used to implant microchips to tag pets and wildlife. I have one. Right . . . here." She poked a spot a few inches above her right hip. "I'm the first human to upgrade, though there are some rats and monkeys that beat me to the distinction of first mammal and primate. But what can you do?"

Paca: "Can they be used for treatment? At this point?"

"You're thinking like we do. So most medicine, like antibiotics, isn't potent. There's a reason they hook you up to a bag or make you take so many pills. Which means we can't really use the tomes for treatment just yet. Right now they're only for biometrics and diagnosis, but we're hoping that they'll be able to do more. I'll pick this thread back up soon."

We strolled among the park benches and lampposts, and Olivia summoned her researchers from their holes. She clearly prided herself on their dejection and fatigue, forcing one or two MIT PhDs to prance tiredly before her guests. This was key to her brand, the round-the-clock, relentless striving, the whole reason why she'd brought us here so late in the first place.

One particularly ragged scientist in her stable, a bespectacled little schlub, she presented to us like one of my dad's begrimed bottles of wine from his collection.

"He has two PhDs. He's only twenty-one," Olivia said, though the emphasis landed less on his education and more on his waning hairline and hollow eyes.

We left these nerds behind and walked through a huddle of boxes draped in black, a washing-machine funeral. The windows behind them were covered, too.

"Please forgive the secrecy. I know it's a little extreme, but we're still in stealth mode. Turns out, you make a lot of enemies when you disrupt an industry, and the boys over at Siemens would take out hits on us to cop our proprietary technology. They actually collaborated with Hitler back in the day. We have to keep the trade secrets secret."

She began another speech. I drifted in and out, letting the torrents of language wash over me. Most of what she said consisted of synonyms for *small* and *life*, with the same phonemes jumbled together over and over. Biomarker, biometrics, biohacking, biomathematics, bioinformatics, biochemistry, biothreat, biotech (duh), microbiology, microfluidics, microfabrication, micro solenoids, nanotech, nanorobotics. It had a soothing, ASMR-like quality.

On our way to the labs, I noticed a familiar song coming out of the speakers, and Olivia gave me a wink. After a few more bars I realized it was an Obnoxious release. It warmed my heart that she'd torture her poor employees with my music.

Olivia stopped at a dingy wooden structure. It looked like an old upright piano, with a book lying open where the sheet music would sit.

"This is a desk from a scriptorium, originally from a monastery in Lyon. Actually, this is a great opportunity to talk a little more about the Gutenberg tech and our big vision for where we want to take all this, if you don't mind."

"Please."

"Every human body literally has a fatal flaw, as we all know. You get fifty good years, and then—probably before then—your body begins the gradual, unstoppable process of breaking down. Why is that? Why, exactly, do we grow old and die? We accept this as a fact of life, but it's not necessarily a given. Bats can be older than forty, while rats usually never make it past two. Octopuses also kick the bucket at two, but the ugly Greenland shark gets half a millennium. It's unfair. And it will get us all. But there are ways to mitigate the effects of this process. I'll explain."

She flipped the page of the book on the old desk, as if reading her monologue off it.

"Really, the body is like a text in a scriptorium. And like any text, to survive the ravages of time, it must be copied. We'll call the copiers the monks. For a while, the monks are on their game, copying and proofreading with precision and zeal. But after a while, these proofreaders get sloppy. The noonday demon gets to them and they slack off. In reality, this is because the selection pressure against late-action mutations is very slight, for obvious reasons, and because some genetic mutations that have benefits early on in life might also have costs later. I'm condensing pretty much all of the work of Medawar and Williams, but that's the gist. Suffice it to say, errors are made, and not only that, they go unchecked, uncorrected. What's worse, once an error gets past the proofreader, it gets copied *again*, and the flaws get passed down, repeated. The text goes from *Ulysses* to *Finnegans Wake*. It makes no sense. The line for skin gets miscopied and you get wrinkles. The line for hair gets miscopied and you go gray. The same goes for any of the suite of errors associated with old age, cancer cells included."

"My monks have been sleeping on the job," the Secretary joked. "Somebody better call the abbot."

"Exactly. That's where we come in. And, Sam, this speaks to your earlier question. Our plan is to move beyond the simple diagnostic function of the nanotomes. Soon they will be home to a volume of nanobots, the Gutenberg II's, and we'll convert the original Gutenberg I's to communication hubs and coordination points for the colonies we're developing. These will be able to seek out the typos, correct them."

She rubbed her finger against the wood of the desk, removing a scuff only she could see.

"Now that's the big vision, and it'll take years to make those advances. Until then, we're focused on detecting treatable illnesses—not that we don't think aging is treatable—with microfluidic assays and real-time results. It won't be long before we're working with a true secondary immune system—something like providing beat cops with tactical armor, drones, and tanks. Or, even better, something like the FBI, looking for long-term threats to the harmony and longevity of the human body. And because the nanobots are modular, they'll be able to function together, cooperating to synthesize compounds from food and drink, supplementing organ function. Insulin synthesis. Hematopoiesis. Hormone production. This opens up a whole new dimension of remote treatment. Imagine an epidemic breaks out, and doctors are able to remotely trigger production of antibodies in patients across a continent, the same way our neighbors in the park might require a software update to combat malware.

"While I'm always vigilant against exaggerated claims, there's no denying that this is the future of medicine. The pilot program with R and W is big. But we're in talks with people over at a certain five-sided building in Virginia, and while I can't say too much about it, I can tell you that there's a lot of interest in the Gutenbergs for use on the battlefield. But I always come back to the flood of letters and emails I get from everyday people, begging for this new technology. For them, for their partners in remission, for their children. This is for everyone.

*They* are who this company is for. I think it goes without saying that this could very well signify a revolution, and not just in medicine. In life, in what it means to be alive."

Olivia's speech abruptly picked up speed. "Anyway, this is partly why I gave the Gutenberg its name, because, like the printing press, it will be the revolutionary technology that will replace this flawed, old way of doing things. But that's only partly why." She smiled at me, then turned back to the medieval desk. "I'll explain the rest later. But let's go take a look at the labs."

As the others moved on, the desk's feet caught my eye, and I hung back to admire them. One was carved into a hoof, one had talons, the third was a human foot in a sandal, and the last had a lion's paw, with claws sticking out. One for each of the evangelists.

I squatted like an ape to take a picture of the lion paw, which had a severe, gothy aesthetic I admired. While I was down there, I noticed something on the opposite leg. A lazy, supine 8—an infinity symbol— had been scratched into the wood. It had thorns poking out of it, hooked like shark fins, and it looked like something had been buffed out behind it. I knew it from somewhere but couldn't quite place it right then.

I didn't have too long to study it. I caught the ding of the elevator in the next room and hurried to catch up with Olivia and the others.

She took us up a floor, where, on the other side of glass panels, men in white coveralls were blasted with air. They looked like beekeepers from the future.

"These are the air showers. They have to suit up like that because of the size of what we're working with. Around here, we think in nano-meters. To give you some idea, this morning, when you shaved"—she dragged an invisible razor from one ear to the other, as if hacking through a neck beard—"by the time you got to the other cheek, the hair where you started had grown two nanometers."

While Paca and the Secretary rubbed their cheeks with new wonder, as if they might feel the faint growth in real time, I put my hand over my throat.

"I can't take you in right now. We can't risk any dust or lint in there. Fortunately, the clinical lab is a little more accessible."

Whereas the designers' "borough" (that's what she called it, though at first I thought she said "burrow") cultivated a cozy, lived-in feel, this lab was a crisp realm of right angles and clean lines, like a maze made out of knives. The machines hummed in low assonance, as if their function was not to test and measure blood but instead to facilitate a gratifying bowel movement.

The same black jelly beans she'd shown off earlier floated in the vials of blood like ugly crustaceans in formaldehyde. Until Kenosis received approval for human testing, she explained, the lab had to make do with plunging the tomes in blood samples, "where they still outperformed anything by Siemens or LabCorp."

"Okay, so this is where we'll test you," she said to Paca. A technician appeared with a needle, and the venture capitalist rolled up his sleeve. When enough blood was drawn, Olivia herself injected it into a vial containing a tiny black Gutenberg.

"It'll take some time for the microfluidic channels to absorb the blood and process the data. I'll just have your results sent up to my office for us to look at when we're done touring the facility. It's one of the benefits—you can transmit the data to any device, so it's as easy as checking your email or taking a peek at the stock market."

The techs, male and female alike, were uniformly overhandsome, like actors from police procedurals. My own employees, though mulleted, were much more naturally attractive, I told myself smugly as I watched a scientist resembling an asymmetrical Hadid sister drizzle fluid into a pan flute of tubes. Nevertheless, their off-brand hotness made them more attainable somehow and turned me on.

I'd become too distracted by the technicians. I heard Olivia say my name and returned my focus to the tour.

"I really do owe a lot to Charles. After I first dreamed up the idea for what would become our proprietary technology, I worked on the project for months, consulting my research team leader, corresponding with biomedical researchers across the country and, in one case, even the UK. But when I took my idea to my adviser, she laughed right in my face, claiming it was science fiction. I was completely devastated. For weeks I practically lived at Widener Library. I reread *Moby-Dick*, reread the *Iliad*. It was a dark time for me."

She looked at me for a while. Her eyes were wet. If this were someone in my family, I'd suspect they'd been studying Stanislavski. But this was real. I couldn't keep up the intimate eye contact and turned away to study the floor tiles.

"I felt I was onto something, but only I could see it. Was it a vision of what the future could and should become? Or merely a hallucination, a pipe dream? I didn't know. Then one afternoon, during a rare study break, Charles and I wandered into the room where they keep their Gutenberg Bible."

As she spoke, three or four other Olivias stared back at us from door-size screens. Each of these Olivias held a Gutenberg between her fingers with a variation on the same deadpan expression, aimed either at her signature device or turned directly toward the camera. Occasionally the three-dimensional Olivia would pass in front of one of her 2D sisters, giving her the momentary likeness of a multiarmed Vedic god or bodhisattva.

"These were the kinds of things I was talking about, there in Widener, when Charles—after patiently listening to my litany of troubles—paused to stare into the pages of one of the first printed Bibles. Charles, do you remember what it was you told me?"

"Of course," I lied. "But you're a much better storyteller."

"'Look at this,' he said. 'This is a technology that changed the world. It wasn't easy for Johannes either. You're in good company.' I needed that, at that exact moment. The next semester I dropped out, and that's when all this really started. It took a while to get things off the ground, but that was when Kenosis was truly born. Thank you, Charles."

The Secretary and Sam looked as if they were contemplating a token of wisdom personally delivered by Ram Dass himself. I'll admit, Olivia's effect on people befuddled me. In public, she had none of the wit I associate with the truly charming—everything she said came after a measured delay, during which her brain calculated its optimal response, and the resulting paragraph was tooled to convey an endearingly geeky vibe while hitting the necessary talking points. She'd slide into a version of what I've come to call smart voice, that vaguely Canadian pseudo-accent pitched down a step or two, an affect popular among provincial nerds, anime fans, insecure graduate students, and roughly a third of all podcasters. While Olivia had occasionally entered this mode during our college years, she had more unfiltered esprit back then. Now this fake Olivia had supplanted the witty one, letting her out only for a rare aside when we were alone. At her persona's core was a politician's tact, but this was wrapped in the tone of a precocious kid's science-fair spiel, brimming with awkward enthusiasm and loaded with facts. I think it might be that her lack of charm was charming—she was a sincere nerd with nothing to conceal her ambition and mission, and this had a disarming effect. But having known her before public life, I could see how this authenticity had been market tested and fine-tuned.

She continued, "That's the other reason why I named our technology after Gutenberg. To remind myself that what we're doing here isn't easy, will never be easy, but we're in good company."

I thought I saw the Secretary wipe a tear from his sunken eye. Impossibly, the hum of the machines seemed to swell under the culmination of her speech, lifting her words to ecstatic heights before setting them gently at our feet. By her closing lines, the devices had gone nearly silent, as if they, too, were taking in the gravity of her utterances. That's how persuasive Olivia could be. I may not have understood it, but I couldn't deny it. She could inspire a machine.

One of the technicians approached us as we made our way out of the lab. He didn't look anywhere as handsome as his peers. He was much older, with a hoary muzzle that made him resemble a geriatric Labrador, and teeth like a pug's. He obviously belonged with the specialists, not among the nubile ranks of the lab techs.

"Olivia, may I have a minute?" He spoke with an Australian accent.

"Mr. Secretary, Mr. Paca, Charles, this is Tim Murnane, our rare Cambridge PhD in a sea of MIT, Stanford, and SNIT boys. He runs the clinical lab."

Tim gave us a perfunctory nod.

"Olivia—it'll just be a minute."

"Tim, I can't talk right now. I'll find you once I'm done with these gentlemen."

Suddenly Clif showed up and ushered Tim off.

"Forgive Tim. I find that, in dealing with the many geniuses we have working here, it's best to treat them like the temperamental artists they are."

Her guests nodded. I thought I detected something behind her calm exterior—a hint of rage or embarrassment in the parts per million, but it came and went unnoticed by her dignitary buddy and potential investor, who didn't know her nearly as well as I did. In any case, I could relate. Though Obnoxious was packed with more poetry and ceramics MFAs than biology PhDs, I knew what it was like to herd talent.

While the two men admired a gigantic model of the Gutenberg II outside the lab (picture a chrome tiki torch mounted on a tripod), I pulled Olivia aside.

"Hey, sorry to bring this up right now, but that guy I introduced you to the other night is still missing. The good-looking guy from my label. Thane. Did he say anything to you about leaving town? Did you notice anything strange? He might be ghosting me as a power play. We think he might have taken off to Falda Linda. His girlfriend is headed up that way tomorrow. But who the fuck knows."

"He might've mentioned something like that. Falda Linda. I didn't spend too much time with him after we left you. I passed him off on someone."

This was exactly what she'd texted me the day before. She was acting cagey, but it had been the same way in college whenever I brought up anyone she was sleeping with.

"I didn't realize he was, you know, important. How important he was to you. I thought you wanted him out of your hair. He seemed kind of fucked-up."

"Yeah, he has some problems. We think he might have relapsed."

"I think we found him an Uber home. But I'm really sorry to hear this. Let me know what I can do to help."

The diplomat and the capitalist joined back up with us.

"Charles, I'm going to take Mr. Paca and Secretary Slobodkin up to my office to see their results and chat a little more. Want me to get one of my girls to let you out?"

"No worries. I'm sure I can find my way."

"Sick. I'll see you tomorrow."

My first shift as the incarnation of my dad's dark, gorgeous money was over. The three of them stepped into one elevator and I took another. Inside the bright booth I slapped my pass against a panel and pressed the button for the lobby. But as I went to stick my card back in my pocket (the only fashion offense greater than the incel Irish newsboy hat is, in my humble opinion, the unnecessary wearing of a pass), I accidentally bumped my elbow into the button for another floor.

After a short trip down, the doors opened. Beyond the cheery glow of the elevator was a pure black rectangle. I smelled stale beer. And it was cold. I could see my breath.

The door began to close, but I stopped it. I was curious.

With one hand still holding the door, I stuck my head out and shined my phone around.

There, on rows of racks about my height, were piles and piles of bags of blood. They flopped over one another like piglets on the teat. Some had fallen on the floor, where they'd ruptured, leaving scabs as big as doormats. As far as I could tell, in the limited aura of my pretty hate machine, the rows of racks stretched about as far as the sylvarium.

I thought I heard something stir far down the aisle. Fear made time skip for a second, like a scratched CD. I released my hold on the door and let the elevator carry me back into the spa-like serenity of the lobby.

## 6

After our road trip, once we'd started taking our second class together, I decided it was time I introduced Olivia to James and Eugen. There was a student play the boys wanted to hate-watch, so I invited her along.

She met up with us right off Mt. Auburn. James was distant, as usual, and Eugen projected some friendliness that to an outsider might seem sincere, but I could hear the irony it was laced with.

"I've read about you," Eugen said. "Are we any closer to a cure?"

She rubbed her head. "I think cancer is winning. But I'll let you know if we manage to come up from behind."

"Then I'll give you a pass for stealing my hairstyle."

She was perfectly concise, giving him nothing to sink his teeth into. We set off down the sidewalk.

The play was in an unventilated black box in the basement of one of the dorms. Eugen and James particularly hated its playwright and star, the daughter of a Grammy winning music producer who, with completely unearned confidence, put on about a play a semester, each with PSA-ready topicality. This one featured not one but two pressing issues: child hunger and sex trafficking. I thought this would be a fairly low-stakes venue for Olivia's introduction to the group, since their attention would be directed toward something other than her for most of the night. But as I sat there watching the personification of Hunger lead a girl to a one-eyed pimp and an obviously doomed life, I knew I'd made a terrible mistake. The walk home would certainly consist of a ritual roast of the production. It would become a test, to see if Olivia could hang and talk shit. Eugen and James would certainly flex the critical muscles our parents had paid so dearly to enlarge, and I knew that if Olivia tried defending the play, she'd stand no chance as part of our vicious pack.

The tragedy ended predictably, with the hungry girl killing herself to end her torment. The death scene took a good five minutes, and there was a lot of fake blood. James pretended to wipe a tear from his eyes. Eugen's stomach growled audibly, a sign that he'd wisely dissociated. I looked over at Olivia, but I couldn't make out her reaction.

We filed out. Eugen shook the writer/director/actor's hand in the lobby, spewing false praise to a point even I found excessive.

As soon as we stepped outside, James and Eugen began their critiques. But before we were even a block away, Olivia fell on the ground and started writhing. We were all freaking out. I thought it might have something to do with her illness, that I'd caused her to overexert herself somehow. Now I was about to be responsible for the death of the girl who would've cured cancer.

But then she started talking, repeating the monologue we'd just heard in the theater word for word. She even managed to nail the actor's intonation. This exceptional performance was delivered with even more brio than the original. Eugen belly laughed. James suppressed a dry WASPy giggle. I'd never seen either of them do that.

She was a hit.

The night after the play, Eugen insisted that I invite Olivia to a party he was throwing at his apartment. It was our regular debauchery den. There was an Algerian-themed café on Brattle, not far from his place, and Eugen loved it so much that he'd lifted its aesthetic. He had a pair of curved daggers on the wall, some silver Moroccan tea sets lying around, and finely carved snuffboxes with gazelles on them, among his many other Orientalist bibelots. This was all tastefully offset by his prized Can and Siouxsie Sioux concert posters (whereas James and I were punk purists, Eugen's love was for Krautrock and the new wave). We liked to make fun of his decor, but only up to a point, as his place was our preferred location for getting high, fucking our second-string girlfriends, and/or drinking until we puked in his toilet, thanks in no small part to the stimulating atmosphere. And Eugen—owing to his Soviet heritage, I figured—could hold his liquor like a still and his drugs like a pharmacy. He'd not only give you the trail mix of pills you required to feel something, but he'd also be there later to get you water or a bucket, a gentle dragoman once the evening crossed the border into entropy.

Our gathering was far from its inevitable joyous obliteration, with only me, Eugen, James, and our extraneous paramours passing a bong around. While I waited for Olivia to show up, I stared at a picture above the couch I hadn't noticed before. I'd been snooping around—I still thought Eugen was a drug dealer, and I'd been looking for his scales and other incriminating paraphernalia. The black-and-white photograph showed two men in frock coats, both with ample, fern-like manes. At first, I thought this was a photo of an OMD or Cure-adjacent duo riffing on Edwardian fashion, or maybe a couple of old-school Teddy boys from the fifties, but as I got closer, I could see it was practically a daguerreotype. The man on the right looked impossibly like Eugen in a wig.

"Who is that?"

"Oh, that's my grandfather. Good-looking guy, huh?"

Before I could inquire further, Olivia showed up, dragging her overstuffed backpack along behind her.

"Want a beer?" I asked.

"I really shouldn't."

"How about some tetrahydrocannabinol?" Eugen asked.

"Sure. Okay."

Eugen rolled her a fresh joint with a level of skill usually found only among European train passengers and anarcho-punks. The two of them began talking about how her research was going. I'd been roped in to mediate some half-hearted argument between James and one of his girlfriends over whether or not the Beatles were any good. James was of the opinion that they weren't.

I kept an eye on Eugen as I nodded along to James. Eugen was definitely making a move, in his blunt Soviet way. It made me nervous.

Now you're thinking, this asshole (me) was in love with Olivia. At a remove, it would make a lot of sense, I get it. But she wasn't my type. More than Eugen or even James, my new friend reminded me of my dad, with her single-minded determination to sculpt out a place for herself in the wet mud of history. I had enough instinct to know that dating someone like Charles Sr. would likely result in a suicidal gesture or two on my part. Besides, she was much more valuable than a mere girlfriend. In my twenty years of life up to that point, she was the first woman who I really felt was my friend. No—I'll say it. She was my first real friend, penis or no. Her pure, Graily quest and teenage proximity to death meant that she wasn't capable of using me, and it changed the usual stakes of companionship. If she and Eugen dated, there was no way she and I could hang on to that. I'd always be seen as (to borrow the language of a later era) some pathetic, friend-zoned beta cuck. I had to do something.

"Olivia," I said, "can I talk to you outside for a moment?"

We stepped out onto Eugen's balcony. He had an old patio table out there, covered in coffee mugs that had filled with rainwater. A few packs' worth of cigarette butts floated in them like drowned worms.

I wanted to tell her about my family on my own terms, before Eugen lobbed something at me and forced me to do damage control. I also thought it might derail Eugen and bring me and Olivia closer.

"Olivia—I feel like we've really become friends, and so I figure I should just lay it all on the table. My family is evil."

I stared into the distance for dramatic effect. My eyes landed on the orange light of a Dunkin' Donuts.

"How evil? More than average, for Harvard? Like, genocide evil? Are they South Africans? Nazis?"

"No, not that. Well, some of them were definitely Nazis, but that's not what I'm talking about. American evil. Rich evil. They're really rich, I guess is what I'm getting at. I didn't say anything at first because I didn't want you to judge me on account of them."

"I mean, I kind of got the idea anyhow. You have a rarefied-air vibe. You said something about Lake Como when we were studying all those Italian painters."

Had I let that slip by? I thought I'd been careful, but some facts were bound to shimmy over my mental paywall.

Olivia leaned against the railing. "How can I put this? Getting sick made it impossible for me to forget how short our time here is, and there's so much I want to do with mine. As a rule, I don't do things I don't want to do. I wouldn't be your friend if I didn't like you, man. Don't worry about it."

I was happy with that. Though I'd hoped there'd be a little more drama, I still felt my confession had jumped our friendship up a level or two. We went inside, and both of us drifted back into the conversations we'd abandoned.

Despite my gesture to force intimacy and dilute their chemistry, Eugen and Olivia quickly became close over the next few months. For growing up in a collapsing/nascent police state, Eugen was remarkably cultured, and I think he did much of the work of catching her up on the humanities. If she ever really did read *Moby-Dick*, it was probably then. I saw her lugging around some John Wilmot (Eugen's absolute favorite), his battered copy of *The Flowers of Evil*, Frederick

Seidel, and a translation of Arnaut Daniel, some long-dead trouba-
dour Eugen was always trying to get me and James to read. Olivia
usually credits me for Kenosis's medieval motifs, but I think it was
Eugen, really, she copped that from.

One evening, as I sat smoking a joint on the high steps of Widener,
I spotted them across the yard. They looked like twins with alopecia.
The pair was headed my way, but they were so deep in conversation
that they failed to notice me flailing my arms at them, so I gave up.
They walked around the side of the steps, resting on a bench about ten
feet below me. Their bald heads shone in the light of the lampposts,
and I could see all the lumps and dimples in their scalps' upholstery.

I was going through my pockets, looking for things to throw at them,
when I realized the conversation was more serious than Olivia's usual
ramblings about her cancer research. Through the din of the anxious
graduate students behind me and a tour group halfway up the stairs,
I overheard Eugen say clearly, "Chuck's just not ready." So the two of
them were dating after all, and they didn't think I'd be able to handle
the news. I tried to catch more, but the tour guide drowned them out
with her trivia about the library's many underground levels.

It was then that I started brainstorming some radical gesture that
would realign their loyalties to me. That summer, Eugen was planning on attending a fancy poetry workshop on some Greek island, and
Olivia was going with him. They hadn't bought their tickets yet, which
gave me an opening I could weasel through. In one partly interroga-
tive, partly declarative, wholly manipulative sentence, I asked if James
and I could go, too, and offered to book Eugen and Olivia's flights.
Gauche, I know, but I was younger then and willing to use any weapon
in my arsenal (the main, maybe only one, being money) to get what
I wanted. My generosity made saying no much harder, and inviting
James gave me extra cover. But after going along with the plan for a
week or two, James flaked. He said he'd forgotten that he'd already
planned a trip to Berlin, but I knew he simply didn't want to go. I'd

rolled right into position as the third wheel, and there was no taking it back now. I prayed the workshop would keep Eugen busy enough so that I could hang with Olivia.

This was about a year or two into Greece's economic collapse, and so everything was cheap. I had dad's assistant book rooms for Olivia and me at the same hotel where Eugen and his poets were staying, and the family fleet had a jet that crossed the Atlantic a couple times a week, so it was easy for us three to ride along. Olivia's eyes widened when she stepped into the cabin and gazed upon its generously spaced armchairs, so I figured I'd at least scored a few points there.

The hotel was a beautifully disintegrating structure, seemingly made of chalk. It left white powder everywhere, though admittedly some of that might have been cocaine. Eugen and I had both independently procured a solid Fleetwood Macload. We were doing everything short of putting it in our coffee.

The poet who was leading the thing, Eugen told us, was mostly known for a poem about a Central American general and a box of human noses. Eugen liked him okay but complained about the idiocy and tastelessness of the other members of the workshop, whose output consisted mostly of fairy-tale retellings, enjambed scientific facts copied and pasted from Wikipedia, and found poems remixed from *Us Weekly* articles. I spotted three of these aspiring bards on the beach one night: two men in tweed vests and a woman in an ugly, almost Victorian gown. We avoided them at all cost.

I noticed Eugen started wearing a silver ring after we'd landed. This shiny bulb on his finger, with a design I couldn't quickly make out, ran counter to his taste, which usually dictated his life ruthlessly. I thought it might be some gaudy mobster heirloom, but I didn't want to ask him about it. He'd been a little sour toward me for crashing the trip. One afternoon, while he was lecturing Olivia on a truly nasty poem by Catullus about face fucking, I managed to get a good look.

Finely etched in the silver, with each line thinner than a hair, it showed a man on the back of a stag, which in turn stood nestled in a crescent moon. The deer rider resembled Attila the Hun, or a member of Pantera. Under all that human fur, at that tiny scale, you could see the family resemblance. It was a good piece.

He caught me looking at his hand. "What?"

"Is that new?"

"It's very old. Used to be my grandpa's. It goes with the knife, which was his, too. The guy loved to hunt. Kind of ugly, and it weighs a ton, but I miss that old piece of shit."

I considered making fun of it, but I didn't want to irritate him further. I suddenly missed James, who'd happily talk shit on Eugen with me.

In the spirit of the class that brought us together, Olivia and I checked out an overgrown Byzantine church and the ruins of a tiny temple to a Phoenician god named Melqart. Other than that, there was almost nothing to do except get high and jitter in the sand.

One night Olivia and I decided we'd return to the temple after hours and get stoned. As we got to the hill where the temple sat, we could hear music and saw shadows gliding across the busted pillars. Hiding behind one of these, we spied on Eugen and his overdressed poets, drinking wine and dancing around a fire to bad techno. While I felt a strong aversion to my friend's literary cohort, I nevertheless wanted to crash the party, but Olivia put her foot down and insisted we give Eugen some space, since the workshop was the reason we were all there in the first place. I didn't think they'd care, but she wouldn't back down. We found an empty cove and got baked there instead.

On the fifth or sixth day, I found myself alone on the beach. We'd partied through the night, and now it was 4:00 a.m. Eugen and Olivia had invited me to join them on a walk just before sunrise, but I'd chosen instead to performatively sulk alone. My plan had failed. If anything, I'd lightened the pressure (socially, financially) of their first voyage together. The wrench I'd gently tossed into their plans had only helped tighten the screws, making their true love run smooth.

I lay there for at least an hour, until an old woman poked me with a stick to make sure I hadn't died. Once she walked off, I checked Get-Together. There was James in a string of foggy underground clubs, posing next to statuesque women with impeccable cheekbones.

Not long after that I spotted my pair of Michael Stipes walking toward me, smiling like idiots.

"I'm headed in," Eugen said. "I need to read the poems for work-shop. We're looking at another with the word *ribcage* in it. Wish me luck."

"I hope it's unflinching," I said.

Eugen smiled and walked over to the hotel.

Olivia sat down next to me.

"Last time we were on a beach together was our San Narciso trip. You were there for me when I thought I might fall apart. This feels like the right place to talk to you about this. I know I can trust you. Charles, I need your advice."

She was acting strange. Her usual self-assuredness was gone. It was just like the night she told me about her deadbeat dad. The vulner-ability was exhilarating, I have to admit. I was thrilled she sought my counsel.

"Look, I know I should have told you this sooner, but my numbers are bad. I didn't want to ruin the trip."

So that was what she'd been talking to Eugen about, outside the library.

"You should have. Fuck. What if something happened?"

"I know. I know. But here's where I need your advice. Eugen's father knows a clinic where they'd be able to try out a new, experimen-tal treatment on me. Stuff that hasn't received approval in the U.S. I won't go into the technical details, but it's unconventional."

More Eugen shit.

"He says we could go straight from here, right when he's done. I think I want to try it. But it's risky, and the side effects could be very long-term. I've done my due diligence, and at least I'm much more informed than your average patient, but I just don't know. What do you think I should do?"

The sun was just coming up. We watched a fisherman bash a giant pink octopus against the side of a boat. He held its tentacles like the stems of a bouquet and kept a pretty steady four-on-the-floor beat until he was positive it was dead.

I wanted to tell her not to go. There was the safety concern, sure, but really I just didn't want her to get closer with Eugen. Hideous thoughts, I know, but I was twenty-one. Death was like Australia: I accepted the fact of its ridiculous existence, but deep down I suspected it wasn't real.

But making my case against the treatment wasn't the best way to get what I wanted. I knew that, in her situation, if someone told me no, I'd want it more.

"I think it's worth a try."

So now you know—the advice I gave her, which she credits for saving her life, wasn't exactly heartfelt. But I don't think anything I said had any effect on her decision. There's no persuading the Olivias or Charles Grossheart Seniors of the world. Like the latter's pet zebras, they can be nudged a little, but they'd sooner kill you than turn around. I have the scars (physical from the zebras, emotional from Dad) to prove it.

"Promise me if I come out of this in one piece, we'll still move to San Narciso together."

"I'm going whether you make it or not."

She threw some sand on me. I shoved her over, and she barrel-rolled to play up the impact.

"You hit me right in the cancer!"

Something fell out of her pocket. I picked it up.

It was Eugen's knife. I handed it back to her.

At the end of the week she and Eugen flew to Moscow (things were happening fast, even by Putin-lackey standards), and I took a lonely jet home.

When Olivia came back, she was cured.

## 7

I pulled up to the gatehouse, where a woman in a performance fleece greeted me with a waiterly spiel:

"Namaste! The light within me bows to the light within you. If you could just confirm that we've received your credit card deposit, I can point you to your cabin and/or Volta charging station."

"I'm with the Kenosis group."

"Excellent. One moment please and I'll let you through."

The gate was your typical slatted steel-disguised-as-wood common among the mansions on the stretch of coastal highway south of San Narciso, something that communicated California laid-back charm while still keeping out the unwashed masses. But this wasn't your average kleptocrat's money-laundering estate, this was the Tamyen Institute. And so in the middle of the gate was the equivalent of a coat of arms for their post-acid, futurist brand. This intricate, heraldic metalwork was divided into thirds, a fancy pie chart displaying the institute's core fixations. The top-left wedge was filled with neurons fondling one another in a starfish orgy. Next to it was a slice of hexagonal tessellation, almost a tidied, abstract rendering of the first wedge. Finally, on the bottom, a cluster of pines and ferns with the occasional deer popping through. Together, these three pieces represented Tamyen's holy trinity of profound human thought (Father), world-saving technology (His sexier, savior Son), and the mystical serenity of nature (the ever-neglected Holy Ghost), respectively. I'd seen this emblem bathed in golden light on Instagram so many times, it was like running into a famous actor—still handsome, sure, but also much smaller and less charming than I'd expected.

The gate slid back, and I drove through, into Tamyen.

I parked my car and got out just as Clif pulled up, blasting Metallica in his Bugatti Veyron. His vanity plate read DAZKPTL. Clif was a troll in every sense of the word. Not wanting him to ruin my first view of the grounds, I climbed the nearest hill and took it all in from there.

Tamyen! There was the redwood dining hall, the dense pine groves, the organic-vegetable garden, the yoga studios, the firepit, the hot tubs fed by underground springs dotting the cliffside terraces like prairie dog burrows. To think, I now stood where several minor Beats had seen God, had their ecstatic orgasms, and/or killed themselves. The very same spot where, decked in robes like stoner samurai, Miles Paranoid took his first koto lesson with Minoru Sawai. (Paranoiacs will know this, but for the more casual fan, this was after Miles had parted ways with Serge.) I could feel my own synapses go into double time off the residue.

They needed the workout. Beyond my presence at the demonstrations, my duties as creative consultant and adviser on ethics could've fit on the toe of one of Olivia's nanobots. It wasn't for a lack of initiative on my end, for once. I did everything I could to show I'd snorted the Kenosis Kool-Aid powder. The day after that first tour, I inherited my predecessor's office and quickly got to work making it my own. She'd left behind a lot of her stuff: books on ethics, a photo of the Dalai Lama, a stone with a Jack Kornfield quote scratched into it. The Buddhist stuff wasn't really on-brand for me, but most of the books were keepable; they'd be useful props in maintaining the illusion that I knew anything about ethics, other than what I'd gathered from Ian MacKaye. I shoved everything else in a box and found a room at the other end of the floor with some leather La-Z-Boys and a flat-screen TV—a makeshift lounge, I figured—and left it there. I spent the rest of the afternoon on eBay hunting decor. I picked up a suitcase record player, a stately walnut coatrack, and a nice Remedios Varo print of some maidens trapped in a tower. It wasn't work, exactly, but I felt a great deal of satisfaction in these finds, knowing I'd taken the first step in cultivating a beautiful space for all the creating to come.

There wasn't much, it turned out. The most creative thing I'd done so far was make a series of intracompany memes about the Gutenbergs using stills from *Police Academy* and *Three Men and a Baby*, and a terse email from Clif put a stop to those. I'd sat in on a couple meetings with the chief creative officer, a Redfordesque man Olivia had lured away from a firm housed in a Michael Graves–designed building downtown. I mostly spent those hours doodling in my notebook (I was creative, after all) as he and his team discussed Kenosis's brand identity. He explained that they were in talks with an Academy Award–nominated director—you know the one, with the quirky movie about the haunted motel in Wyoming—and I used the opportunity to shank my credibility by dismissing the auteur as hopelessly twee. I think the others were grateful when I stopped showing up to meetings, and I figured my best place was by the side of our fearless leader as her shrewd, unflappable vizier. But I soon discovered that my liege's time was in short supply, and that the laid-back college hangs I'd envisioned just weren't in the cards.

I was a creative consultant with nothing to create and no one to consult. A special adviser giving no advice and not feeling particularly special. Usually I would have relished the idleness, but the timing was off. I'd been counting on a reprieve from Obnoxious. Sydney had been a huge pain in the ass ever since she'd come back from Falda Linda.

It looked like Thane had gone up there after all. After asking around at all the hotels and cabin-rental services, she'd finally found a motel that had a record of Thane staying there the night after he disappeared. Just one night, but it was something, the only hard evidence we had of what had happened to him since Olivia's party. Sydney had tried to hunt down the receptionist who'd checked him in, but she'd left to attend a music festival in Jirudo Hills, and her coworkers had no idea when she'd be back.

In the weeks since her trip, Sydney had refused to leave the warehouse, claiming it was too traumatic to have to go back to the apartment she and Thane had shared. She'd been using our office as her base of operations, calling all their friends and family, irrigating Louise's shoulder and the arms of our sofa, harassing the police, and interrogating me. While I was thankful for the occasional distraction offered by the investor tours at Kenosis, these brief excursions weren't enough. Sure, there was plenty of real estate in the warehouse, but just the thought of Sydney, holing up in my office like a gloomy raccoon, sapped the energy out of me, energy that should have been spent finalizing the release of her record.

The Tamyen retreat couldn't have come at a better time. Tamyen was about an hour closer to Falda Linda, so I told Louise and Sydney I'd go back up to the mountains and ask around again, try to track down the receptionist and see if anyone had spotted Thane since he'd checked in that night. My plan was to spend two days at Tamyen, then quickly dip into Falda Linda before I came back and acted as if I'd spent the whole weekend on Thane's trail. I could always use the spotty mountain reception as an excuse for ignoring Louise's and Sydney's texts. This would show I was taking Thane's vanishing act seriously and help me earn back a little of the trust I'd eroded by dismissing Sydney's concerns.

Out my window even the trees looked like they might've graduated from RISD. I'd always wanted Dad to host a Grossheart corporate retreat here, instead of another sweaty big-game hunt, but he thought the staff would lace our oatmeal with LSD and expose us to the dangerous truth of the oneness of man. I was forbidden from ever going. But now I had an excuse! For the next three days I would join my peers on the Kenosis leadership team as we harnessed Tamyen's ambient creativity and . . . well . . . I didn't know exactly what we'd do with it.

Soon we would be meeting up in one of the tubs. Already I could see my shirtless colleagues headed to the hot springs like corporate macaques. I dropped off my bags at my cabin, reluctantly changed into my swimwear from the outfit I'd bought for this creative getaway (a smart Jan-Jan Van Essche getup, a flowing brown jacket with matching pants picked just for this occasion), and walked down to the pools.

I'd left the cabin barefoot and shirtless, thinking it'd be a short walk to the tub. But in my awe of the shimmering grounds, I'd underestimated the distance, grossly. I could feel the talented eyes of Tamyen's many unwinding visionaries on my pale and flabby torso as the rock of the cliffs sliced my feet into sheets of prosciutto.

About halfway to the tub, I eyed a fellow traveler (much leaner, much more prudently dressed) on his way back to the cabins. I was about to look down and feign dignified invisibility, but then I recognized him. It was Joop Hull, the legendary litigator. Probably famous to you for representing the winner of the popular vote / loser of a crucial election, equally renowned for defending the winner of several Academy Awards / loser of his production company thanks to his relentless, systematic abuse of aspiring actresses. Famous to my father for his "poetic" NDAs and their enforcement. Famous to yours truly for helping me out of one of my more humiliating detours on the road to success.

"Joop! It's me, Charles Grossheart."

He gave me a quick glance, like I was a pop-up window. "Say hi to your dad for me." Joop breezed by.

I let my tender feet rest a moment and watched him briskly shrink toward the masseur's bungalow.

I did eventually make it to the tubs, where two Kenosis execs bobbed around like hard-boiled eggs. Speaking of eggs, I could smell some. It wafted off the water. Still, my tenure among the punks had granted me sewer-rat levels of olfactory tolerance. After taking in the laughably gorgeous, citric sunset over the Pacific, I slipped into the swimming-pool-size "conference tub."

I was pretty sure they were just some lesser department heads. One was Equinox trim, and the other could have passed as my body double. The tops of our guts were beginning to redden in sync. Among other things, turning thirty had fucked my metabolism. I had moved from fun-size to party-size, but I'd learned to carry myself with a gym rat's confidence. While my body double lacked my self-possession, he had a thick beard, which I envied, as half my face was covered in the dermatological equivalent of salt flats, where nothing could grow.

"Tyler, from Engineering," the bearded one said. "This is Leif. He's associate director of playing online poker and watching ESPN on the clock."

"Project Management. And, hey, everyone is entitled to his own work style."

I gave a curt nod. Thanks to my family and friendship with Olivia, I was not to be fucked with. I knew my brain would shut down immediately should I task it with making small talk with these human Jet Skis. I leaned back into the ergonomically designed tub wall and listened in on their chatter.

"I just think the obsession with climate change is so shortsighted," the fit one continued, loud enough to make it clear he was performing for me. "We'll have that solved in no time. And then everyone will have been hysterical for nothing. And finally we can move on to the bigger picture."

"Like what?" Tyler asked.

"I mean, the whole Kenosis mission. It's going to be much harder than climate change. But that's why I'm here. My hope is to cure mortality in my lifetime."

"A true believer," Tyler, my torso twin, said, turning to me. I suddenly recognized him as the doubting Thomas I'd overheard the night of the party. And the other had been the one talking him down. "I'm curious about death. I want to die, eventually."

Leif laughed. "Of course *you* would."

I'd heard many similar points before, mostly from my dad. Aside from expanding his vast wealth, his main passion in life was to make sure his life would never have to end. Like many of his fellow tycoons in the 0.0001 percent, he'd been caught up in the whole cryo craze, but I think he was ultimately wary of counting on his boys to defrost him. Lately, he'd shifted his hope to genetic research, but as much money as he threw around, they were still a ways off from killing death, thank God. What good is being an heir without death? I'd be obsolete.

I thought Olivia's talk of immortality was just a hook, an El Dorado that she, a corporate conquistador, could use to inspire her troops on the shore of a vast, tricky continent. Up until then, it hadn't occurred to me to leverage the immortality business. It would certainly give me a one-up on my brother, Peter, the good Abel to my angsty Cain.

The conversation in the tub turned to rumors of CEO bunkers— the latest trend of high-end fortification for the coming class/race war these titans of tech were presently busy bringing about. According to the bro with the minuscule BMI, the founder of a forum popular among neo-Nazis had just purchased half a county in Oregon for him and his Olympic-gymnast wife to populate in the apocalypse's feudal aftermath. The VoltAire CEO, everyone's favorite futurist douchebag, was currently tunneling under a solar farm in Wyoming, and rumor had it that he and his electronic-musician girlfriend were training an elite, all-woman squad of bodyguards equipped with cybernetic weaponry.

"Clif is into that shit, too," Leif said. "He's a real aggro connoisseur. I went out to his place in the desert for a weekend of 'tactical training.' The guy has an arsenal out there. He's got assault rifles in the bathrooms, SIG Sauers under the couch cushions, samurai swords above the beds, even an OG Kalashnikov prototype in his dining room! That gun is his fiancée."

"How'd the 'training' go?"

"We fired off a few rounds, but then mostly we just watched *Bloodsport*."

Olivia appeared, along with a posse of other upper-level Kenosians, many of whom I had yet to meet—or maybe had and forgotten already. She wore a classic black one-piece like the kind you might see on an old pinup. The sun had just set minutes ago, and as she and the others lowered themselves into the water, a circle of braziers around the pool ignited simultaneously, casting our pale bodies in orange light. Whereas for many the sudden illumination was, at best, unflattering, it had the opposite effect on my friend: her arms and shoulders looked cut—you could see every string in them.

The chief creative officer, the swolest of us all, gave me a half-hearted wave. He'd been avoiding me since I dissed the director of his commercial. I'm guessing his thinking was that if he was too nice to me, I might show back up at his meetings. He didn't have to ice me though. There was no chance of that.

"I hope everyone is letting their minds and bodies recharge a little in all this beauty," Olivia said once she was in the tub.

"The brimstone really gets the juices flowing," Tyler joked. No one laughed.

"The baths feed from a stream deep underground," Olivia said. "The mineral content is what makes it restorative."

"No, I really like it." He sank a few inches deeper.

"Clif had to hop on the phone with an investor, but he's not exactly the creative type anyway. Let's get started."

She gave a short homily about Tamyen's history as a geyser of creativity, having spewed forth some of the most important discoveries of the last century, then bragged about Kenosis's successes so far. It was boring as hell, but looking around the circle of transfixed executive bathers, you would have thought she was telling each of them how they were going to die.

"So much here is going so well. We have our CMS approval, our partnership with R and W, talks with the military. But, as most of you know, we've been hitting some minor bumps, mostly with figuring out how to bring this technology to where it's needed most. I know that together we'll not only find the way to get over this human-testing hurdle, but to become a revolutionary force for global health and human rights.

"Some ideas have been floated, but frankly they're all fucking bullshit. This weekend, we're going to open ourselves up and tap into our real creativity. With all the brainpower here, we should be able to take care of this easily."

Tomorrow we'd be assigned "Virgils"—poets who'd been given fellowships by one of Kenosis's backers—to guide us in our creative process. Until then, she encouraged us to get some good rest and refill our reserves so that we'd be ready to get our hands dirty.

"Keep in mind, these hiccups are part of the territory when it comes to leading the field. Don't be discouraged. If you wanted something easy, safe, you'd be working for one of the dinosaurs, pimping people's data. But you, all of you, are driven by a hunger to do something fucking *real*. We're right where we need to be. Remember, rather than problem solve, we problem seek. This is the work."

Before we left, one of the Virgils, their leader, I guess, stepped out of the shadows to read to us. He was tall, bearded, with the side of his head shaved and way-too-long bangs clipped back, a haircut that might have been acceptable in 2010. His poem was impossible to pay attention to. I stared at the surface of the water, imagining how far it had traveled just to heat our gooches, and tried not to laugh whenever our poet repeated the words "my father."

Despite my growing fear that it wouldn't, the poem did in fact end, and while some of the goons lingered to kiss Olivia's ring, I retreated to my cabin. I had the cover of semidarkness this time around, and my feet were already numbed by the pain of my first trek. Still, halfway back, several of my peers managed to overtake me somehow, laughing and running over the razor-sharp rocks like delinquent gazelles. I stepped aside and let them pass, jealous of their bulletproof feet.

As I walked into my cabin, I thought I heard someone behind me. I thought it might be Olivia, breaking away from her sycophants. But when I turned around, no one was there. The ocean was loud, and a pack of execs was still down at the tubs. It was probably just some random harmony between their chatter and the waves. I shut the door and began to brainstorm. Not about Kenosis's problems—I had no clue what these were in the first place—but for ideas as to how I was going to kill the next few hours.

Unlike Olivia and her leadership team, I hadn't exactly been burning the candle at both ends in pursuit of world-changing technology. I had no lost sleep to make up. If anything, I had a surplus. I figured I might join whatever party I could find, but when I stepped out of my cabin, I found that the entire Tamyen campus had gone dark.

There was no way I'd be able to get to sleep before two. I took a hit off a pre-roll, a choice strain called Universal Healthcare, and decided that, in the tradition of the many stoner geniuses that had gone before me, I'd go marijuandering around the grounds.

The cliffs looked like a good place to start. The water clapped and fizzled against the rock a good fifty feet below me. Two bright lights blinked on a massive liner near the shore. Watching the vessel float by, I thought I could make out my logotized surname (what amounts to my family crest, with the last two letters kissing to form a Valentine heart) emblazoned on its side. It wasn't great for my high.

The family business is all nebulous to me, a godlike organism with a mess of demigod bastards, peculiar consorts, goofy and destructive incarnations. Here's what I know, sprayed with a Grossheart Industries polymer coating of self-protective irony. In addition to Grandpa's old operation refining the sludgy remains of prehistoric microorganisms, we pulped trees into both computer and toilet paper, produced a not insignificant percentage of the world's plastic bags and baggies, harvested the earth's subterranean hydrocarbon farts, and dabbled in a little factory farming here and there, employing, all told, 140,000 or so people in about seventy countries. Oh, and there's also Grossheart Unity, which was formed to scoop up some missile defense contracts in the eighties and nineties, but nowadays mostly makes drones. (My dream, after Dad died, was to produce an industrial/drone record in the presence of some of the prototypes, something nearly unlistenable, obviously titled, and loaded with significance.)

I didn't come there to contemplate the dubious sources of my family's income. I turned back to survey the grounds proper, much like Miles Paranoid and the lesser Beats had, when torrents of creativity and amphetamine offered their scintillating brains no rest. I set a brisk pace. My legs felt like two buff lads holding up my brain on a palanquin.

A minute later I tripped over a Buddha and fell face-first onto the rocks. I must have somehow racked up some good karma, because this Enlightened One was jolly and edgeless. He gave me what I knew would turn into a bruise on my shin as I hit the ground, and (I'd notice the next morning) a barely visible scratch on my face.

I lay there collecting myself and thanking the great teacher for the darkness and lack of viewership for my fall. But I might have been wrong about that. Before I got up, I heard a rustling behind me. This time there was no mistaking the source. The sound had come from the direction of the cabins, not the cliffs. I did my best to play it off as if I had no clue I was being watched.

I brushed off the gravel and peeled a flower from my leg. Clearly the smart thing to do was simply address this fellow nightwalker, who was probably just bored like me, or retreat to my cabin, lock the door, and call a guard. But the weed had given my logic an experimental bent.

My best option, I thought wrongly, was to draw whatever it was into the light. One cabin about three down from mine had all its orange lights on, a lonely jack-o'-lantern among the dark pumpkins of the other yurts. I made my way toward it. I could still hear my stalker behind me.

As I reached the cabins, my pursuer picked up speed. I heard it/him/her/whatever getting closer. It began to hiss like a raspy, chain-smoking python, and then I became truly afraid. Something brushed my back, and my heart went into a blast beat. Ignoring the pain of my tender feet, I bolted toward the light.

Now I could see into the luminous rooms of my refuge. Inside, a shirtless Joop performed hanging sit-ups from a bar above a door, all while reviewing a stack of papers heavy enough to double as a medicine ball. His torso was incredibly detailed—it made you think of chain mail, or the gills of a shark.

I rapped on his door, and he flipped down to let me in.

"There's something chasing me," I whined to old, ripped Joop. "It hissed!"

He walked outside fearlessly, moving much as I imagined he had when he stepped forward to argue before the highest court in the land. I figured he'd easily be able to bludgeon my mysterious stalker, be it basilisk or hobo, with the phonebook-thick pile of papers he still held in his hand. But whatever it was, it was gone.

Still silent, Joop picked up his phone and texted someone. In less than a minute, a guard appeared to usher me off to the safety of my cabin. As my escort and I left, I watched Joop grab his packet with one hand, the pull-up bar with the other, and resume his awesome routine. Both Joop and the yawning security guard hated me, but who cares if your protectors hate you? Does the castle give a shit about the slimy insults of its moat? Does gold resent the stony indifference of its vault? The guard stationed himself outside my cabin for the rest of the night. I slept like a monk.

## 8

After a disappointingly healthy breakfast (vegan porridge, mostly chlorophyll), we were paired with our Virgils. Olivia and her people had put together a spread of poets that was about as much of a letdown as the breakfast offerings. There were too many boys. I say this as a feminist and patron of many hard-core artistic women, I swear. Their leader with the bad emo haircut returned. In his company, a man with a flattop haircut, Wrangler jeans, and haunted eyes. An androgynous person dressed like Dennis the Menace. A Black poet in a hoodie and skinny jeans. A pair of lanky, overmanicured twins with stringy blond hair, flannel shirts, and flat-brimmed gentrification hats with springy feathers in their bands (think *Desire*-era Dylan at brunch). Aside from the odd blouse from Target and light vintage cosplay, the women in their ranks looked like reasonable adults, and I hoped I'd be paired with one of them.

The bruise on my shin had turned galactic (purple, green, black, an oddly bright yellow in its corona), but otherwise I was fine. I chalked up last night's scare to a classic bout of pot-induced paranoia and was glad the only real witness was a man I could trust to maintain attorney-client privilege.

The poets threw a marathon reading, mostly to communicate pedigrees, a classic dog-and-pony show of the type my family, thanks to my mother's pet MFA program, is used to. This stuff was fine, I guess, but there were too many sad birds, dead rabbits, and submerged traumas for my taste. Two of the poems were about cutting your own hair.

Then a latecomer showed up to join the mob of bland bards. Her face was familiar—I knew her. Alexandra Liu. She'd dated a bassist in one of the Obnoxious bands about a year ago and had hated me deeply. She still hated me, I was sure of it. The hate people carry for me has a Twinkie's shelf life.

Fortunately, I'd dressed to accentuate my creativity, not my crustiness, and I was wearing sunglasses. I'd also aged considerably in the last year, thanks to some genetic timer running out (lending credibility to Olivia's speeches). That would be enough to keep Alexandra from recognizing me, as long as I didn't draw any undue attention to myself.

She read last. She was going by A. K. Liu now. I hid behind some fellow Kenosians. When she concluded, an assistant showed up to pair off the poets with their pigs. I overheard one of the poets shit-talking—a special frequency I'm attuned to like a female cricket to her boyfriends—and listened in: "I'm sick of this Beat bullshit. The Van Zachs won't stop talking about them, when they're not off hiking or posting pictures of themselves with their shirts off."

I knew exactly who they were: the pioneer twins. And seconds later I was paired with one of them. Things could have been much worse: I could have been partnered with A.K.

I decided to take the lead and guide my Virgil to the remote "Art Barn" on the other side of the campus—a long journey, since my Van Zach kept trying to turn over rocks, and I kept steering him off the path whenever I thought I heard the voice of my poetic hater. Luca? Gunnar? was dense, sure, but not too bad a guy. I asked him about his necklace, which prominently featured, I'd soon learn in the folksy yarn that followed, the penis bone of a raccoon. He riffed about the bone's provenance nonstop until we reached the Art Barn.

Inside, we walked over to a plaque commemorating the suicide of one of his beloved poet forebears, the mildly celebrated Pete Gongfermor, and my Van Zach started reading a poem off his phone in his honor. I'd assumed it was one of Gongfermor's, but the lines about the Kardashians and runs of random patois made me think otherwise.

"That wasn't Gongfermor, was it?"

"No, that was one of mine. Kind of a Gongfermorian homage."

I knew how to fan the flames of artsy ego and, keeping an eye out in case Alexandra decided to lead her exec our way, asked the broet about his work. This three-day residency was the catch for some prestigious fellowship. But since winning this one, he and his brother had both garnered another, even more prestigious, from one of the pharmaceutical heiresses, and they now found themselves among what they believed to be a lower class of poet. They didn't even need the fellowship, he admitted, thanks to some prudent investment in crypto years ago.

"But, hey, it's a great chance for the two of us to see our unpoetic brother."

"There's another Van Zach?"

"Yeah, dude. You know Leif? He's a project manager or something like that with y'all."

I pictured Leif in a brunch hat and vest. I don't know how I didn't see it sooner.

After my pet poet complained about his peers for a while, we admired some of the statuary (babes made from typewriter parts) and bonded over our shared fear of getting canceled.

Being in the presence of such a desperately authentic goofball made me paranoid about my own realness. My life was a beach ball: big and colorful, sure, but also full of air, made of synthetic material, and easily popped. I've seen the Cindy Sherman photos, I know the self is a performance. But as my Van Zach paced among the typewriter babes and frantically jotted poesy in a Moleskine no bigger than a deck of cards, I was filled with disgust. Superficially with him, but really with myself.

We left the Art Barn, and I followed my poet around as he looked for an entrance to the maze of abandoned underground steam tunnels rumored to connect the buildings (legend had it Gongfermor had dropped acid and/or jerked off in them). When it was time for lunch, we parted with faux amicability at the door to the dining hall, and I rushed to put some food in me before I could be recognized.

As I shoved salad into my mouth, Alexandra struck up a conversation with someone next to me. During a pause in their chatter, I could feel her eyes on me. I stared at my arugula as if it were the Talmud. When I looked up, she was gone.

I fled the dining hall. I couldn't risk Alexandra recognizing me, so I played sick and decided I'd trade my Virgil for the many Beatrices available to me on Pornhub. The typewriter babes of the Art Barn, along with the stimulating fear of A.K., had turned me on somehow. I told my sweet, dumb Van Zach the food wasn't agreeing with me, and we parted ways for good.

On my way out, one of Olivia's assistants reminded me that the leadership team would be gathering in the McKenna Lodge in an hour. I asked if the poets would be staying all day, but he assured me they'd be shipped off once our team regrouped.

As I got closer to my cabin, I found Alexandra and her exec sitting about three yards from my door. I hid behind an anvil-jawed bust of Pierce Inverarity commemorating his founding of the institute and kept an eye on them from there, but it sounded like they were composing some kind of complicated ghazal. I listened to their limp collaboration for more than half an hour before they left and I could finally slip back into my quarters.

My horniness had vanished. My thoughts turned to Louise, Thane, and the ever-present barge of shame I always tug behind me. Was I as off-putting as a Van Zach? Did I finally need to be honest with Louise? Kinder to Sydney? Should I at last forsake my vile father and awaken to the beautiful, mysterious, ever-unfolding presence of eternity?

Luckily I didn't have too much time to sit with these useless thoughts. I had to find the lodge.

Despite the elegance of Tamyen's layout, I somehow managed to get lost on my way to the meeting. I had no real excuse, as the lodge was by far the grounds' biggest building, sitting dead center and elevated enough to never be completely out of sight. I simply figured that, given how small our group was, we'd be meeting in one of the cabins by the vegetable garden, not the enormous wooden cinnamon roll that dominated the campus.

This—the contrast between our team's size and that of the lodge's interior—made my late arrival particularly noticeable. On the cover of one of the pamphlets in the antechamber, I saw Neve Olmert, the sexy professor I'd spotted at Olivia's party. I grabbed it for some light reading material in case I got bored and reached for the door, opening it as slowly as I could to keep my entry quiet. This didn't help. The door heralded my arrival with a loud, whiny creak.

Inside, the space was empty, save for another, smaller dome suspended in the center. Thanks to a near-invisible wire, this translucent white tent hung about three feet above the floor, looking like the ghost of a gazebo. Under this levitating skirt I made out a circle of chairs and the legs and asses of my colleagues. It took a while for me to get to them, with each step slapping through the space like the gated snare on a Peter Gabriel record.

Other than Clif (who greeted me with a dead-eyed Putin stare he surely picked up from his mobster buddies), my peers were good sports and played it cool as I ducked under the dome and took the seat saved for me.

"Like I said, no idea is too out there," Olivia repeated for my benefit. She was wearing a black Obnoxious tee, which reassured me that

I wasn't on the outs with her. "Turn off your filters, your editor, your guards, and let's see what we can come up with. This is about flow. We can do this. Some of the smartest people I've ever met are right under this dome."

Tyler, the bearded bro from the hot tub (the one who'd wished to maintain his mortality) was the first to speak up.

"Okay, so this has actually been something of a pet project of mine for a while. It's not going to sound too similar to what we're doing with the Gutenbergs, but bear with me. I think it fits nicely with our mission and core values. I mean, 'Obsess,' right?"

His idea had something to do with working with Indigenous communities to maintain a network of sensors to protect and collect data on delicate ecosystems. While he rambled on, I flipped through the pamphlet I'd picked up at the door.

*The Silk Canopy was cocreated with 6,500 live silkworms in the lobby of the SNIT CoLaboratory,* it read.

> Using cutting edge transgenic techniques, architect / artist / engineer / thought leader / professor Neve Olmert and her team were able to design silkworms that produce spideroin, the complex protein chains found in spiderwebs, resulting in a bioengineered thread stronger than steel and as soft as a scarf. "In more than one way," Olmert says, "a silkworm is a sophisticated, multimaterial, multi-axis 3D printer." Her diverse body of work includes the development of intricate wax sculptures created by hundreds of wasp-size robots, biodegradable camping equipment in cooperation with REI, and a line of high-fashion garments inspired by biological structures.

The pamphlet featured a photo of the impossibly hot professor holding one of the silkworms on her finger. She was LA skinny, and her face was intentionally disrupted by renegade curls. Her lips formed a tiny, beautiful sofa.

Olmert believes these humble worms, each no bigger than a crayon, might be the future of manufacturing. "The Silk Canopy speculates about the possibility to implement a biological swarm approach to 3D printing. Google is for information what swarm manufacturing might one day become for design fabrication." The Canopy is a feat of collaboration on every level—between the worm and spider DNA, between man and nature, and between the very worms themselves. We hope that you might draw inspiration from these amazing creatures during your time here at Tamyen.

The do-gooder finally finished up his pitch. "Anyway, aside from helping local communities and animals and trees, I think this could be great for PR, and it could take the pressure off the Gutenberg technology. At least until it can catch up to our vision."

Apparently, Olivia found this as dull as I did because she didn't give him any feedback, not even a nod. We all sat in her silence as she studied the weave of the dome.

"I think I might have something," Leif said once it was clear Olivia wasn't going to respond to the monologue we'd just been subjected to. "This is more about the human-testing impasse, so if you want me to hold off on that, I can."

"No, Leif, please go. That's really why we're here. Lay it on me."

"Well, I was thinking," the nonliterary Van Zach began. "We're caught in a Kafkaesque, *Catch-22* situation. We know this technology can help people, but—with the animal-testing hiccups—we can't know the adjustments we need to make until we test it on people. And we need something to show for our work, fast. Even with the Secretary and his buddies from the State Department helping us, it still looks like the testing in Uganda is going to have to wait. Then it occurred to me. We could use our unfair advantages here. What if we flew a small test group somewhere, implanted the tomes, and measured the results from there? That could give us some data for R and D to work with, and, more importantly, it'd give us something to tell investors, many of whom despise the FDA anyway. Some rather vocally. Chartering the plane will be easy, and I'm pretty sure we could come up with an island between us." Leif looked right at me.

It was true—we Grosshearts were in possession of a little princedom among the Lesser Antilles, mostly for the tax breaks and occasional rehab junket. And Dad wasn't exactly fond of government regulations.

"We have more than enough to make sure our subjects are compensated, and we've already received hundreds of emails from people begging for the tomes. A lot of these people are already sick, so they have everything to gain here, even if it is marginally riskier than their other options."

"They'd get an opportunity to help push the field forward," Olivia added.

"We're always saying, 'Don't just think outside of the box. Live outside of it.' In this case, I think we're going to have to test outside of it, too."

I could see Olivia conducting a clinical trial of the idea in her head. This was one of the things that made her a truly great leader. She could appraise the value of an idea with no attachment to her ego. She didn't have to come up with it—it just had to be good. Take, for example, the following anecdote from our college years. There was, in those days, a young woman in our circle who would not shut the fuck up about the nonprofit she dreamed of starting after graduation. We'd get drunk, and then, when all I wanted to do was find someone to fellate me, she'd go on and on about this imaginary organization. What was it? Some food-stall thing for refugees (her parents had fled a war somewhere) that would eventually set them up with their own restaurants. By the end of her pitches she was always crying, and some other girl, often the target of my affections, would hug her and tell her how good a person she was. I began to think she was pitching me, and

I was almost ready to write her a check just so she'd drop out and start the thing.

Sometime during our sophomore year, there was a contest for business plans with a special category for nonprofits, started by one of our wealthy alums trying to rinse the blood off his money. Remember, our beloved university had birthed a now-omniscient (soon-to-be-omnipotent) social media monopoly, and so everyone had a plan they were working on, save for me and a few other prudent classmates. For two months every party was a brainstorm session for the competition. And our little philanthropist was stoked. The consensus was that she would win, and the night after the deadline passed, she held court like Meryl Streep during Oscar season.

A month later they announced the winners. Our philanthropist was not among them. But an idea quite similar to hers had won, in a proposal submitted by future Kenosis CEO, Olivia Watts.

The philanthropist was pissed. She was not very sportsmanlike and filed complaints with both the alum's foundation and the administration, resulting in a full review. I was tickled and soon became obsessed. While we waited for the outcome of the case, the philanthropist published an op-ed in the *Crimson* that, owing to its venomous, unproven claims, had to be taken down from the site two days later. Here's the best part: after two weeks spent reviewing the submissions and complaint, the administration and foundation jointly determined that, while the ideas were undeniably similar, Ms. Watts's feasibility plan was superior. Their initial judgment would hold. The alumnus had, he admitted in an email to Olivia that day, been moved by her argument that she'd merely synthesized several models that had been proven to work elsewhere, and that if the board looked hard enough, they'd find that neither proposal was purely original. Had Steve Jobs invented the computer? The mouse? Did Nate Zuckerman, the bloodless founder of *the* social network, invent the idea of a website where you could stalk your exes and post racist memes? Execution, Olivia argued, was the whole thing. How could he disagree? Olivia would keep the ten grand honorarium, and the originator of the idea would finally have to shut the fuck up. That night I threw Olivia a party, catered with food from all the countries included in her hypothetical stalls.

As for the would-be philanthropist, she was so ashamed that she transferred to Obscurity State University. When the dust settled, Olivia decided not to move forward with her award-winning plan. It wouldn't be long before she'd come up with something better. The rich alum, knowing the value of a good pivot, didn't require winners to use the money on their proposed venture, so she was allowed to spend it any way she wanted. I took her shopping, and she spent the rest on weekend trips with me and my horrible friends. I think she even bought my ticket once, but I can't remember. I don't really keep track of those kinds of things.

"Great job, Leif," Olivia said. "Let's look into this as soon as we get back. I'm really pleased with this plan."

Leif beamed. His idea had accomplished our purpose, and after we kicked around a few more indecent proposals to round things out, Olivia let us go. My peers slipped out of the dome like cats through a gap under a garage door.

I decided to hang back and chat with my friend/boss.

"Think your folks might lend us an island?"

"I can ask."

"We've got another investor who has been trying to get me and Clif to come out to his island, so I'm thinking we can hit him up first. He's a bit more showy than your dad, which is cause for some concern, but we might be able to make it work. The scientists have some ideas, too. But we might need a backup."

I unfolded my pamphlet and showed her the picture of the hot architect. "I'm in love."

"I think I told you, we're not tight, exactly. My guess is that she's jealous of our tech, that she's threatened by what we're doing, reimagining medicine. She seems to think she has a monopoly on reimagining fields. She can't get through a conversation without reminding people she went to med school for five minutes."

"I don't know. I'm thinking we could collaborate with her somehow."

"It's not a bad idea. I'm sure I've internalized a little misogyny here. How about I let you take the lead on that?"

I bent over to leave the dome but clipped my back against the rim as I lurched forward. The whole structure began to wobble back and forth like a haunted chandelier. Before I could get out from under it, something skittered down the shell and banked off my head.

Once I was clear of the swaying bug umbrella, I picked up the fallen piece of debris off the floor. It was one of the worms, dried and twisted into a thin white joint.

We spent the rest of the day rewarding ourselves with massages and dips in the tubs. At no point did I see the scientists or Olivia—there was more work to do, but not for me. By dinner I was exhausted with all the deep-tissue work and repeated dilation of my arteries in the hot water. Maybe I'd bring my artists here, I thought. Or just Louise. No, it'd be better to come back alone, to get away from everything.

I got up early the next morning, around eight. Before I'd left for Tamyen, I had Sydney send me the receipt for Thane's stay with the receptionist's name on it. After a quick call to make sure she was working that day, I made my way toward the mountains.

## 9

The drive to Falda Linda is notoriously beautiful. Desert suddenly surrenders to forest, stifling heat becomes air hundreds of times more pure than San Narciso's signature thick miasma. I wondered how Thane had made the trip. Hitchhiking or ubering the three-hour drive from San Narciso proper seemed unlikely. My guess was that he'd asked a friend who had yet to betray him.

I was beginning to worry about Thane. Despite my assurances to Sydney and Louise, it really was disconcerting that we hadn't received a call or text from him yet. I didn't let myself think about what we'd do if he didn't come back.

Past my windshield, majestic pines with bark orange as Cheetos shone in the sunlight. It reminded me of the sylvarium, except overrun with a particularly invasive species, the silver-haired boomer. Falda Linda was home to hippies and libertarians, mostly, people of polar-opposite political beliefs but surprisingly similar facial hair, musical tastes, and attitudes toward the concept of authority.

It wasn't long before I reached my destination, a motel called the Exalted Rose. The place stood in charming, splintery disrepair, guarded by a platoon of chain-saw-carved bears with faces lifted from schnauzers.

The man behind the counter wore an unevenly tie-dyed shirt. The vortex of dye had only made it to one side, leaving the other half white enough for me to see the armpit discoloration.

"Is Marisa around? I called earlier and someone said she'd be here."

"She's in the back. Let me grab her."

Her eyes were bloodshot, and she carried with her an open-faced sandwich, half in each hand.

"I'm not high."

I didn't say anything.

"Okay, I'm high. You got me."

"It's okay. I am, too." I wasn't, but I knew this would be cause for fellow feeling. "So my friend has gone missing." I showed her various pictures of Thane from Google Images. It took a while to find one without any blood on his face.

"Is he famous?"

"Mostly just critically acclaimed." I told her the name of his band, but of course she'd never heard of them.

"Don't take it personally. I've given up music for the time being. I was listening to too much. It wasn't sustainable." She still held the sandwich.

"Do you remember seeing him? It says you checked him in at nine oh three."

"Hmm. I don't remember. Business has been slow. I would have remembered that guy I think. But it's been a couple weeks now. I'd trust the receipt. Here, let me check the computer and see if anything rings any bells."

She set the sandwich halves directly on the counter and began typing.

"Okay. Looks like he paid cash. Hmm. No bells rung. It's weird. I'm good at remembering stuff like that. You might check the coffee shop. There's a good chance he came through there. Tell them Marisa sent you."

I gave her my number and told her to call me if she remembered anything. For proof I'd been there, I took a picture of the dusty lobby before I left.

In front of the coffee shop I encountered a wood carving of what appeared to be a woodsy, interspecies orgy between a bear, a mountain lion, and an eagle, with a placard declaring it WINNER OF A NATIONAL CONTEST.

I went inside, ordered a coffee, and told the barista Marisa sent me.

"Oh, great. She just called and told us you were going to settle her tab."

She owed them $68 worth of lattes and blueberry muffins. I appreciated her guts and paid it, but when I asked the barista if she'd seen Thane, she said she hadn't.

"I would have noticed him. He's hot. Sorry I can't help."

I went back to the Exalted Rose to demand some weed as repayment for settling the tab.

Marisa and her boyfriend, a kind dummy named Brendan, invited me to the back room, where they were watching a long, beautiful infomercial about a knife that could cut through any substance: tomato, bone, pennies.

Brendan sat there explaining weed for a while before rambling about one of the latest conspiracy theories. It was like a plate from a foil-hat buffet, with scoops of the Illuminati and the Deep State, a serving of classic Trystero, a side of Golden Fang. He hit the familiar talking points: how some mysterious megacabal made all the voting machines, picked the politicians, and laced the water with emasculating chemicals.

As he went on, I extended my high consciousness outward, to see if I could detect any signs of Thane. (Tamyen had opened me up.) I envisioned these thoughts as Saturnal rings of mental sonar, slicing through everything like the magic knife before me, until they reached Thane's dense noggin. Would he stay up here forever, hiding away like Syd Barrett? I could imagine myself, encumbered as I was by the weight of my sinister family (part of the real cabal Brendan wasn't Marxist enough to see) and the stress of running a business, restarting at this altitude, hiking in the woods, getting wasted with Brendan and Marisa. But Thane? He had everything going for him. He was talented enough and, as the barista had reminded me, hot. More than anything, he was a musician, and he needed an audience. There'd be no one to witness him up here, and I couldn't imagine him lasting long. Still, Occam's razor, that knife of reason—everything was knife now, as the commercial played—told me I had to go with the hard evidence of the receipt, despite my peculiar suspicions.

As I drove stoned down the mountain, I felt I could see the car from behind and slightly above, as if in an old racing game.

# 10

Over the next two weeks I showed Murdoch levels of scion industriousness. Or to be precise, Murdoch levels of industriousness with
Guggenheim (Peggy, naturally) taste. And while we're at it, why not
sprinkle in a pinch of philanthropic Carnegie, since, as I'd heard
Olivia repeat again and again to our eager investors, what we were
doing was going to change the world forever and ever, amen.

For starters, the label had never been busier. The word-of-mouth
rumors of Thane's disappearance had grown into an impenetrable
kudzu of hype. Objectively, our vanished singer was a medium talent,
a Chevy Chase of punk musicians who I signed mostly as a result of
his connections and affiliations. But with the right story, the proper
framing, a medium talent can elbow a thousand geniuses out of a slot
in the pantheon. Thane knew this much, I thought.

The cherished local station, KCUF, had been playing the two singles on heavy rotation. I'd already arranged (or our pricey publicist
had) for *Sucker* to be reviewed by the last of the venerable music sites—
you know the one, now property of that prestigious publisher of fashion magazines, long-form journalism weeklies, and golf digests—but
the singer's absence had given them more of a story, à la "Free Earl."
After a short news post outlining his disappearance, it looked like now
the site was working on a longer profile of Sydney. They'd already
called Louise, and I eagerly awaited delivering my own heartbroken
contribution to the record's growing lore. Given Thane's volatility
and affection for self-sabotage, he was better to us gone at this point,

and while I still thought he'd probably show once he caught word of his growing pseudofame, I hoped he'd wait it out until interest in the record receded so we could get our second wind.

As for my fledgling career as a technocrat, my duties still largely consisted of courting investors. More specifically, it meant a lot more tours following Olivia through the capital of her fempire. After Tamyen, I thought my workload might shift, but there I was, trotting behind my girlboss a couple nights a week, smiling wealthily at the wealthy, listening to the Gutenberg story until I had it memorized like a Bible verse. During those first plucky weeks, when I was set on proving I was down with the cause, I wore a blazer, shaved adequately, showered, but by the tenth or eleventh tour I started showing up in my cutoffs, in fraying tank tops and denim vests, and Olivia raised no concerns or eyebrows. In fact, she relished my vestiary flexes, complimenting my deteriorating jeans and rank tees as if they'd come from the House of Worth. I was both the (platonic) Grimes to her Elon and the Elon to her Grimes. But really, with my munificent lineage, I was more like one of the trees in Olivia's sylvarium, only watered in money, basking in the golden rays of privilege. I didn't mind. Actually, it was fun, negging the semi-self-made. It reminded me of college.

Sydney was still making Obnoxious obnoxious, and my PI work did little to lighten things up between us. As the album release approached, I began handling my side of the label's business at Kenosis, and it became like a second or third home. (Louise was under the impression I was working at a coffee shop, finishing up a freelance project to make us a little more money.) I liked it there. Olivia had forced some Obnoxious tracks onto the company playlist rotation and bought three boxes of our shirts, so every now and then my spirits would be lifted by the sound of a scratchy riff sputtering out of the sound system or the sight of a Kenosis employee wearing the Obnoxious logo. I took advantage of my pass, which gave me access to everywhere, except Olivia's office (had to try). I even crashed there one night, just for the hell of it. After some bristly exchanges, the guards learned who I was and stopped asking to see my ID, and from then on it was like I was ten again, the boss's kid treating the office as his playground.

Kenosis was like the human brain—we only used about 10 percent of it. While the route of the investor tour bore witness to near miracles of construction and design that would've made Borromini kill himself all over again, the headquarters as a whole was still a work in progress. Entire floors were swaddled in pink insulation and showing their fetal rebar. It was like my warehouse back in La Tristeza, or even my parents' place. I felt at home in all that wasted space. I picnicked on the empty floors, leaving my trash behind and returning later to find it molding unmolested. I'm sure Olivia and her security team knew what I was up to, but her mix of trust and condescension allowed me to continue my meandering like Eloise in her hotel.

Still, I did my best to avoid the sanguineous floor below the sylvarium, which had left me with a traumatic aftertaste akin to what you might get from walking in on your parents' nonmissionary lovemaking. I assumed I'd simply chanced upon a makeshift medical-waste storage site, a temporary depot before things could be properly disposed of. It made sense. A little improvisation for waste disposal was par for the course for a company creating world-changing medical technology, especially one that would save so many lives and, in Olivia's telling, remove all human expiration dates.

One night, after a hasty feast at the company snack bar, I discovered an unfamiliar zone in the Kenosis labyrinth. Having ascended to the compound's upper floors, I was curious as to how low it could go. According to the elevator buttons, that was a cool, dark floor beneath the lobby, a seabed to which all Kenotic detritus fell. Stacks of chairs, dusty computers, three or four Siemens machines. (Olivia loved to complain about the threat of Siemens and LabCorp conspiring to get ahold of our technology, even as we subsidized their efforts considerably by swooping up theirs.)

As I walked the rows of these abandoned items, looking for pieces that might fit my office, I heard someone on the other end of the floor. A technician appeared, turned on one of the commercial machines, and, after a couple minutes, stuck a sample in before disappearing into a service door. While he was gone, I got closer, so that I was only eight feet from the door, lodged behind another Porta Potti–size analyzer. He came back, left again, and then finally stepped out with a shoulder bag and a thermos, leaving for the day. As he walked off, I managed to catch the door before it shut and slipped through.

It led to a stairwell, which I followed down. The air here had an earthy, mineral smell. The hidden floor was dark save for the glow of tiny blue lights inside the processors. As I shone my phone around to find the light switch, I heard a spray of Pomeranian yips scolding me from across the space.

I decided to keep the light off, lest it cause any more noise, and, using my phone to illuminate my path, followed the yips.

A few desks sat on both sides of the long corridor. I shone my light on one and found it was occupied by half a dozen stuffed animals and off-brand Beanie Babies of Taz, the deranged dervish in *Looney Tunes*, all with slightly different proportions and degrees of ferocity. You see these tchotchke-covered desks sometimes, sad shrines to a single species (usually penguins, sometimes frogs), in the cubicles of university administrators and bank managers. As the son of a man with his own sad, though much more expensive, collection, it never fails to fill me with pity.

I was far enough from the door that I figured I could turn on one of the desk lamps. Against the back wall I found a stack of cages housing eight or nine monkeys, each in its own cell, a simian jail. These little guys were clearly afraid. As I came closer, they sprang to the backs of their enclosures, cheeping in fear. So this was where they conducted the animal testing Olivia mentioned in her tours.

The cages were arranged in a loose pyramid, and spread across the top was an old, matted cat bed.

Then I saw the cat bed move. Another monkey's head pressed over its flimsy rim, revealing eyes the color of deli mustard and what looked like a funny hat—my guess was that he'd escaped his cage to sleep in this more plush setup.

Now that I'd woken him, he began to get up, and I could see he was munching on a bunch of grapes. Curiosity and, mostly, fear held me in place to study this beast as he studied me. In this tense inspection, I saw that my brain had smoothed over the deformities. There was no hat; a pair of twisted, bony growths stuck out of his head. As he rose onto all fours, it was clear that what I'd mistaken for fruit was actually a bulbous, fleshy beard.

The creature leaped at me, and now I could see huge Advil-colored folds of skin under its arms, which carried it right toward my face. Its mouth was open wide, revealing a set of butter-yellow fangs.

I screamed in some unmanly octave and ducked before it could attach itself to my face. It passed over my head, its pink feet and tail brushing my hair. I turned and saw the creature scuttle across the tile before vanishing into some hidden hole.

I got the fuck out of there. I needed to get stoned and fumigate the memories of the monkey and the now-resurgent bags of blood out of my brain. After texting Louise and stopping to pick up some provisions, I sped back to the warehouse.

A couple hours later, Louise was showing me a video of two guys on tall, double-stacked bikes jousting under the expressway. We'd holed up in my apartment behind the studio to smoke weed and watch weird VHS tapes from the nineties, but like any gathering of two or more from my generation, it had devolved to a screening of our latest favorites from YouTube. Before us lay a disappearing spread of snobby Whole Foods vittles slumming it with expired bodega fare. We were low on bowls, so I rinsed out two or three old ashtrays.

"In a weird way, I still believe these cookies were made by elves," Louise said as one of the jousters was unbiked by his rival.

"I'm starting to believe in the supernatural. I've been seeing some weird shit."

"Like what?"

"These weird shapes in the dark, when I wake up in the middle of the night. Ghosts, maybe. Or demons? One was definitely demonic."

"That's terrifying. I always thought you were pretty skeptical about that stuff. I've always considered you an atheist and philosophical materialist."

After swallowing the last of a deck of fancy Pop-Tarts, I asked, "What do you believe? I mean, I know you don't believe in God or anything like that, but do you think there could be, I don't know, like demons? Or ghosts?"

She grabbed a handful of M&M's from one of the ashtrays and talked with her mouth full of them. "My guess is that there are beings that exist on different planes, so I don't rule out ghosts, angels, and demons, but my hunch is that they are more complicated than the costumes at Party City. Something more in the Buddhist cosmology might be closer. I'm all for your inquiry into the numinous and would happily take this opportunity to thrust my belief system upon you—"

"Thrust away."

"—but don't you think this has something to do with Thane? Stress is a bitch, psychosomatically."

"Yeah, you're right. Probably not a good time to trade in my worldview. Start wearing a lot of linen and grow out my hair so I can put it in a topknot."

Louise rubbed my head. "I don't know if this barren field could put forth enough fruit for that."

"I'll shave it like a monk, then." I took a hit off our vape pen and passed it to her.

"Want to do a tarot reading? If you're feeling a little superstitious, it could be a useful ritual. Things are fucking crazy right now."

"I just want to get high. Higher. I don't want to come down until the *fifth* of July."

"I really hope it's not Thane you're seeing, with those ghosts. It can't be. Just remember you're under a lot of stress. It's probably that."

She bit the head off a gummy bear and offered me its body. I felt one of those acute, annoying pangs of love and attachment.

In a way that ugly little monkey did me a favor, shocking me out of my idle routine when Louise needed some attention and help with the release. I needed to manage Obnoxious beside Louise, not at Kenosis. When I woke up in the middle of the night haunted by that pink face and scrotal beard, I reassured myself that I was under a lot of stress with the Thane situation and the album release; that was what had chimerized this primate, adding its suite of clichéd demonic features. Besides, now I'd seen every part of Kenosis, and like any naked body, it was bound to have a few flaws.

## 11

By the time I arrived at Nezhmetdinov Hardware for Pro Laps' soft-release show, I'd pushed all this out of my head and focused instead on enjoying the ride on the twin pontoons of success that buoyed me. I was one of my father's prized zebras, free to nibble the lion-free grasslands of their estate in that cultureless rectangle south of the Dakotas and north of Texas. The last burps of adolescent disappointment had finally exited my mouth. I could finally taste success, and in two different flavors!

Now that I was getting what I wanted, I had absolute, illogical confidence that the streak would continue. Not only that, my baseline had shifted, and I got greedy. My old plan to distance myself from my family, which had been one of my obsessions in the year before *Sucker* dropped, lost some of its urgency. I was sure I could passively excel at Kenosis and expand Obnoxious without anyone knowing I was a biological sequel to one of the worst humans of all time.

I had to keep my glee to myself. There, among my label's pungent bands and inert employees, the mood was somber. Conversation consisted of a single topic: Thane's disappearance and its consequences, namely the hype around *Sucker* and (for the more Machiavellian) what that hype and acclaim might do for his discordant labelmates. So somber, but only out of obligation, with notes of excitement, too.

Louise was with Sydney, who'd front the band until Thane came back. Since his departure, the two of them had become close. Right now Louise was sopping up Sydney's tears in the greenroom. I was eager for the tour to start, which would probably summon Thane from hiding and get his girlfriend out of our hair and back into the grimy locks of his. I thought this show would be enough to do it, but it turns out he had the good instinct to wait just a bit longer for the drama to build.

The opener, a band called Satano Veloso, had just closed out their set with a cover of the Billy Barf and the Vomitones classic "I'm a Cop." They'd played with an understandably confused energy. The band's singer, known for his ability to piss into his own mouth onstage, respectfully settled on lacerating his chest with one of the hardware implements ripped off the wall.

Looking at the crowd, sweating through their black T-shirts and denim, I was proud of what I'd managed to pull off in service to the music I loved. Punk wasn't dead, but it wasn't alive, either. It was undead, a zombie genre, still moving but not looking too hot. To put it another way: it was an endangered animal, and it put me in a weird place. Was I supposed to keep the poor creature safe from harm in a little zoo and educate the world? Or fight for more habitat in which it might flourish? Was it my job to preserve the tradition? Or push it forward? The nostalgia, kept up by both collectors and bands themselves, all crate digging through the past, made what was once so cutting-edge seem like it could only look backward. But hybridity threatened to soften a music that, if anything, should be hard. The subgenera were band-specific, not born of scenes. I didn't have to look far to put the blame for the ebb of local scenes: the disruption of the music industry, the ad-driven algorithms of GetTogether, all of the fault lived here, in San Narciso. The best I could do was make a little space for bands and hope a scene might grow organically from there.

As the opener lugged their amps off the stage, I stared at an arrangement of dust-covered hammers on the wall and waited for the headliners to appear. Somewhere in the crowd was a music writer who wanted to talk about the band, so I struck a brooding pose and waited for her to come to me.

Off to the side of the hammers hung a picture of two men. Nezh-metdinov Hardware is just one of the many bars and purveyors of brunch in Kazakhtown named for the enterprises of its previous occupants. (If you're in the neighborhood, I recommend stopping by Tasmagambetov's Fish and Pet to pick up a record or two.) One of the men in the photo was dressed in what I assume was traditional Kazakh garb; the other—Nezhmetdinov, I'm guessing—wore an orange Hawaiian shirt. Each man smiled like a game-show host and held his own microwave. The photograph was absurd. It would look great in my office. I thought about stealing it.

As I considered the logistics of this, someone tapped me on the shoulder. But when I turned around, it wasn't the twenty-four-year-old goth I'd stalked online earlier. It was a man in his fifties or maybe sixties, wearing a white oxford spotted with coffee stains. He looked like shit, as if the late Harry Dean Stanton's corpse had been resurrected for one last, haggard performance.

"I need to talk to you."

"Who are you?"

"Tim Murnane. We met at Kenosis, a few weeks back. I run the clinical lab. We're coworkers, technically."

Now I remembered him, the pesky Australian scientist who'd flagged Olivia down on my first tour.

"How'd you find me?"

"I followed you here from the office."

First an Obnoxious artist had tailed me to a Kenosis event, and now a Kenosis employee had infiltrated one of my Obnoxious shows. I needed to think about taking less direct routes between my lives.

"Oh. Why didn't you talk to me there? I'm busy."

"It's not safe there. I . . ."

Right then Sydney stepped onstage. Since her partner's disappearance, she'd shaved her head in mourning, which meant I now hustled on behalf of not one but two buzz-cut women. Her fetid jumpsuits had been traded in for a more muted black-and-gray palette befitting her grief, which also contributed to her resemblance to Olivia.

"Can we step outside for a minute?" Tim pleaded.

I ignored him.

Sydney didn't acknowledge the audience at all when she sat down to play. She simply tapped the snare, fucked around with a drum key, and counted her bandmates in—the first time I noticed them at all. Much to my worry, Patty, the one who'd narced me out to Thane the night he vanished, had wormed her way into Pro Laps since his departure. It was only a matter of time until the shit she talked about me fertilized Sydney's vague dislike of me into pure hate.

Sydney went full Phil Collins, with a gooseneck mic craned over the kit. The songs were slower now, and the tossed-off lyrics of the original arrangements took on new, dreamy meanings that I knew for a fact were nowhere to be found in the album cuts. Her eyes were wet, her singing and playing charged with the kind of energy maybe most easily comparable to that classic Nirvana MTV set. I wanted to snort her sadness.

This was my time to enjoy the fruit of all our work, to stand proud as lord of my little scene. And Tim was fucking it up. As the set began, I thought I could inch away from him and no one would associate me with this sloppy uncle. But all through the set he kept poking my arm and uttering things I could barely make out over the music. I caught only stale and sour snippets.

"*Mmmmun*CONSCIONABLE*mmmmm*CHICANERY*mmmmm* MUFFELETA*mmmm*!" That last one seems unlikely but I swear that's what it sounded like. He was an unsightly accessory, a backpack on my suit. By the fifth song I figured it was time to take him outside to hear him out and get him off my back.

I took him to the smoking deck past the bar, an overgrown courtyard where someone had tastefully graffitied over the original, handpainted NEZHMETDINOV HARDWARE sign so that each letter was its own slithering leech or phonetic centipede. Many nights have I sat there, mystically fucked-up, staring at this insect alphabet as it crawled in and out of meaning along the hundred-year-old bricks. Everyone was inside, enjoying (or at least pretending to enjoy) the event I'd painstakingly curated, so we had the courtyard to ourselves. Suddenly I could relate to old Nezhmetdinov, having someone usurp the thing I'd worked so hard to put together. I knew just how he felt.

I sat on one of the lawn chairs, but Tim stayed standing, accidentally kicking over one of the old flowerpots functioning as an ashtray.

"I'm sorry I had to track you down here," he said as he righted the pot. "There was just no other way. I tried to get hold of you at Tamyen, but they kept a pretty tight watch on us."

"Were you the one who was following me that first night?"

"Sorry about that. Every time I tried to get close, you picked up speed, and then I think I scared you off. I tried whispering your name, but you couldn't hear me."

"Thank God." My worldview didn't have to collapse just yet. One more of those inexplicable encounters would have sent me following the YouTube algorithm to its inevitable lizard-person, ancient-alien, anti-Semitic end point.

"I know how all this sneaking around must look, but I had to be sure we were completely alone. They've been keystroking me. I think I may have even been followed here."

He was clearly having some kind of nervous breakdown. My best stratagem was to hear him out and pacify him.

"So what's going on?"

"That's what I'm trying to figure out. Nothing makes any sense. We're actually making some interesting little theoretical advances here and there, between my team, engineering, and a few of the guys down in the borough, but it's never enough for Olivia. We're *years* out from the kind of tech she's telling investors about. It's all very dodgy. The tomes we show off are just props. When they give those tests to investors, Olivia always ushers them off so we can sprint to do the actual test on a Siemens."

As he spoke, he kept inching closer to me and now stood right at the foot of the lawn chair.

"As it stands, the tome is much too small. It has to intercept blood samples, run an entire microfluidic assay, process the information, and transmit data. We pushed for something about the size of a strawberry and she lost her shit. Even this peanut is too big for her. And the lab! We have a real clinical lab one floor down that I run. She and Clif call it the 'cynical lab' because I'm always telling them to slow down, to wait till we have more data. Nothing too special, certainly nothing like the shit she's put together upstairs. The lab she shows off is pure Disney. We don't have a working product! The tome can do seven assays. Seven. Not the fifty she's claiming, and we're not even remotely ready to put it in a human. But we're still receiving more and more blood and tissue samples."

I recalled the conversation I'd overheard when I was about to piss myself in the cloister a few weeks back. And the weird floors I'd stumbled onto, full of blood and monkeys.

As if reading my mind, Tim went on: "They've been running illegal animal testing, too. From what I can tell, all the monkeys in the first round died except for one, and he has serious health problems. I think they're trying more, now. My best guess is that she's trying to jump right to the nanos, and that's why all these poor things died."

So that was why that monkey looked so fucked-up.

"Why would she do that?"

"I don't know. She keeps us all so separate so that she's the only one, she and Clif, who have the whole picture. It's bizarre. Last year I heard some people talking with Australian accents in the lobby. Turns out they brought in a scientist from Tasmania and didn't ask me to show them around or anything. They don't want anyone to know anything more than they have to. I have a sense of their regulatory strategy, though. She thinks that our CMS approval and the military contract in the works will be enough to work around the FDA. That's *not* a viable regulatory strategy—at least for any other company it wouldn't be—but with Olivia and her superboard, who knows? She seems to just bend reality around her like it's taffy anyhow."

In college, I avoided taking a required expository writing course for so long that, as I neared graduation, my adviser was forced to call the dean, who was more than happy to flex his clemency for the sake of the family name. Olivia, with all her connections to the deans of American commerce, diplomacy, and warfare, must have hoped for the same dispensation.

"From what I gather, Olivia's under the impression that once they try them on humans, they'll work out the bugs. But I don't know why she refuses to pare things back and take a little more time. Especially with the nano shit. I mean, it wouldn't be fast by Rancho standards, but we'd at least have a product. But that's beside the point. I'm here to tell you that you *cannot*, under any circumstances, let them use that island. People could die. I know there's another investor who has one—I caught wind of a chat in the hall—but I haven't found him yet. The guy I heard thinks it'll be yours. Please don't let them test there."

"I don't know, man. This is a lot. You're one hundred percent sure about this?"

"I don't do this lightly. There's a lot more I could show you, but it's too complicated to go into right now. I don't feel entirely safe. Can we meet tomorrow?"

"I don't know if I can."

"Just call me at this number." He handed me a slip of paper. "It should be secure. Use a pay phone."

"Where am I going to find a pay phone? I guess I can get a burner."

"That'll work."

He slapped his arm. A mosquito had sampled him right before he

flattened her. He studied his hand for a moment, then wiped the bug
and blood on his pants.

"Either Asian tiger or Australian backyard. I usually like to spare
the Aussies, if I can, out of patriotic duty. They came to San Narciso
around the time I did."

My neck was starting to get sore from the reps of slow, empathetic
nods.

"You're my hope here. Your parents are investors. I think if you tell
them, we can bring these issues to light before anyone gets hurt. I'm
on some of the patents, so I think they're going to keep me around to
rot, but we burn through so many people I wouldn't be surprised if
they let me go soon. We need to move on this."

We heard a terrifying, dying-animal screech from over the fence.

"What the fuck was that?"

I stood on a chair and peeked into the next lot. An ugly kid with ear
gauges and checkered Vans was taking out the trash.

"Did you hear that? Is everything okay?"

"Oh, sorry. I was just practicing my scream, for my band. Are you
playing the Nez? Do you want to set up a show?"

I ignored him and returned to Tim.

"Just some kid." I gave Tim a Sam Waterston stare, the arcs of my
eyebrows bending toward justice. "This is very serious. I'll do whatever needs to be done. I'll be in touch."

Just as I'd suspected, my attention sated Tim. He calmed down
some. The years subtracted from his face before my very eyes. I now
had the room I needed to wiggle away.

"Look"—I put my hand on his shoulder like a wise football
coach—"I need to take care of things inside." Louise had appeared
behind my distressed Australian zombie. "Go home and get some
sleep. You're very brave to alert me to all of this."

He surfed my stream of bullshit right out of the courtyard, through
the bar, and into the night.

"Was that him?" Louise asked. "I thought he'd be cooler."

"Who?"

"Our benefactor. Our tech Medici."

"Oh, yeah. That's him. Don't tell anyone."

"He's really embraced the normcore aesthetic. Did Jillian talk to you? I think this piece on *Sucker* is going to be good for us. I just hope Thane gets his shit together and shows up soon. I'm happy to be there for Sydney, but I need to get to work on my record if I'm going to keep my sanity."

"Maybe I should go inside and make the rounds then."

We turned to leave the deck, but before we got inside, there was another scream.

Sydney, her face slick with snot and tears, ran over to Louise. "They found his body."

She collapsed onto my girlfriend.

## 12

We were named Best New Record and Album of the Week and What I'm Listening to Right Now. Thane's body—according to what Louise relayed to me during her brief escapes from her now-constant companion—was found by joggers in Clemans Park the morning of the release show. An actress (most famous for her role in a show about bisexual bank robbers) tweeted her condolences to Sydney and posted a link to our title track. The corpse had mostly been mutilated by coyotes, who'd done much of the work of exhuming the body, but a good chunk of an arm remained surprisingly intact, enough that his tattoos, in concert with dental records and Sydney's relentless harassment of SNPD, allowed investigators to identify the body within hours of discovery. A British music site founded by a former critic from *The Guardian* made *Sucker* their lead review, with their managing editor declaring, after dedicating some respectful words in memory of the singer, the album could have been "focus-group tooled to win my instant love."

After five weeks, the arm was remarkably preserved. It had decayed so slowly it almost could have been reattached, the only signs of trauma being several holes, one of which was almost certainly from a syringe, the other two at the wrist, either the work of a particularly large coyote or, improbably, the elusive Clemans Park mountain lion, a creature with a GetTogether fan page who had for years now sustained a huge international following. It seemed nothing about Thane's death wouldn't draw a few clicks.

I managed to get some good pictures for Instagram at the funeral. Sydney beside the sarcophagus, red as a pimple. The deceased's uncomely Midwestern mother, a woman completely interchangeable with the mayonnaise-filled denizens of my official (but seldom visited) hometown. Like Olivia's cloister party, this was a very Catholic affair, and I snapped some quick pictures of the proceedings' papist wizard as he cast his spells over the closed casket. ("Nothing is lost," he lied. "It is only changed.") But all these felt a little gauche. I considered posting a photo of Thane's face on the brochure, but it didn't feel true to his aesthetic. I swiped through Google images of him, and while I did find a bunch of good options, most of them captured him in poses not exactly appropriate for a somber in memoriam. The pictures of him covered in his own blood after smashing his face with a brick, however dynamic the composition and lighting, were simply too evocative of the circumstances of his death to use for this kind of thing. There was a good one, though, of him spitting his own piss onto his audience that I just couldn't resist (these guys weren't too original when it came to bodily fluids). So I settled on the brochure with a bit of kneeler and pew in the background and posted this and the piss one together, hoping they might balance each other out. The condolence comments and teary-eyed emojis came rolling in right away.

This was a time of mixed emotions at the label. I resolved, in loving memory of our visionary artist's extinguished flame, to forge onward to make sure his last statement got its due.

Ah! Where would I have been in those trying times without Louise, my rock, the Mary to my William, the Sarah to my Lawrence. Louise was the one with the good sense to arrange for the live recording of Sydney's release-party set, and with the tasteful mix of the soundboard, an atmospheric room mic, and subtle overdubs, we had enough tracks for a live album. We'd start trickling out tracks once they were mastered and drop a vinyl pressing next year to extend the tail of the relative meteor the record was shaping up to be.

In light of her partner's untimely end, Sydney wanted to cancel the upcoming string of shows we'd booked to support the album, and while I was convinced one or two dropped nights would be good for us, I made her play the New York, Philly, and Chicago gigs. I guilt-tripped her some, telling her that the best thing to do to honor Thane's memory was to keep his songs alive on the road. She caved, but only with Louise's promise to accompany her as a human emotional support dog. I decided I'd have to find a way to reward Louise when this was all done. Maybe by paying off her student loans, or with an actual dog of her own, one of those perpetually popular Chihuahua-mix rescues that crowd the alleys and pounds of our city.

The shows yielded dozens of perfect photographs of Sydney and her grief. The photographers captured her anguish so completely that, despite their having been shot by different people over several nights in far-flung venues and cities, the pictures could have easily been assembled into a lacrimal flip-book: tears welling up to polish her eyes, spilling down her cheeks in exquisite rivulets, then a blotting out on her sleeve on the upbeat. A few reviewers used Sydney's performances as an opportunity to write essays on grief itself, leaving the quality of the music as a given. Skimming the luminous press, I was vindicated of my doubts about my insistence she play the dates.

I passed along my record of Thane's stay in Falda Linda and told the cops how Thane had accosted me at the cloister. They didn't ask what I'd been up to, which was a relief. They were more concerned with his behavior, and I answered their leading questions, confirming that he did seem fucked-up.

The next day I met Olivia in the sylvarium and told her about my conversation with the cops. She cut in before I had the chance to finish.

"Did you mention me?" She looked afraid.

"No. I didn't think it was relevant. I just wanted to let you know how things are going, I guess. I feel bad for bringing you into it."

"I'm sorry. I'm sorry this happened to your friend. I'm just a little out of sorts with all the bullshit I have to deal with."

I was still debating whether or not I'd tell her about Tim's paranoid rant at the show. I had no confidence in Tim as a person, but his tirade and my spooky discoveries had pooled into a suspicious aquifer at the bottom of my brain. Having been raised by a man of bottomless ego and suspicion, my gut told me that simply entertaining Tim's doubts might constitute betrayal in Olivia's eyes, especially now that she was so stressed-out.

Honestly, I didn't think much about all this and had faith that the authorities would find their answers, Kenosis's dubious corporate practices would get tidied up, and all of this would blow over. My worries about the investigation, my grief over Thane's death, the nightmarish visions in my employer's secret floors, all of this occupied just a sliver of my mind, eclipsed by another feeling, something so foreign it would have been frightening if it weren't so serene. I felt a great peace about things for the first time since Olivia hired me, a serenity that dwarfed that short pause between tribulations.

Humor me here, for I know what follows might amount to looking a gift castle in the moat. But life hasn't all been lacrosse, gap years, and crystal stairs for me. The shadows of my father's, grandfather's, and—not to neglect Mom's side—great(plus)-grandfather's legacies have blocked out the sun for me, making it impossible for anything of my own to grow. My entire bloodline envies and resents my frictionless path through the world, but at the same time, any hardship, any obstacle I put in my way to prove myself only amplifies their disdain for my ingratitude for the golden road they've lubricated for me. Now, miraculously, I could have it both ways. My label, the one thing I'd made on my own, was thriving *and* I'd achieved something on their terms, which is to say capitalism, by way of my involvement with Kenosis. Soon the investigation would be over and any risk of being prematurely exposed as a Grossheart would be gone. The album and Kenosis would be undeniable successes in their respective realms of art and commerce.

But of course every time I begin to enjoy my hard-won triumphs, someone shows up to pull down their pants and shit on my dreams.

This time it was Sydney, waiting for me on the couch in my office, thumbing her phone like a petulant teen. She and Louise had just come back from the Brooklyn and Chicago dates and spent the last day recovering on the second floor, lying around in their pajamas and watching cartoons among the rusty file cabinets and old munitions boxes. (Louise insisted on staying out there, hanging on to her youth and showing solidarity with our employees. I bought her a decent mattress so she'd stop complaining about her back.)

"How are you holding up?" I asked in a Bob Ross–soft tone. I crumpled my face into an expression of deep sorrow. After an unnerving incident with a nanny (marking the Grossheart boys' discovery of the devious applications of catfish bait), my parents became rightly worried that Peter and I were baby Bobby Dursts and had hired us an empathy coach. He'd been nominated for a Tony, back in the eighties, for his performance as a priest trying to rehabilitate a wounded fox, and he brought a mix of pastoral gravitas and Catholic discipline that made it easy to see why. Thanks to him, Peter and I could convincingly counterfeit just about any of the regular human emotions and even cry on cue. I owe much of my sexual career to that washed-up thespian, as well as a couple key mentions in my grandparents' wills.

Sydney: "Have the police come by yet?"

"No."

I thought she'd been playing a Candy Crush–style game on her phone, swiping her thumb around in quick zigzags. But now I saw the yellow slug sticker on the back.

"They found Thane's phone." She showed me the lock screen. "They're going to try to get the location data, but they told me to try to figure out his PIN. It's not anything obvious though. He was kind of weird about passwords. Still, I'm pretty sure there's a piece of paper somewhere with all of them on it. I don't know. Louise said there's a tech guy who supports the label that could maybe help."

"He might be able to do something. I'll ask. I can take it to him, if you want." The video of me with Olivia was on there.

"I'd rather give it to him myself, if that's okay. Something feels fucked-up about all of this. I think this could be the missing piece."

"I totally understand. I'm scheduled to talk with him this afternoon. I'll mention it then."

"Thanks."

I started going into the details of the next string of shows, but she just sat there swiping pass codes into the phone for a minute before interrupting me.

"Look, I need some rest. We can talk about all this stuff later. I've got a lot on my mind. I'm sure you understand."

"Please, do whatever you need to do. We're here for you."

She left, still staring at the dead man's phone as she walked out the door. A few minutes later I could hear her and Louise's footsteps on the floor above me, plodding about the industrial firmament like angels that hated me.

## 13

About ten seconds after walking into the lobby of the SNIT CoLaboratory, I bumped into what looked like a six-story sculpture of a tube worm. I watched the vibration work its way up the shaft and waited for a reprimand from a security guard or receptionist, but lucky for me no one noticed anything. I backed away and pretended to answer a phone call.

Such was the state of my mind. I'd spent the last two days hiding in my Kenosis office, obsessing over Thane's phone and the video inside it. I'd told Sydney our fake patron said there was nothing he could do, but she remained undeterred. According to Louise, Sydney and Thane's apartment contained mountains of paper—piles of songs, old set lists, decade-old flyers, press clippings, terrible poetry, and drafts of a science fiction novel set in the fourteenth century. While I was glad his untidy effects had bought me some time, I also knew that the password quest was Sydney's only grief channel and that she might at any moment find the combination that would unlock her rage. I didn't think its contents would help much. My guess was that he was likely killed by a fellow addict down in the park, someone who wouldn't have left any trace on his phone. It couldn't bring Thane back; it could only hurt me. I considered telling Sydney that I'd seen him making out with someone the night he vanished, but now I needed her loyalty to him. I got so down that I brought the SAD lamp to my Kenosis office so I could bid on guitar pedals I'd never use in its perky glow.

My obsession with Thane's phone makes little sense now. Getting outed as a Grossheart would've sucked, but I might have been able to weather it. Plenty of good artists have problematic parents: investment-banker dads, CIA-operative dads who've broken up democratic governments, lobbyist dads who fought for the rights of corporations to supersede those of people. We don't blame them for the geopolitical sins of their fathers. Now I know I fixated on the phone because my unease about Kenosis and all of Olivia's Secrets of NIMH felt too big to handle. My worry had found a more comprehensible object.

I convinced myself I had no bandwidth for Tim. I believed Louise, that the weird shit I'd encountered was a symptom of stress. Tim was just another hater, like Dad's wealth manager, Renata, like Peter, like Mom. Olivia and I were artists, and anything that disrupted the old status quo was bound to rile up these negative types. Tim would be proven wrong soon enough, and his case against Olivia would fizzle out. The best thing to do, I thought, was blow off the whistleblower.

When the UV rays and therapeutic shopping failed, I downloaded a meditation app and visited the sylvarium. There, in the shade of the indoor pines, I toggled through Scottish, Welsh, and South African bodhisattvas, watching my breath, scanning my body, and noting my cognitive sputters, respectively, but after thirty seconds of each I'd find myself flattened like a penny under trains of thought bound for Thane's phone. It was better to simply fuck around in Olivia's wood like a child looking to gorge himself on a house of sugar. Though I'd visited many times, I'd never ventured off the path, leaving most of Olivia's personal microclimate unexplored.

Kicking up the pine needles, I eventually stumbled upon a thin stream, no wider than my shoe, gushing from a spring just past the tree line. I followed it, curious to see where it emptied, and discovered a pond populated by a pair of gray frogs and spotted with lily pads. I sat down, thinking I might try another meditation, then saw some movement on the other side of the pond. Out of the trees, a deer stepped forward and bent down to take a drink.

I'd never seen a deer like him. His fur was silver, with a shaggy scarf encircling his fat neck. And he was fucking huge. His antlers could have held up a tree house.

"You've found Fyodor." The voice came from behind me and sent the beast running back to the cover of the trees. Its owner was a young man in tan coveralls bearing the Kenosis logo, a groundskeeper. He had that Tony Hawk complexion, California white.

"Fyo's usually pretty shy. It's a miracle he let you get so close." The groundskeeper peeked around a pine to make sure no one else was nearby. "Um, if you don't mind, could you not mention this to Olivia? Clif will skin me and turn me into a pillow. He said he would do that, when I was hired. He is, no offense, a huge dick. Please don't tell anyone else, either. This big boy's not here legally. We don't want the animal rights people on our asses."

"No problem."

With the basement monkeys and now this giant deer, Olivia's compound was crawling with exotic fauna. But Olivia's pet stag wasn't as unusual as it might seem. It's an ancient flex. Caesar dragged a giraffe back from Egypt after getting to know Cleopatra in the biblical sense. Pope Leo had his white elephant, Selassie his lions, Teddy Roosevelt his hyena, Michael Jackson his traumatized zoo. Back in college, in a course on Japanese art, I learned of one official during the Tokugawa shogunate who put a koi pond above his home's glass ceiling, so people dropping by would stare up in awe at the bellies of fish. My father engaged in this practice, too, though I would prefer any of the above creatures, any beast plucked from Lucifer's menagerie, to the contemptible striped horses he keeps around.

I stopped in the little white room just past the sylvarium. I'd barely noticed it on the other tours. It was mostly empty, save for a column of drawers resembling file cabinets. Having nothing better to do, and being nosy as fuck, I opened one.

It smelled like the stinky heart of Morcillo. Inside were the compacted bodies of birds, a frog or two, countless insects, and at least one squirrel.

"You don't want to see that shit, man." It was the deer boy, following me out. "This room sucks out any creatures who might contaminate the other floors. They get processed into fertilizer at least, the whole circle-of-life thing, but it's not pretty. The sound is as bad as the smell."

After that, it was almost comforting to think about Thane and the phone. But after a few more hours caught in this loop, I decided that the best thing to do was to substitute one fixation for another. I still had the pamphlet from Tamyen and would stare into the eyes of Neve Olmert, the gorgeous prof, whenever my brain conjured up the numpad of the phone's lock screen. But, as is the case with any source of pleasure, I built up a tolerance, and eventually the picture in the pamphlet no longer soothed me. I turned to her TED talks and a series of long, fawning profiles written by journalists as smitten as me, almost exactly the same panels and publications I'd found had featured Olivia, during my Kenosis cramming. With each video, interview, and article in this marathon, my resolve to touch the hem of her genius grew, and I put a plan together to visit her at her SNIT lab under the pretense of a Kenosis collaboration.

The drama with Sydney and Thane, along with the ever-present threat that the increased attention would out me, had been giving me so much stress that I'd been entertaining the idea of doubling down on my Kenosis career. I'd prove the creative director, Olivia, my parents and brother (pretty much anyone who ever knew me, I guess), wrong and show that I could actually amount to something. I could see myself in ten years' time parlaying my achievements at Obnoxious and Kenosis until I was a creative guru sought out by the Caverns' biggest companies, all while multiplying my wealth with shrewd VC investment. Plus, if Sydney and Patty brought me down with the phone, at least this way I had something to live for. Meeting with Neve was a kind of test run, my first real act as creative consultant and proof that I could bring the same resourcefulness and ingenuity I'd used at Obnoxious to my position at Kenosis. A partnership with Neve, one of Olivia's fellow patriarchy-shattering woman geniuses, seemed perfect, and it had the added benefit of getting me close to her.

So this was why I was at SNIT, bouncing off the sculpture. The towering lobby worm I'd nearly toppled was, it turns out, one of Professor Olmert's creations. It had two brothers and with them formed a crimped trio resembling pubes tweezed off a titan. They'd been made by "spinnerbots," which, like the dome back in Tamyen, were part of her grand swarm-manufacturing vision. Up close, they seemed to be made entirely of fishing line. When I was sure no one was watching, I brushed my fingers against the strings, then wandered back toward the doors to take in the lab.

In the years since I moved to the city, the San Narciso Institute of Technology had grown in tandem with the industry it fed and fed off of. As minds (carried by soft, usually white, almost exclusively male bodies) migrated from its campus to those of the nearby tech companies and cash flowed back into its military-budget-size endowment, SNIT had come to look more and more like the businesses dreamed up in its dorm rooms. No place embodied this more than the CoLaboratory, with its standing desks, exposed pipes, and white-walled minimalism interrupted by the odd Crayola accent. As for the layout, it was a kind of boxy Guggenheim museum, and from the atrium I could see all the floors of the CoLaboratory stacked high above me. The effect of the tube worms in the space was like that of seeing a daisy sprout out of a MacBook.

Somewhere among the futuristic vending machines and the juice bar was the worms' mesmerizing creator. I approached the front desk.

"Hi, I'm here to see Neve Olmert. Can you point me in her direction?"

"Do you have an appointment?"

"I'm with Kenosis. Um." I'd assumed I could just catch her in her office. One of the major disadvantages of my upbringing is that I don't know how anything works.

"I'm sorry, but I can't just let you up there."

"I mean, you could, right? Technically you could."

"I really can't allow unscheduled visits. I need to help the gentle-man behind you."

"Okay."

I hung back and watched as doughy geeks flashed their passes and walked through the plexiglass turnstiles. I considered retreat, but my mind returned to Thane's phone, and I knew that another day back at my office or apartment would result in an anxiety attack. I pretended to take another call and speed-walked a few laps around the worms, waiting for an opportunity to slip past the desk.

I didn't have to wait long. A film crew showed up, some five or six people toting cameras and microphone cases. Seeing them, the receptionist smiled and let them through.

When she turned to help someone else at the desk, I slipped behind a short woman with a boom. She looked at me for a moment, but I gave her a confident nod. I knew that, with my single-breasted wool Wales Bonner jacket and unfortunate Republican skin tone, I looked like I belonged in this hall of learning. The gate shut behind me.

As I walked down the hall, peeking into the sterile rooms of wires, computer monitors, and unshaven dweebs, I heard one of the crew mutter the professor's name. I overtook them before they reached the elevator and, stepping in first, took the spot by the buttons.

"What floor?" I asked.

"Five."

"Oh. Same as me."

I held the door for them as they filed out with their equipment.

When I pictured Neve's lab in my fantasies, I imagined it would look like the inside of a cicada shell, or the set of a Björk music video. A biodegradable dream. I was sorely disappointed. Her wing was made of glass, steel, and plastic—the very materials she denounced in her viral YouTube lectures. With the exception of some translucent tan sculptures here and there, the rows of computers occupied by serious nerds could just as easily have belonged at my brother Peter's offices over at Grossheart headquarters.

The professor and the rest of the crew were gathered at the other end of the room. To get there, we had to pass a line of plinths and display cases showing off the architect's greatest hits. "Experimental fashion" pieces resembling iridescent intestines. 3D-printed glass columns from an installation at the Smithsonian. At the end, a wooden chaise longue lined with pink nubs of artificial coral, a reef of nipples.

Once we were past these displays, I grabbed a clipboard off one of the vacant workstations and made my way toward the shoot.

"I love a good verb," the professor pronounced to the camera in an accent equal parts Israeli and elvish. "In fact, I think all nouns should be verbs. For example, *naturing* as opposed to *nature*. I often ask, 'How can we *nature* this building into being?' Also *Mother Nature*. We have the responsibility to *mother* nature. Languaging can presuppose the paradigm of our creative horizons, but it can also be a way out of those stiff paradigms."

I positioned myself just far enough from the film crew that I could pass for an interested colleague in their eyes, but close enough to the action that the professor's minions might take me for a production assistant. Behind the crew stood a line of supplicant postdocs and grad students, each presenting their own orb, flap, or cube, all seemingly composed of fingernails and dead leaves, to their empress.

Neve took one of these offerings, a dinky wishbone, and appraised it like a jeweler, turning it in her fingers for the cameras.

"Here, we believe in the future. A time when we will not build our houses, places of business, our hospitals and schools, but rather, we will grow them." She paused, conscientiously leaving room for editing. "Mind if I provide an elaboration? Something a little longer?"

"That would be just perfect," the director said. I'd picked him out right away. He wore a blue pajama shirt and had the bloated dandyism of Julian Schnabel. He might have actually been Julian Schnabel.

Another beat of rest and facial reset for the edit, then she began:

"We are working on something very big, a project that will change architecture forever. For centuries, humans have relied on brick, on wood, on materials like glass and steel. Whatever the material, the paradigm has been pretty much the same. Mine, build, mend. *Building* buildings. But we don't want to build at all. We want to *grow* our buildings. To usher in the age of the biodomicile." As she spoke, I experienced a little slap of déjà vu. This monologue was, rhetorically, syntactically, identical to Olivia's spiels, though with less performative geekiness and more performative artsiness. "Imagine, instead of painstakingly assembling a house, you simply plant a seed. A large one, sure, compared to, say, a mustard seed—we're thinking about the size of a small refrigerator, or a washing machine—and the house shoots up like a dandelion. But it doesn't end there. Biodomiciles will do much more than that. They won't need fixing. They heal. They don't need AC. They breathe. Instead of a security system, a nervous system. We've been working with our colleagues here at SNIT and already we've found promising combinations of cephalopodan, fungal, and arboreal DNA patterns. We're talking about a new, truly symbiotic relationship between *Homo sapiens* and the domicile."

After a few more shots of the professor examining the ugly baubles and reciting her go-to koans, the director spoke up.

"Okay, I think we have enough of this for now. We're going to move on to our interviews with the research assistants. Neve, you were great. We'll see you tomorrow at the museum."

"Excellent."

While the crew began packing up, a skinny young woman appeared at Neve's side to usher her off. I followed.

I'd held out hope that Neve's office would make up for the banality of the rest of her lab and be the Apple Store made of moth wings I'd envisioned, but again I was let down. Just a bookshelf with its volumes organized by hue, a hundred colored pencils lined up on a wooden desk, and a pair of black candlestick holders on either side of them. Through the big (and according to Neve's lectures, technologically obsolete) glass windows, I surveyed the office and watched Neve and her assistant chat for a while, until finally the professor was left alone. I gave her a second, then rapped on the glass.

"Neve? Hi. My name is Charles Grossheart—I'm a creative consultant at Kenosis, and I was wondering—"

"I'm sorry, but how'd you get in here?"

"The receptionist let me in."

"Huh."

"We're trying to do a lot of the same things as you, and I think we could join forces. I'd love to bring your ideas to the field of medicine." I quickly rattled off the pitch I'd practiced all morning, but I wasn't exactly getting the deep, slow nods I'd envisioned.

"You work for Kenosis?"

"Yeah."

"I'm sorry, but if you want to set up a meeting, you'll have to talk to my assistant. I have a lot on my plate right now. We're filming a documentary—did you see the crew? And I need to prepare my keynote at Thinkcubate. I'm sure your boss doesn't take walk-in appointments, either. You understand."

I apologized for wasting her time, left her office, and sulked behind the nipple chair. I'd fucked up yet again. My mind wandered back to the lock screen on Thane's phone.

Now that I'd broken off from the film crew, some of the research assistants started giving me the stink eye. I made my way to the door, snatching an ID card off a desk before slipping out.

While I was here, I figured I might as well check out the rest of the lab I'd spent the past couple days researching. I put the abandoned pass around my neck and set out to explore the rest.

I circled the tube worms until I came to a door with forbidding signage. I tried my pass on the pad next to the handle and, with a click, was let through.

The room was fairly typical of the labs I'd peeked into on my way up. Racks of processors along the back wall fed into a couple desktops by way of thick Rapunzel braids of wires.

Toward the back sat an arcade-game cabinet painted with green amoebas wearing bandit masks. Its name, BioShot, was written across the front and sides in blue electricity. It looked like a new indie game, trading in nostalgia for the era of Galaga and Donkey Kong. Arcade games were standard at start-ups, to trick the boy-men into never leaving the workplace. Growing up, Peter and I had a rotation of these devices in our rooms, and I was eager to try this one out. I turned it on.

The title screen was a classic bit of 12-RGB pixelation, followed by screens of credits and exposition, but the simple joystick didn't seem to require a tutorial so I skipped through them.

I thought the gameplay would keep up the retro graphics, but what came after the tutorial looked like the view from the eyepiece of a microscope. As the 8-bit score played, cute, squarish cells (a loosely rectilinear grid, like a map of counties) began to populate the perimeter of the screen. The joystick guided a blue amoeba with crosshairs over its nucleus, and when you pressed the button, your micro-avatar spat out caustic goo that ate up the nearby green cells. It was essentially Whac-A-Mole, but your character was limited by convincing physics and randomly needed to absorb the remains of his blocky victims.

I completed a level and watched as food was sprinkled around to nourish my foes before I could start again. I beat back three or four more waves before I got bored and quit. The play was redundant, but the visuals were undeniably cool. I thought about buying my own console for Obnoxious HQ and restarted the cabinet to see if the opening frames had any contact info for its creators:

**BIOSHOT: Play the first living video game! You control a REAL, living microorganism beating back a wall of ACTUAL dividing cells. While this may seem like a toy, BioShot is a GAME-changer, with wide applications in medicine, science education, and biological research.**

There was more about just how the "game" worked, which I skimmed until my stomach started hurting. I'm not squeamish, especially about violence in video games. I've run over countless virtual pedestrians, leveled the barrels of every kind of gun at the heads of zombies, cyberpunk mobsters, and innocent digital children. And these were just cells, after all. But it made me queasy.

I turned to go, but as I was walking out, a tsunami of foamy orange puke gushed out of my mouth, breaking against the braid of wires on the floor. The resulting mix of cords and vomit looked like a still from a Ridley Scott movie. I wiped my mouth on my sleeve and got out of there.

I felt better right away. With all the stress I'd been under, a little high-velocity regurgitation was both inevitable and cathartic. I picked up where I'd left off in my lap around the atrium. Nothing struck my fancy. More pasty dorks transfixed by computer monitors while their pores begged for exfoliation.

I'd nearly made it back around to Olmert's fief when I heard music playing in one of the labs. Just then, across the atrium, a young man stepped out of the forbidden corridor and started shouting into his phone. The lab I'd filled with puke was his, I was sure.

I ducked into the room where the music was coming from and shut the door behind me. This one was dark, too, save for an illuminated platform in the middle of the floor. I felt like I was back in one of the black box theaters with Eugen and James, snickering through our classmates' performances in some Americanized Pinter, bungled Wharfinger, or an all-woman production of *'Tis Pity She's a Whore*.

Three people stood on the platform, swaying to the music. Now that my eyes had adjusted somewhat, I could see the group consisted of two women and a slightly hunched man. They wore giant VR goggles, and blue nodes blinked on their hands and feet.

Despite my deep investment in punk, I'm a listener who takes pride in my broad, multicultural palate. But even I couldn't pin down the peculiar sounds coming through the speakers. There were snatches of Fela Kuti beats that, as soon as I registered them, vanished under Xanaxy trap hi-hats. In an instant, Tuareg guitar noodling pivoted to what could only be a Van Halen neck-tap flurry. At any moment, the pieces fit and sprang naturally from the previous notes, but the feel and time signatures were always shifting. I would have found it awe-inspiring if it weren't so disorienting.

As my brain ran its own analog *Shazam*, I noticed something strange about the people on the platform. No matter how they moved, they stayed in time with the music. When the man jerked his arm around in the arrhythmic Caucasian style, a trumpet spurted forth a few jazzy notes. When one of the girls whipped her hair back and forth, the drums added a short fill.

The rhythm shifted constantly, the key kept modulating, and a different instrument might pick up the melody halfway through a phrase. And somehow the dancers' every movement fit perfectly, predestined. As I tried to piece this all together, a fourth figure emerged from the shadows. His face appeared briefly in the glow of a tablet, and all at once the lights came on and the music stopped.

"Excuse me, sir, but can I help you?"

While I mumbled some excuse and apologized for my intrusion, the man who'd been dancing slid his goggles up to his forehead and looked me over.

"Charles?"

"Oh, hey." Who was he? I couldn't place him.

"It's good to see you, buddy. How've you been?" He and the others picked the nodes off their hands and feet like they were ticks.

"Good. Nothing to report, really."

"We were just checking out this omni-thing."

"Omni-theremin," the man who killed the music said.

"Pretty cool stuff they're doing here. Oh, and these are my assistants, Katie and Bella."

"Hey," one of them said. She had long blond hair that went down to her waist. The other had removed a lollipop from her purse and busied herself with peeling off the plastic.

The goggles and mind-bending music had thrown me off, but his "assistants" were the clue I needed—I suddenly knew who this was. I was a fan of sorts, or the opposite of a fan, devoutly hate-watching the movie of his disgusting life. The man who stood before me was something of a legend to me and my brother, Peter; no Hercules or Paul Bunyan, more of an anemic Hades. He owned an island near ours and was always trying to get an audience with Dad, who, like Peter and me, hated him. But while Dad's hate manifested itself in his signature gelid indifference, my brother and I relished the sport of this creep's gauche idiocy like ESPN commentators. His long head, nineties jeans and button-ups, and default leer had earned him a nickname among the Grossheart boys: Nosferatu Jerry Seinfeld.

"What brings you here?" NJS said. "You looking to donate? You guys should have reached out to me! I'm tight with just about every-one around here. All the important people."

"I was trying to get a meeting with Neve Olmert. Do you know her?"

"Of course! I've sponsored a couple of her projects. How'd it go?"

"Not very well. She didn't really have time."

"Seriously? Does she know who you are?"

"I came here for Kenosis."

"Oh yeah! You guys actually have a chunk of my money. I think you might be using my island sometime soon." One of the assistants took a hit off her Juul (decorated with Hello Kitty stickers) and loudly sighed out the vape smoke. "This is awesome! What a coincidence. Not really too much of a coincidence, I guess, since they let me hang here a lot. I'm this close to getting them to build a little apartment for me somewhere in here. But still. You know what, why don't we go and get this all sorted out? Girls, let's go."

"Can we just stay here?" the one with the lollipop asked. She'd pulled a cootie catcher out of her bag and had started telling her friend's fortune with it. "We need to finish this."

"No, I need you guys with me."

NJS led the way, followed by me and the man who'd rebuked me. The girls ran around us playing a spasmodic game of tag, with each trying to poke the other's ribs.

Over the years, we Grossheart brothers had, thanks to the contribu-tions of various friends and associates who'd done what we couldn't bring ourselves to do and actually hung out with the aging socialite, become a repository for a vast oral history of anecdotes on this ass-hole. We'd learned, for instance, that in his closet could be found a pallet of white Lacoste polos (retail $89.50), which, after a single shift on his nasty body, were used as rags by his unfortunate maids. A guy I knew from Dewey Willson told me he'd once wandered into the playboy wannabe's bedroom and found himself surrounded by a mix of Swedish porn, extreme-martial-arts DVDs, and a Teenage Mutant Ninja Turtle's arsenal of loose swords and nunchuks on the floor. NJS had caused an ecological disaster on our shared private archipelago by bypassing local government inspections and importing a shipment of lumber containing a dozen mating pairs of a particularly raven-ous species of toad (ours was just barely spared, as Dad had naturally picked the most isolated rock in the chain). And, obviously, there were the girls, two of which presently wove between me, the so-called phi-lanthropist, and his SNIT guide.

The poor guy. He was clearly embarrassed by our parade. Behind his glasses, which looked as if they'd been stolen from an intellectual tortoise, he wore an expression of muted, painful exasperation com-mon among my father's handlers.

Just before we got to Neve's wing, NJS stopped us.

"Shit, Charles. This is Michael Monteverdi. He's the director."

The nearsighted turtle gave me a faint nod.

"Neve!" NJS shouted once the director let us in. "Neve!"

The professor came out of her office. "I didn't know you were com-ing by. What can I do for you?"

"Can I have a word? It'll be quick."

NosJer, Neve, and Mr. Owl ducked into Neve's office while the girls and I hung back on the other side of the glass to watch the silent movie of their conversation about my family tree and the money that grows on it. NJS's girls provided their own commentary, with the long-haired girl pulling double duty as Monteverdi and Neve, and the one with the lollipop (a real talent) delivering a pitch-perfect, whiny imper-sonation of her (tor)mentor.

"Want some of my *munny*?" she said.

"I do indeed. Indeed I very much do."

The two of them were killing it, I have to say. Someday they'd come forward with unnerving allegations and get great book deals, I was sure of it.

NJS stepped out of the office. "Neve's up-to-date on things. She has a little time now, if you want to chat."

"Thanks. I appreciate it."

"Just keep me in mind if you're looking to donate. And my invitation to Little Saint Victor is always open—you know that."

*"You know that,"* one of the girls expertly echoed.

Monteverdi herded him and his pubescent interns off, and I went into Neve's office.

"Hey," she said. "I'm sorry I was so brusque earlier."

"No, it's fine."

"Here we practice radical honesty. It's the only way we can purify and execute our ideas. I'm going to be honest with you now. I looked into the Kenosis tech when your boss first started getting buzz. I just don't think you guys can deliver on that. I think you're overvalued, grossly. You're probably aware I went to med school before I became an architect. Biomedicine isn't the same thing as tech. This isn't the kind of stuff you can throw together in your garage or code on your laptop. There's no way a dropout would be able to pull off what she's claimed to have achieved. Maybe it's one of those things where she throws enough cash at her pipe dream that it comes true, I don't know. But I do think there might be other ways for the two of us to collaborate. I've heard about some of the things you're doing over at Grossheart with biodesign, and I think we could help."

Truth, the purest form of party poop. The doubts I had about the company, the things Tim had told me, the whispers I'd overheard, the strange floors—I'd kept it all compartmentalized. Neve finally made me put all the pieces together. Kenosis was fucked. My oldest friend was either a scammer or an idiot, and now I'd brought my parents into it, setting myself up to be even more of a disappointment in their already piss-poor estimation.

Another sour realization hit me, too. The only reason I was in the room, taking a pitch from this freakishly hot icon of design, was because of my last name. It was the only reason I was hired at Keno-sis, too. I'd been aware of this, of course, when Olivia made her offer, but I'd gotten so caught up in the glamour of the industry that I'd forgotten this fundamental fact.

I couldn't rely on a corporate backup plan. The label was the most important thing, the one thing I'd created without invoking my family name, and I'd lost sight of what that meant. As I nodded along to Professor Olmert's silver-tongued ramblings, I recommitted myself to my artistic pursuits. I'd do something about the phone and get through this drama. I'd bust my ass until Obnoxious took its rightful place among the very best independent labels, reducing my family to a footnote or fun fact.

I thanked her for her time and left the office. I wouldn't follow up on the Grossheart Industries collaboration. But Neve (as you might expect) was much more tenacious, and it turned out that my meeting would bear some bioengineered fruit for the family business, though I wouldn't be the one to pluck it.

As I walked toward the elevator, I heard a buzz coming from the nearest tube worm. There, about ten feet above me, at the tip of the structure, was one of the spinnerbots. Its head/body peeked out just inches past the mouth of the tube it had built. I caught a glimpse of a little red light before it retreated into its tunnel.

## 14

I heard the Kenosis origin story so many times during my first months there that, after a while, I began to dream about it. I could see myself there in the library, listening like a kindly parish priest as Olivia spoke of her troubles. I gave the same little speech over and over, pointing to the Gutenberg Bible as my sermon reached its climax. I could see Olivia's face as she absorbed my wisdom and filled herself with renewed resolve. Every detail was perfect. Which is funny, because it was all bullshit.

Not that it mattered to me. I knew that, like any etiology, the story wasn't about accuracy, but more about feeling. The Googlers have their garage. Nate Zuckerman has his now-cliché dorm-room bullshit at our shared alma mater. These nerds know a story is nothing more than a bit of code with a job to do. You carefully string together your commands and cues, then let it loose to program whoever runs it (okay, I admit I know next to nothing about computers, but bear with me). Olivia's origin story was properly sequenced—it referenced her elite education and venerable dropout status, chronicled her tear-jerking struggle with cancer, and alluded to an obvious genius forebear—and it served its function well, namely, to hack into people's wallets by way of their hearts. I was never under the impression that it should be true.

Much more important to me, a question I still ponder, and probably will forever, is whether or not she believed her own story. Was she knowingly lying? Or had she suckered herself, too?

I didn't see Olivia for months after the trip to Greece. I spent the rest of the summer in New York crate digging, guzzling down nano-brews, and deciding if I wanted to be addicted to cocaine. Whenever I reached out to see how my friend was doing, it'd be days until I received a brief reply. I figured she was recuperating.

We returned to campus that fall and marveled at the new Olivia. Learning about her cancer's comeback had caught me completely off guard, and since we'd parted, I reviewed the preceding months and couldn't come up with any evidence of her illness. It took the shock of her sudden transformation for me to fathom how sick she must have been, and it made me wonder if she'd ever actually been healthy the entire time I'd known her. It was truly a thing to behold. Olivia carried herself with the poise and coiled energy of an athlete (and not some runt Ivy League quarterback—a real, state-school jock). She was still pale, but it looked like while they were at it, the Russians had her skin enameled, and it now possessed a lunar sheen.

I tried to organize a party to celebrate, but Olivia didn't want to make a big deal about it. She told me she was worried it might come back, and she didn't want to jinx it. I kept trying to settle on something less hedonistic—day drinking down by the river, a weekend excursion to MASS MoCA—but she resisted. A little hurt, I pressed her on it.

"I don't know. It's something I felt when I was in remission that first time. I guess I feel guilty, leaving everyone else behind. I need to work hard now, more than ever, to find a way to help them."

It was the typical melodrama she dipped into whenever she got going about cancer, and like bringing up a dead child or third-world poverty, it didn't leave too many rhetorical countermoves available. I didn't push back.

For the first couple weeks or so after that, we barely saw her. But soon she hit a wall, and all of a sudden she was with us almost every night.

Eugen didn't come back with Olivia. She told us he'd found a publishing gig in London and had worked out some deal with the extension school. My guess was that the life-or-death stakes had been too high for him, and that he dumped Olivia once it was clear she'd recovered. After we found a new drug dealer, we barely missed him. By then, Olivia had absorbed his best qualities and had inherited at least one of his coats. From a distance, you wouldn't have been able to tell the difference between our original trio and our new one.

She did, however, lack Eugen's ability to keep us in check. Without Eugen to talk us down, James and I began our proper codependent rivalry, a battle with many theaters: the Yard, the Square, the dorm rooms in the House where a hot young FDR probably received his second or third blow jobs. What transpired between us, then, was a contest only two boys at the top of the social order could participate in. A duel to see who could most elaborately scorn both our parents' monies *and* the wealth-encrusted university we reluctantly attended. I mutilated a Brunello Cucinelli sweater with a pair of Fiskars and safety pins. James took a Sharpie to a surf-green, American-made Fender Jazzmaster, defacing it with a dripping, girthy speed, then, with an array of fuzz pedals that would make any shoe-gazer look up (he owned *two* Klon Centaurs), blasted a ten-hour noise drone from his dorm room during finals week, daring his roommates and neighbors in Adams to challenge him.

I scored only small victories. For a month James tried to defeat me by going straight edge and forsaking all pharmaceutical pleasure, but I mocked and hounded him relentlessly until his nose was no longer clean.

Olivia was both audience and accessory to our displays (accessory as in *accessorize*, a smart handbag or a purse), perfect for our purposes. Thanks to her father's downfall, she was the ideal spectator to appreciate the nuances of our performances, a groundling who'd once been an actor herself. On top of this, she was hot and stylish, sporting a prototype of the looks she'd hone as founder of Kenosis. My and Eugen's influences had refined her style into a thrifted, soft-goth look long before it became the uniform of every millennial and Gen Z practitioner of the liberal arts. We were like a band, with Olivia holding down the rhythm and James and I trying to out-solo each other.

Which brings me back to Olivia's origin story for Kenosis.

We were in Widener, that tall shrine to a wealthy corpse flexing its Gutenberg Bible. It was finals week, I think, though such concerns only affected me peripherally, as in how many of my friends would be down to party. I took Valium much more seriously than I took school. (I have to say, graduating from H—— was almost as easy as getting in. My profs and adjuncts would, in response to the watery procrastinated vomit I turned in, only go as low as a B.)

Back then Olivia's project was a mystery to me. Not because she kept it secret—I just couldn't bring myself to care. In those days, every kid at that school had some half-assed scheme to change the world, save the planet, and ultimately get famous. I vaguely recall Olivia's plan and the obligatory nods I gave her as I tried to avoid falling asleep. I'm guessing I did a lot of this that day in Widener, but the sage wisdom is a feature exclusive to Olivia's telling.

In mine, James was there, too. We weren't studying. I got my hands on some ketamine, which I'd only done once before, and which caused me to strip naked in front of an already Chuck-weary friend group. I suspected that dose wasn't exactly pure, and I was eager to experience some of the long-term, positive effects of the drug. Olivia had promised to look after us while we got high, to make sure I kept my clothes on this time. But she was taking too long studying, and so James and I went to get her.

Eventually we peeled her from her table in the library's legendary reading room. Before we left, James snatched (with perfect, enviable confidence) the computer of a particularly humorless kid we'd known at Dewey Willson who was also something of a rival of Olivia's. (He's at UNICEF now, ever the do-gooder.) We loved fucking with him— pounding on his door late at night, catfishing him with made-up profiles of ambitious, bespectacled young women.

I watched it all play out. James calmly walking back with the Mac-Book under his arm. A few seconds later, far down the vast chamber, a squeal. Our studious dweeb screamed at the people around him, all too focused on their own performed rigor to have noticed anything.

The sight of the three of us would be enough for him to figure out what had gone down, so we left before he could spot us and ducked into the Gutenberg room. The Bible lay before us on its pedestal, its open pages a maze of spiny Latin (no way of knowing if it was actually turned to the chunk of Philippians Olivia credits as the source of her company's theological name, but it's doubtful). Outside we could still hear our nerd shrieking at some librarian or guard.

This was clearly a point in James's favor. I did not want to be outdone. As Olivia rambled on about her then-imaginary company, I scanned the room, frantically searching for a way to show off my own devious ingenuity. Then it occurred to me.

I dumped the ketamine onto the glass above the Gutenberg Bible and chopped it into lines with my student ID. I made it so the powder and the Latin verses were lined up, then snorted half through a $20 bill.

"Your turn," I told James.

"Man, I'm good. I don't want to do that here."

I won. I tried to pressure him more as Olivia kept blabbing about her vision, but then all of a sudden I lost track of where my body ended and the rest of the room began.

"Holy shit," a thoroughly dissociated Chuck said.

Olivia: "Administration by way of snorting facilitates quick passage through the nasal mucosal membranes and a relatively rapid crossing of the blood-brain barrier when compared to smoking and other methods."

I could see myself as if I were in a movie. Patterns I'd taken for granted were now perfectly clear. I looked at James, standing by the Bible, still clutching the stolen laptop, and felt as if I could really see him. He radiated pain. It rose off him in shimmering, steam-like waves.

But Olivia's drug-inspired aura dwarfed his. She stood surrounded by a flame made of shadow, which tapered to a point whipping around the heights of the chamber.

I observed myself at a remove as I launched into some mind-blown bloviation:

"I see you, Olivia. I see you. It's terrifying, but also awesome. But terrifying. You have this power. There is this awesome, terrifying power inside you. Or like, around you. It's dark. How did we not see it sooner? We should be afraid of you! I see you, what you really are."

I understood something else about her, in that moment. She wasn't merely our friend—she was studying me and James, to see how we worked. All this time, we were her master class, tutors and subjects both in a course available nowhere else. Except maybe Yale, Princeton, Oxford, or Cambridge.

As I moved on from the subject of Olivia's power to a homily about reality's hidden, glittery levels, James and Olivia grabbed my arms and took me to the lower-level stacks to ride it out. When I was in a better place, we returned to sea level. Olivia escorted us to the door but hung back at the library to do a little more work.

By then the effects of the ketamine had diminished to something peaceful and antidepressive. Outside it was one of those days of perfect sun and breeze, weather that presaged the immaculate comfort of our futures. The Square was packed. We found a trash can near the health center and dumped the laptop there.

## 15

I tried to convince myself Olivia was being lied to, that she might be someone else's pawn, maybe Clif's. I did some research on the Kenosis CFO. His Russian mobster taste in clothes had confused me—I hadn't been sure if he was a thug playing businessman or a businessman getting his rocks off as a thug. While I suspected the former, it turned out to have been the latter. He'd worked for Microsoft for a while in the nineties before starting two software companies of his own, a voucher-like alternative to regular money for online purchases and a website for selling pet food and accessories. (Actual Russian mobsters appear to have been involved in the first one, allegedly using it to launder their ill-gotten gains, so my read was not entirely off.) Thanks to some crafty, semilegal moves, he'd netted himself about $20 million selling off his stock before the dot-com bubble popped. I thought maybe Clif, with his sketchy history, explained the unusual things I'd noticed at the company. Olivia might just be the pretty lady carved into the bow of Clif's pirate ship.

So I was leaning toward this pawn theory, but I wasn't so much of a chump that I ruled out her fucking us over. I wanted to talk to Olivia, but I was afraid that none of this was news to her, and I worried she'd deny everything and confirm my biggest fear: that she was trying to dupe me and my parents. I needed more information.

I called up Renata (Dad's right hand / tight fist) to see just how much we had tied up in Kenosis. I'll say this: it approached the net worth of the kind of actor who shills tequila as a side hustle. If Kenosis went bankrupt, it obviously wouldn't be enough to change anything about the Grossheart family's collective lifestyle in any way, but it would certainly rankle my Scrooge McDad enough that I'd never be able to wash off the minus signs. If I moved quickly enough, I could save him some precious money and maybe even boost my standing in the spreadsheet of his mind. I had to be sure, though, lest I preemptively fuck things up for myself.

I texted Tim. I didn't heed his order to use a different phone—Tim was being paranoid. We arranged to meet in Fennario Wharf, at the aquarium. If it was clear Olivia was being conned, I'd share Tim's findings with her. If it looked like we Grosshearts were the ones being played, I'd take them to Dad.

Before I left my office, I checked in with Louise. I needed to be sweet to her. She was doing all the heavy lifting, managing the entirety of our operations and the tear monsoon of a grieving widow / our only remotely profitable artist. Last night, to make up for my recent unavailability, I'd taken her to a new restaurant that had seized on the medieval trend Olivia had helped start in the city. They served pottages, Dark Age bacon, and, in keeping with the old Catholic prescriptions, on Wednesdays, Fridays, and Saturdays offered exotic fish courses of roast lamprey and eel pies. I particularly enjoyed the blood sausage, which, according to the hefty book-of-hours-like menu, had been made in such a way that didn't kill the cow. With a cut above the leg, they could extract the blood and spare the beast's life, just as the villeins did back in the reign of King Edward.

Needless to say, the bill was enough to finance a long war with France. I let Louise see it, though I acted like I was trying to conceal the princely sum from her. Two of the guitar pedals I'd stress-bought had arrived the day before (for you gearheads: a nice Tube Screamer clone, a bitcrusher), and I gave them to her when we got home. I'd made sure to ask her some questions about her songwriting and how she was coping with the Thane crisis, and while she seemed skeptical of my gestures at first, I could feel her affection for me regenerate somewhat with the attention.

"Need anything while I'm out?"

"No, I'm good. Though I think that food from last night gave me gout. I can't feel my toe." She shook her foot and gave me a cute, mock grimace. "Hey, you might want to give Sydney some space. For some reason, she's convinced herself that you want Thane's phone. She's got it in her head that you were trying to steal it from her in her sleep, and now she's keeping it in a lockbox in her van."

I *had* tried this, the night after I visited Neve. Sydney had woken for just a second, but I hadn't thought she'd been able to see me.

"I've managed to talk her down some and convince her that you're not some psycho, but I think she's made you her emotional scapegoat in all this, and the less you're in her face, the better."

"That won't be a problem."

This felt good. Louise was still loyal to me. I was amazed, given how little I'd done to earn it. After her dad died, I flew Louise and her mom to Ireland to scatter his ashes and stare sadly at the snot-green sea. In her mind, the gift represented much more than the infinitesimal shred it was. They were economy tickets. It turned out to have been a shrewd investment because that, and putting out her record, had convinced her I was good deep down. I was inclined to let her keep up the misapprehension.

"I'm getting worn out," Louise said before a trust fall onto the couch. "Thane's death has fucked everything up. It's fucked me up. I'm still grieving my dad, and now I feel like he just died again. And everything is falling on me. You need to do more, man, or hire another person. I didn't want to say all this last night because we were having such a good time."

"Thanks for letting me know what's going on. I was going to tell you this later, but I've been saving up, and when Sydney is doing better, I'm renting a place for you in Palm Springs to get away and write. But until then, here." I gave her some money to take herself and Sydney to a spa, then left to see Tim.

The Inverarity Aquarium sat on the site of a palatial bathhouse and amusement park complex built over one hundred years ago. Louise and I had heard a podcast episode about it on a road trip during our relationship's first flush. It was the white elephant of one of the city's more eccentric city-fathers-turned-mayor, Pierce Inverarity (his son or grandson of the same name had founded Yoyodyne—like us Grosshearts, like all ultra-high-net-worth families, the Inveraritys have no creativity when it comes to names). You had to admire the man's sense of pizzazz. They had to gut most of the structure in the nineties to accommodate the network of tanks and pipes for a modern aquarium, but they'd wisely hung on to the marble façade. This housed the most intact expression of the naughty nautical iconography found all over the decaying compound, a parade of voluptuous mermaids and sea nymphs, with the occasional phallic, leering beluga. It was enough to inspire some real *Ruinenlust*.

On my way there, I reached my hand into my pocket and found the eye patch I'd stolen back when I reunited with Olivia. I put it on as a gag. It messed up my depth perception—I nearly impaled myself on a concrete narwhal as I stumbled toward the entrance.

I found my cheap Deep Throat at the first big tank, staring at a turtle. The thing was about the size of a Volvo and looked like it had a spaceship growing out of its neck. After the San Narciso mountain lion and the cockatiels of nearby Inverarity Heights, it was probably our town's most famous creature. Its original right fin had been hacked off by a boat, and in a savvy PR move following some unfortunate leaks about user data, Zuckerman had donated a fully functional prosthesis to the poor beast. Now you could watch a livestream from a camera in its armpit.

"Notice anyone following you?"

"No. I think we're okay, man."

"And you're using the burner?"

"Of course," I lied.

"What the fuck are you wearing?"

"I thought it was funny."

"Take that shit off. This is deadly serious."

I peeled the eye patch off my head and stuck it back in my pocket.

"You took your time. I was starting to think I'd never hear back from you. Or that you were going to rat me out."

"A close friend died. It's been hard."

"God, I'm sorry." Tim wore a tie covered in golfing mice. It was so ugly it was cool. I should have offered to buy it off him. "I'm not myself. Friendship is important. They say it's the whole of the dharma. I could use a friend right about now."

I thought I caught a whiff of some sea lion or dolphin shit, but I traced the scent to Tim. He was drunk and clearly hadn't showered in a while. In the blue fish-tank light, he looked like the last, hypothermic survivor of an ill-fated expedition.

"When I moved out here, I thought I'd be living the true, carefree California lifestyle. I'd learn to surf, which is something I could've done back in Melbourne but never really got around to. We even bought an old Volkswagen van. Now I feel as boxed in as this turtle."

I didn't need the sad-dad vibes. A melancholic Frenchman or Englishman I could handle, but a depressed Australian was too much. Australians (and I still doubted the existence of their country, for the record) were made by God to strike up friendly conversation in hostels and jovially fistfight at music festivals, not mope. It was like having a gloomy golden retriever.

"Don't look, but I think that guy is following me. The one with the notebook. Let's go outside, to the Sea Walk."

I turned and saw a dopey old man sketching the cyborg turtle. I doubted he was surveilling us, but I was grateful to get out of there before Tim pointed out any other objective correlatives among the marine life.

The shore was gridded with concrete pools that had been the aquarium's original attraction. Together they formed a gray, half-eaten waffle. In addition to the saltwater pools near the building, Inverarity had built a couple retaining basins out here, so people could gather round and gawk at trapped sea creatures. Tim led me out along a narrow pier that divided two of the pools.

We sat down on a bench, but not before Tim peeked under it to check for listening devices. In the sunlight his skin was the color of eggnog.

"R and W's backed out."

"What?"

"Rome and Wieger. I was worried they were going to use the tomes on patients in the so-called pilot project, so I dug around. It turns out the whole thing was really just a validation study, used only to assess the effectiveness of Kenosis tech. They were going to set up the tomes in blood samples like they do in the clinical lab, to use alongside normal Siemens machines to test their potential. Needless to say, it didn't work. I thought this would slow things down, but Olivia has already leveraged it to raise money, to get us into other, potentially more dangerous projects and contracts. And the second round of testing with the monkeys failed, too. I couldn't figure out why they were dying when it's just a little implant."

He dabbed his forehead with his mouse tie. It was only about seventy degrees but he was sweating through his shirt.

"But now I think it must be tied to something else I found that I still can't quite make sense of. I've always joked that there were two companies: the real one, and Olivia's fantasy. But now it seems like there really are two operations. It turns out a small group of scientists has been working on a different model of the tome. I found the diagram of one in a colleague's workstation, and it's baffling. At first I thought it was for integrating the Gutenberg I's with the nanobots, but that doesn't quite explain it. There are far more microfluidic channels, and the unit houses a tiny compartment to hold something, some kind of living tissue. I have my hunches as to what it might be, based on some of the documents, but I can't say for certain just yet. I have a trove of files I still need to sort through. It's been a real job of work. Almost a second job."

"What can we do? How can we handle this?" Now I'd absorbed his stress.

"I'm getting to that. So about two weeks ago one of my friends in engineering gave me the heads-up that he'd overheard Clif and one of his nephews—he's hired at least three of those fucking oafs—mention my name and something about security. He told me that, judging by the tone, it probably meant they were going to conduct another one of their autocratic security checks over at the lab and see if any of us were hanging on to sensitive material containing their holy 'trade secrets.' This has happened before, about three months ago. Clif and his gestapo raid your office for printouts or thumb drives, then check your computer for any suspicious activity. Clif has a cybersecurity expert who reports to him only. His own one-man Stasi. Some Russian hacker prodigy. Clif likes to brag that when this kid was twelve, he used to hack his way into power grids and turn off his enemies' electricity—*overseas*. He can do anything.

"Anyway, I'd just sent some more complaints to Olivia the week before, so I figured it was either a raid or I was going to be fired. Way back when Kenosis was starting, I got one of the tech security guys the job. He's not one of Clif's fascists, so of course he was fired. But we saw that coming, and he gave me a sneaky way into the system. I haven't sifted through all of it yet. But knowing there's no limit to their paranoia, I zipped everything onto a CD and then took that down to the borough, thinking maybe even Clif would be paranoid enough to check a CD if I left it lying around in my office or even go through my bag. I stuck it in the hot dog stand, figuring it would be safe down there."

"The stand is fake?" I couldn't hide my disappointment. I'd seen it on our tours and assumed it was operational, that it was always closed before we got there. I occasionally daydreamed about dropping down to the borough to wolf down a dog or two.

"Oh, yeah. They had a guy running it for a week, but Clif was worried he was too much of a security risk. Anyway, my thinking in putting it there was that if they searched my office, I'd be able to pick it back up at the end of the day and take it home. And if I was fired and they made me walk out and leave my stuff, I could ask one of my friends among the specialists to get it for me. I received a message from Clif that afternoon, telling me he wants to see me, and I think, that's it, I'm fired. But it was stranger than that. I'd been demoted, though of course they didn't put it in such straightforward terms. I'm officially a consultant now, which is their way of keeping an eye on me. They took away my office. They gave my parking spot to one of Clif's lackeys. But here's the dumb part: the very moment I stepped out of his office, I found they'd limited my access to the clinical lab only. I can't go down to the borough without permission, and it's clear I'm on the outs now, so even my so-called friend in R and D won't answer my emails. I'm sure the CD is still there. It's labeled *Dark Side of the Moon*."

"All I need to do is grab a CD?"

"Your pass should let you down there. My guess is that Clif doesn't want any conflict with you. Has he ever searched your bag or anything?"

"Of course not."

"Then this will be easy. If you can get me that CD, I'll compile everything I've got, and I'll be able to demonstrate beyond a doubt what's been going on. It'll be undeniable, to your father, to the FDA, to CMS, to whomever. This is going to be tough. They've got Joop Hull on the board, which gives him a personal stake in what happens with the company. He's going to be even more of a pit bull, if that's possible. One hundred ninety percent pit bull. But I believe we can do this."

Tim froze. "Shh. I think it's a drone."

Tim took off his glasses, shoved them in his pocket, then covered most of his face, as if he were about to sneeze.

High above us hovered a massive black bird. It looked like a pterodactyl carrying a cow heart.

"It's a frigate bird," I told him. I'd seen plenty of these before, gliding around our island. My dad, a man indirectly responsible for the disappearance of, I'd say, roughly an eighth of our planet's fauna, nevertheless showed great interest in the avian life of his island and often forced Peter and me to go birding until our necks nearly snapped off from the Bible-heavy binoculars he encumbered them with.

The frigate bird dove at a passing seagull, nipping at its tail feathers and causing the poor thing to tumble in the air. After a few more attacks, the gull vomited into the water and the frigate bird, elegant as a fencer, slashed its beak across the surface and tweezed up the regurgitated hunks of fish.

## 16

I made my way down the indoor sidewalk admiring the expensive graffiti of the specialists' borough. I'd been to this geeky Sesame Street plenty of times in my months of tours and demonstrations. But it had always been the same stretch of that simulated Brooklyn, the same park benches, lampposts, brownstone stoops. I'd never ventured off the path and seen where the scientists actually worked.

I caught a snatch of Scarface coming through the borough's hidden speakers. Olivia's gangster rap thing has me embarrassed on her behalf. Predictably, my hip-hop tastes lean toward the brainy East Coast jazz rap of the midnineties. I'm a Tribe, Digable Planets, De La Soul guy who occasionally fucks with Vince Staples and Freddie Gibbs. Olivia was (ugh) more into Mobb Deep, Raekwon, and, every white girl's favorite, Biggie, whose corpus she treated like a self-help book (at least two of her Precepts were lifted from the sayings of the late Christopher Wallace). I figured it was mostly tactical, something to endear her to the finance bros and broadcast her youthful savvy to her elderly board, for whom a few bars were as baffling as lines of code.

I poked my head down an alley and found an actual dumpster, which, I had to admit, drove home the naturalism. But it turns out that was the last bit of virgin simulacra I had yet to see. Everything else beyond the tour's Potemkin village was terribly dull. Cubicles, whiteboards, fluorescent lights. It was practically an adjunct's office down there.

In one of the cubicles, I saw another *Looney Tunes* Tasmanian devil, this time in sticker form. Someone had drawn over the sticker in red ink, dotting Taz's body-chin with bright acne. Curious as to how it might relate to the shady operations of the secret floor, I rooted through the papers on the desk, which were apparently the cryptic results of some biopsied tissue samples. I couldn't make sense of them.

My phone buzzed. It was the label's accountant. I couldn't worry about that now—I'd call him back once I completed my mission.

The hot dog stand was next to an algae-covered fountain and a statue of Einstein. Once I was sure no one else was around, I opened the stand's steel hot dog drawer and found it packed with garbage. Cigarette butts, faded receipts, a shriveled roach or two, and balled-up handouts from what appeared to be a team-building exercise. No weenie had graced the drawer with its steamy, processed presence in some time.

Pressed against the side, all but concealed by the detritus, was a green jewel case. Tim's handwriting looked like a teen's, and he'd even drawn the album's signature prism in Sharpie. The object inspired in me a fondness for simpler times, when our nation's youth devoted their evenings to pirating music and quaintly burning it to these beautiful rainbow discs. So transported was I that, as I walked away from the stand, I nearly collided with Clif.

He'd been busy accosting a young woman. My arrival had upset her hold on her emotions, because as soon as she saw me, she began to weep. Clif's face, veiny and maroon with rage, looked like a kidney.

"What the fuck are you doing down here? What are you holding?"

The excuse I'd prepared—that I'd come to the borough to better understand our technology and brainstorm ideas for brand identity—was perfectly acceptable in this situation. But I wasn't Tim, and I didn't have to report to this turd.

"Excuse me?" Then, to turn things on him, I addressed the girl. "Are you okay?"

"This is a security matter," Clif said, his skin losing some of its egg-plant hue. "Why don't you let me handle this."

"I just don't think Olivia would appreciate all the noise while her team's trying to work."

"She knows what I'm up to. Everything I do has her approval."

I had him on the defensive, a good place to leave things. I raised my eyebrows and headed toward the elevator with my CD, but not before grabbing a lamppost and swinging around Gene Kelly–style, just to show I didn't give a shit.

I fumed in the elevator, hotboxing my hatred of Clif. He had to be the one responsible for all the fucked-up shit I'd seen, and Tim's account of authoritarianism and bullying seemed to put Clif as the cause. It made a lot of sense for him to use Olivia, an unsullied prodigy, a cancer survivor, a prophetess with little care for profit, as his ethical beard. I needed to talk to Olivia and let her know what was going on.

Instead of heading back to my office, I pressed the button for Olivia's floor.

Don't get me wrong. I knew she wasn't a saint. But with all she'd been through fighting cancer, I knew she *did* want to help people like her, on top of her understandable desire for ridiculous wealth and cultic worship.

On the way up I texted Olivia.

"Are you at Kenosis? There's something important I want to talk to you about."

She said she was at a conference all day but could make something work later in the week.

The elevator doors opened. I thought I'd be dramatic and leave the disc in her office with a cryptic note.

She had a classic setup from the golden age of secretaries, lifted—like so much of the culture in the Caverns at the time—from the anti-hero's office in *Bad Company*. There was even a vintage intercom box on the desk, looking like a guitar amp for a musical gnome. Her secretary leaned into the decor, wearing a plaid pantsuit and a polyester neckerchief. Beyond being on-trend, the nostalgia was a smart move considering most of the board's salad days were tossed half a century ago.

"I have something for Olivia."

"I'm sorry but she's out right now. Can I take a message for her? Or set up a meeting?"

"I found an old CD she'd burned for me, back in college. Could I just leave it on her desk? She'll get a kick out of it."

The secretary let me in, and I shut the door behind me. I leaned the CD against Olivia's intercom box and grabbed some Kenosis stationery to write a note. I went through two sheets before I came up with something sufficiently mysterious and suspenseful:

> *There's more than Pink Floyd on here. Someone is trying to push you off a cliff. Call me and I'll tell you what I know.*
>
> *—Charles*

Before I left, I took the opportunity to examine the decor. I'd been in there only once or twice before, and always under Olivia's watch. I couldn't resist the *Room Raiders* thrill.

Most of the wall space was dedicated to Olivian/Kenotic promo: photos of our benevolent founder with a charcuterie-plate variety of Global Southerners, playing marbles in a circle of scrawny scamps, standing next to a shabby school with a shovel, reading one of the chubbier volumes from a series about an orphaned wizard boy to a bunch of actual orphans. Her bookshelf was an obvious, Buttigiegian display of smarts. *The Odyssey, Moby-Dick, War and Peace, The Bushido Code*. I flipped through *Finnegans Wake* (frequently name-checked on the tours) and wished the wake were mine.

As I put the book back, I noticed something else on the shelf. A display box holding Eugen's old hunting knife, the one with the antler handle. I picked it up to take a closer look, and a tiny button clicked up from the spot where the box had been sitting. Another, louder click followed on the other side of the room.

A hidden door, about as wide as an ironing board, had opened just slightly, peeling away from the wall behind the desk.

I opened it, but instead of the GlenDronach and Japanese whiskey I'd expected, I found a small room, completely white and with no windows. Six Doc Martens lay scattered nonmonogamously on the floor, and her almost entirely black wardrobe hung along a rack in the back.

Between the dark sleeves a swatch of fabric caught my eye. I slid back the hangers on either side and discovered it belonged to a Hawaiian shirt with flip-flop print.

I knew this article. Thane wore the same one on the night he accosted me and vanished. I remembered she'd liked the shirt. Maybe she bought it off him or ordered one right after she saw him. It was a classic Olivian move, to ruthlessly pilfer someone else's style like that. She'd done it with me and Eugen back in college, and she'd gone on to perfect her aesthetic thievery on the corporate scale, with her remixes of the greatest hits of Steve Jobs and Nate Zuckerman.

In the corner sat a minifridge. I was hungry and, knowing Olivia wouldn't mind if I helped myself to her likely trove of brain food and probiotic snacks, opened it.

Inside, in neat rows, were dozens of bottles of what appeared to be pomegranate juice. It might have been some kind of fancy kombucha, a big fad in San Narciso at the time, or some off-brand Soylent. Whatever it was, it looked too healthy for my taste. I shut the fridge door.

Next to the refrigerator lay a balled-up flannel blanket. She'd been sleeping in her office, probably on the couch, and stored the blanket in here. While others might appreciate her Spartan existence as evidence of her single-minded dedication to her vision, she was my friend, and I saw something else. I pitied the emptiness of her life. This was all she had.

The closet/cell was too depressing. I shut the door, then checked to make sure the knife looked like it did when I discovered it. As I moved it back, I saw a little glyph on the blade I'd never noticed before—the same barbed infinity sign I'd seen under the desk.

Long purple curtains took up an entire side of her office. Standing by her desk, I peeled one back to peer out the window from her God View—the peach, postsunset sky over the parking lot of Teslas and Prii, the café tables, the Kenosis sign—wondering what it must be like to be Olivia or Dad. I found myself filled with great sympathy for the two of them and their responsibility-sore shoulders. Then, as if my musings had summoned her, I spotted my friend crossing the lot with some underling in tow.

Riding my wave of affection, I pulled out my phone and called her, ready to give her a few earnest, goofy waves through the glass.

I could see Olivia four or five stories below as the call, finishing its journey to space and back, reached her. She pulled out her phone and, seeing my name, rolled her eyes, shook her head a little, and put it back in her pocket.

I was still processing this when I saw Clif crossing the lot to meet her. His head was like a pencil eraser. He waved the assistant away and then, thinking no one was watching, did something that utterly perplexed me.

Clif took Olivia's hand, pulled her behind an SUV, and wrapped his arm around her waist. He whispered something in her ear, and she laughed. Then the most traumatizing sight. As he turned to walk her back to the building, she squeezed his ass.

Immediately my newfound empathy and loyalty voided me. She

and Clif were fucking. Whatever was going on, they were in it together. My vision of Clif as the mastermind, using her as cover, was the product of denial. It was still possible he was manipulating her, but the shock of this disgusting revelation made me finally see around my affection for Olivia. She was too shrewd to be played like that. And me? I wasn't a confidant—I was an annoyance, a tool that had landed her a big check or two. I'd known all this on some level, intellectually, but now my gut knew it, too, and that big boy had my absolute trust.

Everything that Tim had said, everything that I had seen, fit into a picture. Olivia wasn't a chump. Everyone else was.

I grabbed the CD off her desk, pocketed my Hitchcocky note, and prudently fished the earlier drafts from the waste bin. Once I made sure there was no sign of my snooping, I got out of there.

I went to my office and rooted through my desk. I barely used the thing, so it didn't take long to find what I was looking for: a stray business card from my ethical predecessor. I stuck it in my wallet.

Feeling like I might collapse and wanting to lie down, I remembered the room with the big leather armchairs where I'd dumped my predecessor's shit and headed there to get some rest. It turned out the box, with its Buddhist contents, was exactly where I'd left it. But now the room was occupied. Two big men filled the armchairs, half-heartedly playing some first-person shooter where you rove through a postapocalyptic cityscape firing bazookas. With their burly frames and bright pink, sunburned skin, they could have easily fit in among the corn-fed farm boys of my home state. They had a sluggish quality about them, as if a little drunk or high. My guess was that they were a pair of Clif's incompetent nephews, nominally employed like me.

"Gimme two more minutes and we'll be right down," one of them said at about half the normal tempo for regular speech. He looked as if he'd been carved from Spam.

"Wrong room. Sorry."

I ran off to the freshly stocked company snack bar to eat my feelings. In this instance, my medley of resentment and anxiety took the form of sriracha-glazed almonds, organic knockoff Cheez-Its, and Gouda-dusted kale chips. A haggard scientist joined me, and together we filled our plates, munching and grunting in tandem like two polar bears feasting on the carcass of a beached whale.

While dining, my hungry partner knocked over his water bottle, flooding the table.

"Oh, shit, I'm sorry. I'll get a rag."

He found a black one by the sink and began sopping up his mess. As he wiped away the last of the water and drifting crumbs, something on the rag caught my eye. Printed on the scrap of fabric was about half the Obnoxious logo.

## 17

This was not the first time I had to reckon with the evil ways of someone close to me. My wavering and avoidance were the results of years of conditioning starting with my preadolescent awakening to the fact that my dad wasn't exactly Superman and actually had much more in common with Lex Luthor. It's no coincidence that this was around the same time as my first, failed attempt to prune myself from my family tree.

One night, when I was eleven or so, I typed my own name into the bar of the search engine. This was just a year or two after most of America had gone online, and soon I would be toggling between seven or eight different accounts and identities in my harmless deceptions, a tiny fry that would soon grow into a hefty catfish. But at that point I mostly used our primitive computer for games, dipping my toe into the internet only occasionally, checking message boards for bands I liked (this was my short-lived, humiliating nu metal period) and timidly searching for porn. Dumbass that I was, I thought the search engine would be something magical, that I'd be able to trawl the megahertz for the very Truth itself. Naturally, I started with me.

My name being the same as my father's, the results for the more renowned Charles Grossheart filled the screen of my Acer. I learned he was famous, for terrible reasons. I'd always known he was above average as a person. Grossheart superiority, not our nominal, lukewarm Methodism, was the family religion, along with Reaganomics (for Dad, the Laffer curve is sacred geometry). But my last name was my baseline, and as a given, I had no context for it. I assumed everyone's dad was a remote billionaire running a multinational empire. But now I could see the exact areas in which he particularly excelled: evil, mostly, by way of pollution and eroding our already shaky democracy.

I saw his many subsidiaries listed among the most noxious polluters of land, air, and sea. I read a long, accurate, and devastating profile of him by the journalist who would eventually make her career with books about my dad and uncles. *The Washington Post* had obtained a secretly taped speech of him addressing his fellow oil industry insiders, urging his co-emitters to wage an "endless war" against environmental lobbyists and labor unions through "exploiting emotions like fear." The only evidence I have of his emotional intelligence to date. While he was nowhere near as notorious as he is now, he was already the major foe of climate science, laying the elaborate network of lobbyists and hollow foundations to overturn even the most minute effort to cut emissions or curb our nation's reliance on the fossil fuels he happened to refine.

I even searched for *charles grossheart good*, but nothing turned up to scrub his name.

It was clear. The world thought him despicable, a molester of humanity, an exploiter, a scoundrel. A world historical motherfucking son of a bitch (sorry, Grandma).

For another week I kept typing his/my name into the search bar. I'd wake up with the resolve to run away and live my life as someone else. By lunch I'd decide on loyalty and unconditional love. Then, at night, just as I was sweeping the shards of evidence under my mental rug, they'd blow back out.

There was a farm nearby, only a mile from the family compound. There were only farms, really. A mix of Cargill estates and smaller family tracts. The family that lived on this one had had a boy my brother's age who'd died a year before. He'd been fucking around in a grain elevator with his friends at night and stepped into the nothingness of the shaft. His name was Trent or Travis—I don't remember, though the image of him falling down the shaft was enough to keep me away from grain elevators even as I grew into a demonic teen.

They had two barns: one was functional and relatively new, the other had been built during the lifetime of John Brown. I liked to sneak out of our family compound (this was before Dad paranoically bulked up the security to UN levels) and walk over there. I usually just read magazines and devoured whole bags of Cheetos. More than once I cut the fingers off my gloves and pretended I was an orphan hobo. The man and woman who ran the farm had wide, flat faces and an unpronounceable Czech last name. I like to think they, having lost a boy, enjoyed my presence on their property, but it could just as easily have been that they knew I was a Grossheart and had no choice but to allow me to squat in their historic barn the way serfs had no choice but to offer their scant food and drink to a lord out on the hunt.

This was where I went to contemplate my paternal theodicy, the camel-through-needle's-eye odds he was even a halfway decent person. After a week spent on the computer, I took my moping over there. I'd wander over to the barn in the mornings and hide out until dinnertime. Given that I was often described by both parents as "obnoxious" (a word I reclaimed with my label, as a fuck you), I think my parents enjoyed the silence my absence allowed.

While in that bleached and dissolving barn, I discovered a box containing a run of archaeological *Playboy*s, a rusty pocketknife, and a smashed pack of Beaconsfield cigarettes. These, I believed, were the effects of my fellow mischievous predecessor, the one who'd fallen down the dark shaft. I diligently read the old *Playboy*s cover to cover without distinguishing the ads from the articles, then returned the box to its corner. This I remember clearly and have since looked up to confirm the details. July 1992: a Michael Keaton interview, "20 Questions with Nicole Kidman," "Super Mario! A revealing look at Mr.

Cuomo." But even "a pictorial tribute to nurses" was not enough to distract me from the sins of my father.

I decided it would be best to take my information to Mom.

"Is Dad evil?"

Mom had developed the necessary dissociative skills to survive a twenty-year marriage to a tyrant. In seconds, she could vanish into her own haut little monde, then be right back when the notes of cognitive dissonance had been absorbed into the walls and floorboards. But she didn't have the self-awareness to impart this crucial gift directly. Mom answered my question with a long list of the charitable foundations he'd started or supported. She told me he was one of the biggest patrons of the arts in the country, and that "millions" of people depended on him for their livelihoods. I should have left it there, but now his goodness was my obsession, so I followed up with some research and found articles explaining how most of the charities were lobbying arms—Americans for Pollution, Citizens for Corporate Greed—and schooled myself in the tax code regarding donations. When I came back with my findings, she whacked me with one of the statuettes she'd carted out as evidence of my father's charitable nature.

I ran off to my barn to lick my trophy-induced wounds. This time I brought with me a cigarette lighter (my mom hadn't dropped her European habit just yet) and forced some of the Beaconsfield's smoke down my throat, as my dad, despite being an antiregulatory bedfellow with Big Tobacco, hated smoking.

The next night he called me into his study. On the wall hung various trowels and scissors from their respective groundbreakings and ribbon cuttings, plaques acknowledging his philanthropy, loose change from the empires of Darius and Alexander, along with a collection of honorary degrees given in return for his money (with enough strings attached to knit a cardigan for the moon). Oh, and also a letter from Calvin Coolidge to his boat repairman.

My father, I already knew, was a human abyss. Talking to him was like shouting down the grain elevator the neighbor boy had died in. It was this very emptiness, something I'd feel my whole life, that convinced me there was truth to what I'd read on the baby internet.

"Your mother says you've been on the computer and now you're interrogating her. You think I'm evil?"

"Are you?"

"That's a fucking stupid question. No one thinks they're evil. But everyone is evil. Except your mother. You like ribs? Pepperoni pizza? Where do you think that comes from? We can't waste our time fussing over what we have to do to survive. You can bet your ass a pepperoni would eat you if it had half the chance."

He pulled back a little, then spouted what would gradually harden into his stock answer, as the question of evil became more frequent in his interviews.

"I'm not perfect. But I want everyone to be free from oppressive government. I want to give everyone a job. To change the world, you have to break a few eggs or legs or whatever it is."

He let me go.

The next day I went to the barn again and began my first attempt at cutting myself off from my family. I had a bag of clothes and snacks packed, some matches, and one of the ceremonial shovels from Dad's wall, for self-defense. I'd also worn my fingerless gloves, even though it was at least eighty degrees. I pictured myself warming my exposed fingertips on garbage fires, using them to nimbly hoist myself into railcars and guide a harmonica across my shivering lips as I slouched among the straw and cargo. That was how I imagined homeless life.

To truly start anew, I needed to burn any identifying documents. At the time, I carried with me a vinyl *Ren & Stimpy* wallet containing a library card, a D.A.R.E. ribbon signifying my pledge to be drug-free (lol), and a miniature, laminated copy of my birth certificate I had Brad, our estate manager, make me when I got the wallet.

I crumpled up two or three pages of a *Playboy* around the rest of the pack of cigarettes. After a couple weak strikes with the matches, I got the fire going and threw my mini-birth-certificate and library card on it. I practiced warming my hands hobo-style above the flames, and then, seized by the spirit of pyromania, I tossed in the whole wallet.

The vinyl melted into a burning puddle, and now the dry planks of the floor were catching. I tried to smother the growing fire with the clothes I'd packed, but the child wallet was incredibly flammable, and the windbreaker I threw on there was a combustible blend of nylon and polyester.

I grabbed the ceremonial shovel and got the fuck out of there but hid in the tall grass nearby to see what would happen.

Not only did the fire consume the historically significant barn—it spread to the new one. The flat-faced man and woman stepped out of their house and began to scream, and not long after that the fire department showed up.

One of the firemen spotted me huddled in the grass with my shovel. It didn't take long for them to put it all together.

"Who are your parents?" the fireman asked.

Gone was the despondent kid who'd burned his wallet and pledged to make his own way in the world. I had to own up to my parentage then. My old life looked much better than a new one in the juvenile detention system. Brad picked me up ten minutes later, and my dad handled everything and settled the issue privately, presumably with a big check. Now that I had my own fate to worry about, my fixation on my dad's terribleness was gone.

It was a problem I didn't have to solve. A problem that solved me. The best thing I could do was not think about it at all. Dad was like Dante's God in the *Paradiso*, and I let him stay just shy of my contemplative range. Years later, I found some relief in the nihilist strains of punk and hardcore, which imbued me with the beautiful notion that nothing fucking matters. In the end, I came full circle: my coping mechanism, cynicism, made me even more like the man with whom I had to cope. I know Freud would have plenty to say about all this, but fuck him. I always preferred Lucian to Sigmund anyway.

As for those tragic farmers, my fuckup was their ticket out. I think they moved to Florida with the money from the settlement. For a long time, I avoided driving past their sad plot if I could, and then years ago, once all guilt had exited me, I went looking for it, setting out on foot the way I had as a kid. I'm not sure if I got to their property or not. Their land had been absorbed by the vast industrial fields abutting it. I couldn't find the old farmhouse, or any trace of their small, unlucky lives. The sun was starting to go down, and far away I could see one of the grain elevators against the pink-and-purple sky, a castle on Venus.

## 18

Tim had the CD and promised he'd compile something for me soon that I could take to my dad.

In the meantime, I locked myself away in my Kenosis office and basked in my SAD lamp. The relief offered by traditional employment was gone, and the hole it'd covered over had only grown deeper with the realization of Olivia's deceit. Her scamming of investors, pharmaceutical companies, and the U.S. armed forces didn't bother me that much. That was the game, as far as I could tell. And I already knew I was being used to some degree and tolerated that under the premise that we were a pair of old friends helping each other out. But seeing the look on Olivia's face as she ignored my call had made clear something I'd already suspected. I wasn't her friend, really. I was only a prop. I'd been manipulated in ways that triggered my deepest fears and insecurities, seen as a mere extension of my dad and his money, a gilded drone who couldn't think or act on his own.

This insight let me reexamine all that I'd shoved aside over the past weeks: the mumblings of her disgruntled employees at the cloister party, the blood floor, the deformed monkey, Tim's monologues. I was done with my half-assed Hardy Boy meddling. I decided I was going to help Tim stop Olivia. I wanted the pure ethical rush of saving lives, sure, but I also wanted to get back at her for leaving me out of her scheme. And I needed to make sure I wasn't humiliated in front of my family. I'd rat her out to my parents (which would help me do a little damage control for my standing with Dad), and word would spread to the other investors from there.

The next night, Tim met me back at Nezhmetdinov Hardware and handed over two copies of a Bible-thick packet detailing Kenosis's malfeasance.

"I've been able to go over everything, and it's worse than I thought. It's better if you go through it in order, piece by piece. Look closely at the part about the ones that host living tissue and call me when you get there so I can field your questions. I've also uncovered some stuff that I think might allude to some human testing already underway, too, but I can't say for sure. This is terrifying."

"I think Clif and Olivia are fucking."

"That's news to me. Investors should know about a conflict of interest like that. If we get more evidence, I'll make an addendum. Can't say I find the mental images that conjures too appealing."

I was instructed to store the second copy in a safe place, should Olivia and Clif find us out and employ their dubious methods. I took it up to the third floor of the warehouse and hid it inside the largest of the furnaces. I spent the next day poring over the contents of the packet.

Tim was no dummy. He'd laid everything out perfectly, artfully arranging memos, photographs, and emails so they showed obvious lies. He'd annotated the dull spreadsheets, which were footnoted with citations to the emails whose claims they disproved. There was even an abstract! And an index! But what really surprised me was the cover. In a move of unexpected irony and wit from the dour Aussie, he'd lifted the cover from a biography of Johannes Gutenberg.

The dossier was packed with his own notes, which often served as illuminating prefaces to the cryptic data and inscrutable reports that followed. It was, I'd discover, sequenced in such a way that you could track his own discovery of Kenosis's shady dealings, peeking over his shoulder as he made sense of things.

In one daring raid of the specialist borough, he'd managed to photocopy a bundle of bizarre documents about a rare cancer among Tasmanian devils. Here's a bit of his exegesis:

> Loads of research on transmissible cancer among *Sarcophilus harrisii*—tazzy devils. In 22a you'll see K. has paid consultants from the University of Tasmania who specialize in this tazzy cancer. I can confirm this myself—I overheard an Australian accent in the lobby and made conversation with a professor from Hobart, though they did not disclose their purpose or specialization. [Tim was careful about concealing his identity throughout the text, but a scrupulous reader would pick up on this clue. I was sure Tim, with all his resistance and difficulty, already topped the list of suspected leakers anyway.] While much of the K. mission is ostensibly to detect cancer, why so much on a disease irrelevant to human health?

This explained the *Looney Tunes* merch, but little else. I looked up this weird cancer on my phone and discovered a batch of pictures of miniature bears with growths resembling pizza cheese on their sad faces.

Tim's estimation of Clif made for the most entertaining reading in the whole thing. I admired Tim's healthy application of shade:

> He expects Kenosis employees to be at his beck and call at all hours, day or night, on weekends and holidays. Every morning he checks the security logs obsessively to see when employees badge in and out, and every evening, around 8:00, he makes a flyby of the labs and engineering department to make sure people are still at their desks. But he lacks the discipline and intelligence he demands from others. His knowledge of science is on the high-school level, perhaps less; during a meeting with the engineering team, he wrote the atomic symbol for potassium as P (not K). On more than one occasion he has claimed his IQ to be

nearly 200, "second-highest in the company" only to Watts. A more reasonable estimate would place it squarely in the average range.

Tim clearly hated Clif and had no reason to downplay his wrongdoing. While Clif was the source of most of the toxicity in the company culture, he wasn't the mastermind I'd thought he was.

Though Tim had trouble understanding just *why* Olivia would lie about Kenosis's operations, the introduction laid out the corporate malfeasance pretty cleanly. There was no denying it any longer. Olivia had crossed the thin line between tech CEO and scammer. I might have been proud had I not remembered just how much of my family's money (and my standing with my folks) was tied up in Kenosis.

Still, I had trouble believing she was out simply to con people. Was she faking it till she made it? Or just faking it? It didn't matter either way, money-wise, but it meant something to me, as someone who once considered her a friend.

Since the handoff, Tim had been texting and calling constantly, to make sure I was still on board, to go over the details of Olivia's malfeasance like a nervous SAT tutor hoping for his bonus payout. I mostly ignored him or kept our conversations short, which probably only made him call me more.

Somewhere in this flurry of calls from Tim, I got a text from Olivia, when I wanted to see her least. She said it was important and asked if we could meet right away.

Did she know what Tim and I were up to? If she and Clif were as paranoid as Tim said, it was entirely possible they were following the sad Aussie and found out about our communication. I'd play it cool and let her tell me how much she knew.

In the years since Kenosis first sprang up, Olivia's headquarters had, in that culture of conformist disruption, spawned a litter of lookalike buildings scattered about the Caverns. The gigantic compounds remained the same, but the newcomers were almost uniformly Keno-sian. Trystero, a company set on disrupting the postal service, had sprouted a high, gargoyled tower. Another, a hyped company devoted to some esoteric wisp of cloud infrastructure, had appropriated Keno-sis's geological design, with a Noguchi-like mountain on the roof that made the building look a bit like a robot wearing a toque. Even they had to give in to Olivia's medieval sensibility, too, adding a half-assed buttress to the amorphous stone mound. What had taken Abbot Suger a lifetime took these titans of digital industry a year or two. But Olivia's had been first among these ergonomic castles, and now I was getting ready to lay siege.

I tried to ignore these cramps of shame as I drove past Kenosis HQ. I wasn't headed there today. Olivia wanted to meet me in the Caverns, the big hole in the dirt after which the tech hub was named.

I hadn't been there since my psilocybin excursion a couple years before, and I have to say, without the mushroom-fed undulations of the rock or mystical insight into my father's wickedness, the place was much less exciting this time around. The mouth of the cave blew cool air, and just a few yards in the daylight gave way entirely. For a moment I was blind, until my eyes adjusted to the faint red footlights that ran the length of the tunnel.

According to the legend, Hippolyte Bouchard, our city's founding corsair, hid out here to dodge the Spanish authorities set on hacking off his head. Hippo was undoubtedly a badass—I'd strongly consid-ered getting a tattoo of the guy, but it was only a matter of time until HBO put out a critically acclaimed miniseries about him that would render those etchings upon my shitty body passé.

As I walked down the drippy passageway, I bumped into a withered old man limping his way back to the entrance. He wore a straw hat about the size of an umbrella and under it had a face to which the skin had only loosely been applied.

"''Ello," he said, in what I took for an Italian accent. Another eccentric European tourist, here to judge my countrymen's obesity and scar teenagers as he bronzed his junk on the beach. I nodded, and he hobbled off.

As I started texting Olivia to see where she was, I heard a rustling behind me, like someone hugging a bag of potato chips.

"Charles."

"Holy fuck!"

Olivia was right there, only feet away.

"Sorry to make you come all the way out here. They're doing some repairs on the sylvarium. A squirrel got stuck in one of the irrigation pipes. I thought I'd get away and clear my head, see if I couldn't solve a few problems. Why don't we find a place where we can be alone."

We were the only two people in the tunnel, but I followed her anyway.

"God, I love it down here. It's the only place where I can truly be alone. Clif can't stand it. He refuses to set foot in the caves. They freak him out. He has a limited capacity for awe and mystery." She waved her hand around, churning the ambient atoms of mystery. "My security team hates it, too. They say it's almost impossible to secure. I don't really think anyone is out to get me, though. Not like that, anyway."

Her fingers grazed the tunnel wall as we walked. "Since we helped them out after the cutbacks, the parks people let me drop in anytime I want. It's a great perk."

I stepped over a condom wrapper. "It really is something."

"You know what? Why don't you take this?" She pulled a key off her key ring and handed it to me. "This will let you get in after hours. I've got an extra copy in my office. If anything, the place might be good for taking pictures of your bands, or even recording something. They've been really generous in letting me use the space. I think we might host a party down here when we go live."

Not a bad idea. I was jealous I hadn't thought of it.

"I heard a Siouxsie Sioux song on the way over and it had me thinking about Eugen." (Really it was the knife in her office.) "What ever happened between you two?"

"Nothing," she said. "We're still in touch, actually." I could tell she didn't want to say more about him, so I let it go.

"I heard you met Fyodor. Beautiful, right? He was a gift from one of the members of my board who loves the sylvarium even more than I do. He says it's an homage to Tycho Brahe, the astronomer, who had a tame elk or moose. Once we put him in there, it just made sense, added a wild authenticity to the space. I've really bonded with him. The droppings are unfortunate, though. The dude can eat."

The groundskeeper must have told her. I bet he didn't trust me to keep my sighting a secret and wanted to break it to her himself before I blabbed.

She led me down the trail to the big showpiece, Hippolyte's Crypt, a vast chamber with so many stalag-whatevers above and below that it looked like the maw of some sinister deep-sea fish. She took me up to a rail and, after bringing a finger to her lips, hopped over to the maze of tree-size spikes on the other side. We wandered between them until we found a clear patch far from the trail.

She stared up into the dark, her eyes darting around like she was on acid. This was a different subcategory of Olivian pause from the beats of rest that peppered the scores of her speeches. This variety was almost certainly lifted from TV detectives and blockbuster geniuses (Benedict Cumberbatch, basically), a trick to make her audience think she was privy to a set of floating, translucent data no one else could see.

"How are things going over at Obnoxious?"

"Honestly, better than I could have imagined. Given the circumstances. I just got the album art for a new thing. Want to see?"

This was for the vinyl pressing of Sydney's album-release set. The live tracks we'd put out were already more popular than the original, belabored recordings, thanks to the lore and audible sadness. I pulled up the picture (a gloomy collage with grainy bits of Sydney, Thane, some orchids) on my phone.

"Oh, that's great."

A text came in. It was Tim, whose number I'd lazily saved under *Australia Tim* (with a couple koala emojis). I swiped it away before I could read the message. It was on my screen for a quarter of a second at most. There was no chance Olivia registered anything.

"Really on-trend," she added without any hint of suspicion. "Chuck, there's something I need you to do. It's a big favor."

"Whatever you need. Of course."

"I trust you'll keep this between you and me only. The stuff we talked about at Tamyen—it's worse than that. R and W have put a temporary pin in the pilot project until we get the bullshit blessing of the FDA, and things are taking a lot longer than anticipated to bring the Gutenbergs to clinical trial. I thought we'd be using one of our investors' islands, but from what I've gathered, he might be facing some real PR problems soon. He reassures me it's nothing, but we're already pushing the envelope with this, and I don't want any extra sketchy shit to blow back on us. So now I'm in a jam. Would you be willing to visit your parents and see if they might be persuaded to loan us their island after all? Soon? I know this is a big ask. But I also know how your father feels about regulators, so I don't think it'll be too hard to convince him to help. I'm asking a lot from you, and them. I'm sorry."

Looking into her eyes, which now seemed about as big and shiny as doubloons, I felt I could trust her more than anyone in my family, more than I could trust Louise. Even though she was bullshitting my parents, the U.S. military, and, I don't know, America. It didn't make any sense. There was also something probing to it, a searchlight sweeping through my brain. Now I understand the cause of this advanced emotional manipulation, but there, in the cave, all I knew was the extreme cognitive dissonance. Had I been reared in a kind, loving home, I might've snitched on the snitch right there, but thankfully I'd learned from an early age to never, under any circumstances, fully trust anyone, so there was always a cartoon safe in my brain kept well above the high-water mark of these corny floods of sentiment.

"I can do that. I'm happy to."

This was perfect. I could bring Tim's files to my parents under the auspices of asking about the island. And just then, with the traces of Machiavellian savvy I'd inherited from Dad, I figured out a way to solve the problem with Thane's phone.

"How soon can you do it?"

"Maybe two days?"

"Wonderful. Keep me in the loop." She flashed her high-beam eyes at me again. "We have a good thing going. I think if you kept in touch with any of our old buddies from school, you'd find that you've accomplished so much more than they have, both with me and Obnoxious. At best they're evil Wall Street assholes, or at one of the VC firms out here. They've all cleanly fallen into line, but not you. You should be proud of that. We're renegades. It's how we relate."

"Definitely. And you know I'm grateful. You've been like a father to me. A good father, I mean."

She put her hand on my shoulder and gave it two quick squeezes, the kind of thing an affectionate father would do, or so I've heard. I felt guilty already.

"My assistant is sending you some information about one of Ralph's shows next week. Ralph Langenburger, my mentor. If you're back from your folks by then, you should go. I need a Kenosis face there. I think it will be interesting. You might bump into someone familiar. You'll see what I'm getting at."

"Sounds like a good time. I'm intrigued."

"I know you're busy, Charles. I won't keep you. I'm going to hang back a bit longer. I still have some things to turn over. Keep me updated."

I managed to find my way back to the entrance without the assistance of the National Guard, and whatever strange feeling that had tested my resolve back in the cave now evaporated in the sunlight. Half an hour later I called to arrange my flight. It was time to see the old sire and dam.

## 19

The next day I was on an airplane, one of the many jets in the fleet that regularly migrate from our nation's major cities to the private airport a stone's throw from my father's house.

Before I left, I broke into Sydney's van with a brick. I grabbed the lockbox and, to keep up the ruse of random theft, a stray guitar amp, tossing both into the ocean on my way to the airport. For my alibi, I'd bought a ticket from Delta so I could forward the information to Louise (I told her my mom was getting her hip replaced), and that flight had been scheduled an hour before my mini-heist. By the time Sydney got off work at the library and discovered the break-in, I'd be with my family, playing our traditional mind games, the closest we get to Settlers of Catan and Apples to Apples.

My plan was this. I'd hand over Tim's dossier and explain things to Dad in private. Once I'd convinced him of the validity of my source and his findings, we'd bring in Renata, who'd take the first steps in extricating us from Olivia's scheme and alert the other big investors. If things went according to my plan, my former best friend would never know I'd betrayed her. My story would be that I'd come to ask Dad about the island, and he'd caught me off guard by confronting me with the whistleblower's findings.

I started skimming the sour facts of Tim's dossier again. The next thing I knew—thanks, Xanax!—I was riding through the gates of the family fortress. Despite being a near-invincible pig, my father has hung on to a fear of leftist terrorists he'd picked up in the seventies, and sometime after 9/11 the fortifications became an exercise in overkill (behind closed doors he'll tell you it was environmentalists, not Osama, who orchestrated the attack). My driver waved at an ex–Green Beret, who opened the gate and granted us entry to the fief.

Anyone visiting their childhood home knows why the old Greek rhetoricians came up with the house as the perfect mnemonic device. My default memory palace just so happened to be an actual palace. Over there was the knoll where our German nanny, the stern but beautiful fräulein who messed me up so bad, taught my brother and me, a twelve-year-old already sporting an early dad bod, about the many achievements of Frederick the Great. (Though, judging by her authoritarian tendencies and the anti-Semitic remarks I caught here and there, I suspect there was another German leader she was even more fond of.) There, just down the slope a piece, was the sculpture garden where, as boys, my brother and I would chase each other between the tubby Miró and a lumbering Henry Moore. Where, years later, during our fresh, Ralph Lauren adolescence, my brother would fuck his high school girlfriend while I watched, rolling magnanimously on Molly. But the most charged memories had nothing to do with these fond recollections of an innocent American boyhood, no. The warm nostalgia was but a garnish on the larger cocktail of enmity. For the grounds were still populated by my most ancient and hateful foe: the fucking zebras.

"I'll pay you ten thousand dollars to hit one of those zebras," I told my driver just before he let me out. Dad had bought them as soon as Peter and I were no longer cute, surely an upgrade in his view. (No coincidence, this was just after I torched those barns.) He adored them with the special, grandparental love his friends lavished on their children begotten with second and third wives.

"God, I wish. But don't repeat that to your father."

My phone started buzzing. It was Louise, probably calling to tell me about the break-in. I'd wait until after I ratted out Olivia to call her back.

My family was waiting for me inside. Mother, quaintly shrouded in her usual Hermès, with the casual beauty of an aging Bergman muse. (A woman for whom, growing up, sprezzatura was more important than the Golden Rule.) Dearest brother, his flowing blond ringlets loosely bunched like a bouquet at the nape, the curls showing under his mostly unbuttoned shirt the exact same color and length of those on his head. Finally, in the back, letting the physical distance reflect the emotional one, my father. Looking much older than last time, wearing a suit now far too big for his shrinking frame, like a prom-going teen. Essentially me, or Peter, but crumpled up in anticipation of the only significant decline in assets in his whole life. I'm talking about death, if you haven't guessed.

You might be wondering why it's me, and not my older brother, who bears our father's name. Dad was second-born, and to emphasize that his children were vessels for his identity, he named Peter after his older brother and gave his name to son number two. A decision, like that of spawning me in the first place, I'm confident he now regrets.

We exchanged the usual greetings. A fitness appraisal and a joke about my smell (Peter), quick kisses and a scoff at my outfit (Mom), and a few more venomous scowls (Pops).

Brad, our estate manager, was there, too, and gave me a big hug. In the nineties Brad had lived an enviable existence as a rent boy for a retail magnate, and while the breakup had left him penniless, he'd found a career that could put to use his deep, firsthand knowledge of life's finer things. Among my alloparents, he balanced out Renata's mind of serrated indices with a huge heart that pumped Chablis.

I dropped my bag in the parlor and set Tim's book on an end table. I could feel their eyes all over me, like chiggers. Peter and Mom smiled with faux tenderness. My father leered at me like a mean little cat in a window.

I was proud (maybe too proud) to have shed most of the trappings of wealth in pursuit of an authentic, poverty-lite existence. But you miss the small comforts of home. Veronika ironing the sheets in the morning, Brad anticipating your breakfast preferences, the cathartic luxury of channeling your emotions into a spicy tirade at either of them when Dad gives you a silence that makes God seem chatty. I was happy to be back, even with my unfortunate mission and the negative presence of my family to contend with.

"Is Veronika around? I have some clothes."

I'd brought with me some choice articles—a rubberized trench coat, a silk bathrobe I will never part with, a denim jacket bearing an embroidered black widow—to hand off to Veronika for a good dry cleaning at our in-house setup. I only trusted her with these flashier prizes of my otherwise machine-washable wardrobe.

Mom summoned her. Dad had his bland assistant, Charlotte. Mom had Veronika. Theirs was a long, high-decibel codependence, a shark-and-wrasse dynamic much more like a marriage than what Mom had with Dad. I suspect that when her attendant dies, Mom won't be far behind, and not just because she won't know how to feed herself.

Veronika arrived, and after a brief, routine explosion of simultaneous monologues in Slovak and German as she and Mom chewed each other out in their respective mother tongues, she lugged the bag away.

"Peter was just about to show us something from Unity," Mom said. The Unity division was Grossheart Industries' defense-contracting branch, a duchy helmed by my more conventional brother. "Why don't we go see what they've been up to?"

The journey to the lawn took ages. Dad, hobbling on a cane that had once belonged to Otto von Bismarck, set a tectonic pace while the rest of us tried to walk as naturally as we could so he wouldn't notice our accommodating him. This involved a lot of zigzagging, like dolphins surfing the bow waves of a cruise ship. From time to time my mom offered an arm to right him with a tenderness I rarely witnessed and suspected might be part of some psychosexual scheme.

Ever since I was a teen, I always thought my parents should have

gotten a divorce, just so I could fit in with my Dewey Willson buddies. It would have given my sadness some object and direction, lent
me a little more pathos, and possibly netted me a hot stepmom to
awkwardly pine for. (This replaced my childhood fantasy of the two
of them being murdered by a poor person so I could be raised by a
butler and become Batman.) But here they were, still together, when
my school friends' dads had gone through more wives than Henry
VIII and John Huston.

"I saw your boss on the cover of *Prosper*," Peter said as we veered
around our waddling progenitor. "I was almost proud of you there."

"Aw, shucks." It was the nicest thing he'd ever said to me.

"It sounds like you've weaseled your way into the next big thing
somehow. Can't wait to see how you fuck it up."

If things went according to plan, it would happen within the hour.

"You know, since you reached out to them, we've been in talks with
Neve Olmert, over at SNIT. It's actually looking like something might
come of it. There's a lot of money on the table, so we've accelerated
things. Her company lost a bid with the Israel Defense Forces, and it
turns out there's a lot of overlap between our projects. It's all moving
very quickly. Neve and I have really hit it off, too."

Louise was calling me again. I turned off my phone, along with
the chunk of my brain that would produce images of Peter and Neve
doing anything other than negotiating.

I told Peter I'd seen Nosferatu Jerry Seinfeld when I was at SNIT.

"Anything to report?"

"Olivia says there might be some kind of scandal in the press soon,
but people are always saying that. When I saw him, he was just dangling money, treating the place like it was his frat house. Gives off a
very Rodney Dangerfield in *Back to School* vibe. If Roman Polanski
directed. Or was in it?"

"I'm a true sicko. I'd watch the shit out of that."

One of Peter's Unity flunkies waited for us just past the slouching

Henry Moore. On the ground in front of him lay what appeared to be some kind of mechanical condor.

"What the fuck is that?" my father and I pronounced simultaneously.

Peter responded with the indifference he'd spent decades practicing on the two of us in particular. "It's an ornithopter. This is the next generation of surveillance and recon. If things go right, the sky will be full of these little fuckers."

Tim hadn't been that crazy, then, when he suspected that frigate bird of eavesdropping.

As Peter and his assistant fired up their mechanical bird, I examined my father to appraise his mood. My brother's folly was perfect for my surveillance and reconnaissance of just how pissy my dad was.

With a few uncannily naturalistic flaps and the buzz of twin shoulder propellers, the bird was airborne.

"We've managed to replicate bird flight to the point where our 'thopters can adjust wing thickness, like a falcon does when it dives. This guy can go for days if the pilot can find the right updrafts. We're working on albatross, kestrel, and even bat models for nocturnal recon."

The shadow of the robocondor passed over us and slid toward the house.

"Beautiful," my mother said.

My old man's face was an expression I'd describe as groggy animus. I was lucky—this was a good day.

Peter inflated before us like an air mattress. "We're very close to avian indistinguishability, though we are hitting some issues on the materials side. Coming up with something strong enough that doesn't fuck up the density has proven a little challenging, but we're getting there. We've started working with the people over at SNIT. Charles actually helped with some of that. It's looking like they're going to push us *years* forward, and we'll pick up the added benefit of biodegradability, which would cut the risk of interception and make the devices disposable. Which means we can make a ton of these guys."

The bird landed, and my mom gave a half-hearted clap. As I turned to Dad, prepared to bring up Olivia's deception, I heard some commotion behind me.

"Fuck!" Peter shouted.

A zebra had discovered our animatronic vulture and came charging right at it, baring its gums and fucked-up Giuliani teeth in a display of pure hate. Before anyone could do anything, he was stomping on the wings, kicking robotic chunks high into the air until they rained down upon us like the world's most expensive confetti.

By now my brother had already summoned the zebra man, a white South African who I suspected had moonlit as an apartheid operative, though I was still building my case. The freckly Afrikaner languidly loaded his tranquilizer rifle.

My dad raised a shriveled hand. "No. Let him finish."

Peter: "What?"

"Tranquing can be rough on the joints," the zebra man explained without invitation. "This one, Xerxes, he's your dad's favorite. Weighs a good three hundred and twenty kilos," the Afrikaner added proudly. "He's getting addicted to the darts anyhow. Building up a tolerance."

A quick diatribe on zebras:

Reader, whoever you are, I think it's a safe guess that your father never took such a liking to zebras that he decided to import a herd of them to his estate for his daily enjoyment. So you, unlike me, have had the real privilege of only observing these fiends at a distance at best, or filtered through David Attenborough's narration. But in my quest to understand my father, I've looked at zebras from both sides now (all sides, actually, including on top and underneath), and let me tell you, a more vile creature has never been born. Excluding man, naturally. Perhaps a more intimate portrait is required.

Imagine, then, a cross between a donkey and an alcoholic penguin.

Our Creator took a perfectly fine organism, the noble steed, sawed a bit off his legs, trimmed his mane into a tacky Mohawk, and endowed His new abomination with the demeanor and teeth of a xenophobic soccer hooligan. A divine affront to taste only forgivable if you figure He worked in alphabetical order and was down to the shitty leftovers by the time He hit $Z$. Long ago, after years of close observation of these striped fiends, I came to a conclusion I stand by to this day, the only explanation for my father's love for them that makes any sense: they are the ultimate flex, the perfect beasts to tow the chariot of his incontrovertible, bitter whimsy.

Peter did his best to keep his cool and waved his assistant off. We tried to go back inside and leave the brute to do its thing, but my dad was content to watch his pet settle the definition of *smithereens* once and for all. We were there a long time, until even the zebra got bored and trotted off to his stinky harem. I'd wait to break the news later.

After dinner seemed my best bet. I spent the rest of the afternoon reviewing my treacherous speech's bullet points and following my mother around as she tabulated the imperfections in a batch of new paintings she'd commissioned. Just last year, for no reason other than to stick it to his wife, Dad had donated the whole of their art collection to the nearest decent museum in return for its rechristening with the Grossheart name hyphenated into it. (They'd kept their Picasso sketch, thank God. I'd throw a fit if they ever removed that ugly little face from its home in the downstairs bathroom. He'd been a real companion through so many lonely adolescent shits.) To placate my mother, Dad ordered detailed facsimiles of each work to replace those treasures. I'd urged her to simply buy contemporary works. The closest thing she had to contemporary art (other than her portrait with Dad) was a pair of Derwatts she'd bought from the estate of some

Texas oil baronet, and now these were nearly old enough to collect Social Security. Whatever my issues with her stagnant taste, these copies were good and likely racked up a bill hefty enough to purchase a Lautrec or two. Give me Wayne Thiebaud or Nancy Graves over my mom's paint-by-number dullards any day. My task now was to put institutional weight behind my mother's perceived imperfections so she could compile and forward them to the professional forgers, thereby extending the project essentially forever in order to enact her sly vengeance on my father. It was fun.

"That boat is wrong."

"I thought it was a dead seal," I added helpfully, mama's boy that I am.

Veronika and some of the other staff ran by with brooms and one of Peter's old lacrosse sticks.

"Some swallows got into the house," Mom said. "Maybe one of them could shit on these. It might improve them."

As we nitpicked our way down the house's main artery, my snotty ancestors scowled from their places of honor above the landscapes and sex workers. Through a multidecade intimidation effort, Mom and Dad had managed to get their hands on the finest portraits of the more prominent figures in their respective bloodlines, enlisting painters to fill in the gaps where no portrait existed. Such was the case for my dad's grandparents, an indigent German printshop assistant and his busty wife, flatly rendered here by some sentimental hack and looking like a pair of human Easter eggs. Their son, my grandpa, is depicted with much more regality by the same artist who did the official presidential portraits of Truman, Eisenhower, and Nixon. His is the finest of the patrilineals and even holds its own next to the quality pieces on the maternal side (literally a side of the hall—I'll get there soon). He deserves it, as it was his oil wells in the USSR, along with a few projects approved by Hitler (many American businesses did this, Dad will tell you), that buoyed the family finances and established the empire Dad and my uncle would inherit. The portrait, unlike the empire, couldn't be chopped up and went to my uncle Pete, who surrendered it to my father about two years after Grandpa's death. They'll tell you it was a trade, with Dad handing over a subsidiary, but Peter and I would bet the zebra ranch it was some Palm Springs bathhouse kompromat. Mom and Dad—at Mom's urging—were done by Andy Warhol, who made them sit for just fifteen minutes on a bed in their apartment on the Upper West Side back in 1975 as he took his Polaroids. The resulting print has them looking much more hip than they are, and while Dad always used to vow he'd get another in his old age, the picture's significant appreciation in value (recent and nineties dips aside) silenced him on the matter.

But my favorite side, in both senses, has always been Mom's. With Dad's money, she was able to strong-arm a cousin into giving up a likeness of her great-grandpa, a man who'd saved the life of Franz Joseph during the Battle of Solferino, earning him a barony and the daughter of a fellow von as his bride. In the portrait, he stands fully upholstered with his epaulets tasseling onto my monochromatic great-great-grandma, decked out in a white dress to match the shade of her skin and hair. Mom's grandpa was a government bureaucrat, and it's hard to tell if the scant personality in his picture is the artist's fault or his own. It was during his lifetime that the Austrian nobility was abolished (don't start Mom on that), and thanks to his son, it didn't take long until the family's holdings were gone, too.

Grandpa's portrait was taken late in life, right here at my folks' estate, and in it he looks senior to his dad and grandpa. After an undistinguished career as a drunken soldier, he became a drunken engineer, which is how, at a Hamburg refinery in the spring of 1934, he met my dad's dad and formed the friendship that would eventually bring about the union of my parents and produce your humble narrator. Of all my ancestors, he seemed the least judgmental, and I always felt close to him, in his lucky ineptitude. I never got the chance to meet him—he died just a month before I was born—but I like to imagine we high-fived on those twin mall escalators in that big dark, as I was coming down and he going up. Or, more likely, the reverse.

Then it was time to eat. Rather than sport my usual uniform of defiance, I wore a boring black oxford, a pair of vestigial horn-rimmed glasses, and even manipulated my hair into an orderly loaf.

At the table, my mother (who has never failed to maintain a high standard of Tyrolean glamour) made no disparaging remarks on my clothes, which amounts to a glowing review. My brother kept looking at me like I might suddenly lay an egg or produce an automatic weapon. But I kept my eyes on the prize, the little man at the head of the table pickling in his own malignity.

First I'd check the wine bottle to suss out his mood. Beneath our feet lay a catacomb holding a Temecula worth of wine, a collection with a gaudy emphasis on bottles that had, at some point, found their way into the hands of the Great Men of History. Here, in the dank maze below my 1982 Doc Martens and my mother's Tibi flats, could be found bottles once officially owned by Franz Joseph (in honor of the Hero of Solferino), by Napoléons I and III, by James Monroe, Winston Churchill, and John Locke. Dad was a big fan of the enclosure movement.

These beautiful bottles were right there, ready for consumption as these giants paddled the rivers of History. Vintages statesmen and autocrats drank, or would have, had the Course of Human Events not demanded a sober mind and a moderate disposition. Just think! If Nelson had reached for another glass of port, or had Himmler (yes, Dad had one or two bottles from the less admirable Reich) taken one more for the road, these bottles could have been cause of famous, perhaps even world-changing, hangovers. This sad, small-minded hobby still gives me one of those tender pangs of embarrassment particular to seeing over your father's head.

The real prizes of his collection were not even remotely drinkable, but there was a narrow band of wines, the former property of, say, some mustachioed German general, or a macho novelist remembered more for his alcoholism than his prose style, that, when in a wistful mood, my dad might occasionally whip out and share. (It should be noted these notable bottles weren't all we drank—they were merely celebrity guests at the table. We'd take a quick sip of History's vinegar and then move on to glug more mundane vintages.) If it was just some run-of-the-mill Bordeaux we were dealing with, I'd hold off on bringing up Olivia's chicanery and dodge the risk of a tirade. But if our wine had passed through the hands of a man of consequence, I'd know it was time to shoot my shot and tell him the bad news.

I waited for Brad to emerge from the cellar and explain just what it was we'd be choking down. If I could have, I would have descended along with him to divine my fate and see what Pops had selected, but I'd long since been banned from our basement after a vengeful busting of a Millard Fillmore bottle.

Our typical mealtime conversation consisted of arc-less recounting of minor inconveniences. Inconvenience, so rarely experienced among my kin, held an almost mystical fascination for them. But tonight I was spared accounts of multi-minute waits and mildly unsatisfactory customer service experiences. Mom's mind was on the paintings. She went on about the fraud Monets and I passively nodded my assent, eager for the bottle to drop. When at last Brad reappeared, my eyes went straight to the cataloging label.

I was in luck. It was a Spiro Agnew. Brad gave us a brief book report on its provenance while I plotted my approach.

". . . housed at his estate in Ocean City, Maryland . . ."

"That's enough," Dad said. "I'm hungry."

We ate our salty repast, and I waited to bring up Kenosis. I wouldn't have to wait long. My brother, whose only previous interest in me up to that point was as a lightning rod for my parents' disdain, now seemed to show some genuine curiosity about my nascent tech career.

"I want to know about your new boss. What's she like? Is she really the next Jobs?"

For a normal person, this would have been a good place to allude to my doubts about the company and lay the groundwork for what I'd tell Dad later. But I'd learned to speak by one-upping my brother to win a scrap of my dad's attention. The flow of idiotic talk that followed was completely involuntary and churned up from some primal cove of my gut, a kind of brag reflex.

"She's better than that turtlenecked diva. This is medicine, not kids' movies and phones to watch TV on. It's like comparing Florence Nightingale to P. T. Barnum."

"But is the tech really there yet? We've toyed with nano at Unity, and the conventional wisdom is that we still have a ways to go before we're looking at anything practical. Neve mentioned something along those lines."

"That's the thing. Nanotech is the long-term vision. She's really changed the game with microfluidic assays, which is our bread and butter right now, and that'll lay the groundwork for the nano shit. Which certainly has a ways to go, but not as much as you think. For us, anyway. But you're right, development is hard, especially when you're the only one this far out in front of the pack, encountering problems the rest of the field hasn't even *predicted* yet. We want to do things right, and that takes time." I released a noble sigh. "And the FDA isn't helping things, either." I looked to Dad, who couldn't hide his contempt for government regulations of any kind. I needed to shut up, but I couldn't. "We're securing more funding right now, so we can have the runway we need to do all this. We'll be able to land government contracts once we jump this next hurdle, so we're focusing on that."

One of the swallows, the trapped birds the staff had been hunting earlier, flitted through the door, then quickly looped back out, a black boomerang.

"No, I guess that makes sense."

I looked over. For the first time in my life since I made my gooey debut thirty years ago, I had my father's undivided, nontoxic attention. He didn't say anything, but he was studying me—listening, even! I felt like a bottle of Moscato owned by Julius Caesar.

But the true vessel metaphor for me, at least when I'm around Dad, isn't the bottle. In my father's presence, I become a colander. So, dipshit that I am, I had to bring up my other achievements, totally, stupidly cashing in all my saved-up dignity and converting it into the unstable currency of his approval.

"Things are going pretty well with the label, too. We're in the black now. We're making a profit for once."

"Really?" Mom butted in. "I thought you quit that with the new position."

"I didn't have to. It's a well-oiled machine at this point."

"We'll have to listen to the big hits after dinner, then," Peter said.

"Sure." I couldn't imagine Mom lasting more than a second into even our mellowest release. It was why I liked the music in the first place.

We returned to the subject of the bad impressions of the Impressionists. While Mom complained, I savored the moment, repressing all thoughts of the lies I'd just perpetrated. My parents were proud of their prodigal, and my brother seemed genuinely jealous. As I sat there in our cavernous dining room, surrounded by phony Monets, the play count on *Sucker* was steadily climbing. I could've kissed a zebra. I'd let myself have this moment of tranquility, and tomorrow I'd show Dad the dossier outlining Olivia's bullshit.

I floated from the dining room to the parlor, just about as happy as I would ever be in that life (or the next, for that matter). I glimpsed a dark flash in the hall—it was the swallow again. I admired and related to the little creature's tenacity.

I plopped myself on a plump sofa, one of the few remaining pieces of furniture from my childhood, the rest having been replaced by a new Jeanneret armchair and a Royere set resembling a family of over-fed polar bears. But in my tranquil brain, even these ugly, overstuffed chairs had their charm.

Brad and the zebra man joined us by the fireplace, the former cradling a guitar, the latter with a violin, and as we sat down, the two began to play a sweet, sad tune. Brad started to sing in his signature soulful tenor, and his Afrikaner buddy Garfunkeled in for the chorus. My mother sipped her wine by the mantel. My father idly turned the pages of a book on his lap. My brother checked his email on his phone. For the first time ever, I felt at peace among them.

> *I don't ever want to feel like I did that day.*
> *Take me to the place I love, take me all the way.*

An old folk song, I assumed, though sometime late in the night I'd realize what it was—a Red Hot Chili Peppers hit. But that's okay. The music soothed me, taking me farther down my path of serenity.

"What is this?" my father asked me.

Only then did I see just what book he'd been reading. Tim's dossier. The cover, the image of Gutenberg with history practically growing out of his beard, had struck Dad's fancy. This was not how it was supposed to go down. My boasting at dinner was either going to make it look like I was in on the scam and dumb enough to leave the evidence lying around, or too stupid to see it for what it was.

Just then one of the original cuts sung by Thane came shooting out of the sound system, drowning out another tender duet. Mom put her hands over her ears. My brother sat smiling, phone in hand, having clearly spent the last half hour waiting for the perfect moment to pull the trigger.

"THIS IS CHUCK'S MUSIC!" he proclaimed.

Veronika came in. "WHAT IS THIS SHIT?"

"TURN IT OFF," Mom screamed. "I'M DYING!"

The good son obeyed. Dad's eyes remained fixed on the Kenosis exposé.

"What the fuck is this?" he yelled, and chucked Tim's dossier at me. It bounced off my shin and landed on the rug. "Are you fucking with me? Are you and your little friend trying to rob me?"

Mom and Peter (still beaming from his dump on the chest of my dignity) took the hint—she led him off to denigrate the paintings, and Brad, Veronika, and the zebra man slipped away behind them. I was tempted to go outside, grab one of the guard's guns, and litter the turf with incarnadine zebras.

"Dad, I've been trying to talk to you about this. It's not exactly like what I said at dinner." I blanked. The chatty spirit that had possessed me earlier now ghosted me.

But then I heard a knock at the door behind me. A member of the staff wouldn't knock, and it was entirely impossible for an unexpected visitor to show up without a guard intercepting them. Mom, Peter, Veronika, and the zebra man all followed Brad back into the room to watch him get the door, and even Dad looked surprised.

"Charles!"

Out of the shadows stepped Olivia. Tim's tome-to-end-all-(nano)-tomes was still at my feet. I kicked it under the sofa.

## 20

"Sorry I'm a day early," she said, seeing the confounded looks on my family's faces. "Charles didn't tell you I was coming?"

"How'd you get in?" Peter asked, but Olivia had already dived into conversation with my mother. Olivia's German was Goethe good, even better than mine and Peter's, and with it she was able to disarm Mom right away. I watched as she moved on to my still-stunned brother, then finally came to greet my dad.

"Mr. Grossheart—I'm so delighted to meet you at last. I can finally thank you in person for your faith in our mission."

My dad stayed silent, but I could see his rage had melted away, leaving him hollow.

"I've long heard of your legendary cellar and have always wanted to see it." She was speaking in the overformal register most people automatically used when addressing him, the way a defendant would talk to Judge Judy. "Any chance you could give me a tour?"

Their eyes met. I had no reason to think my father would want to show her around under these circumstances. But after a few seconds of silent valuation, his face reanimated, as if he'd just been asleep with his eyes open and now found himself suddenly, embarrassingly awake.

"Oh, certainly."

He rose and began his slow journey to the cellar door. I tried to follow, but Olivia waved me away.

"That music was terrible," Mom told me. "I was prepared to take my own life." Fair enough. I'd been about to Young Werther myself, too, but for other reasons.

We waited a long time for them. I was on the verge of a psychic break. How the fuck did she get here so quickly and make it past Dad's Praetorian Guard? Did she know about Tim? More important, what was she going to do with me?

I considered grabbing the telltale report and hiding it somewhere more secure, but I didn't want to draw any more attention to it and figured it was just as safe under the couch as it would be in my room.

Sweat from my armpits was flooding my love handles' chubby deltas.

"What was Dad saying? About you robbing him?"

"I was trying to get him to put some real money into the label. I have a hunch it won't happen now."

"I need a cigarette."

I wasn't a smoker in San Narciso, but when I came home, I usually picked up a pack of Beaconsfields at the QuikTrip. It gave me an excuse to duck away from my family at regular intervals, and it drove my dad delightfully insane.

"Don't burn the house down, Carrie." Peter had called me that ever since I incinerated that poor couple's barn.

I stood out there sucking on a Beaconsfield and puzzling over Olivia's strange arrival. Nothing about it made any sense. Even if she'd figured out what I was up to, how had she followed me? I had a panicky, childlike fear of her, the same feeling I used to have awaiting the administration of punishment from the man currently with her in the wine cellar.

I received a call from Louise. This was, at least, conflict I could handle. It was time to play dumb, the role I was born for.

"Someone broke into Sydney's van," she said. "She had a panic attack, and I had to take her to the hospital. They took the box with her phone in it and, like, a stupid Orange practice amp. Not even a tube amp, just solid-state."

Louise started sobbing. She sounded like a choking sea lion. "Chuck,

I'm so fucking tired. This isn't what we agreed to. I love you. I love Sydney, too. I miss Thane. But I need some time to myself. Just, like, a day. Two days. I'm going to fall apart here."

"I'll come home as soon as I can."

"I'm sorry. How's everything with your mom? How are things at the farm?" she asked once the last sob was out of her. When we met, I told her my family lived on a ranch. Which they did, technically, if you counted the zebras.

"She's fine. Everything's fine. It's very pastoral. Hip surgery is pretty chill nowadays. I'm going to go rebook my flight back so I can be there for you. I'm sorry it's been so fucking awful."

"Are you okay? You sound kind of, I don't know, weird. You're talking really fast."

"I'm just worried about Sydney. And there's my family. You know how it is. You miss them, and then it only takes about ten minutes of quality time before you start looking longingly at ledges and sturdy rafters."

"Please get back as soon as you can. I'm starting to go crazy."

Back inside, Olivia and Dad reappeared, each carrying a bottle of wine. As Dad settled into his chair, she came over to show off the fruits of a very productive half hour.

"Your father has just agreed to double his initial investment in Kenosis. And it turns out he hates the FDA as much as I do, so the island will be no problem. Oh, he gave me this, too."

I looked at the label. The bottle had belonged to none other than John Frémont, the first presidential candidate from my father's beloved party. I'd have been jealous if I weren't so afraid.

"Sorry to drop in unannounced like that. I decided to bow out of a conference at the last minute." She studied the bottle of Frémont, then smiled widely at my mother. "I thought you might need some backup."

Betrayal and humiliation have always been the major dialects of

Dad's love language, and I worried he'd blabbed about Tim's dossier down in the cellar. I was completely perplexed by Olivia's skill with him. As someone who had never persuaded the man—the only trust he ever gave me being of the fund variety—I was curious about her methods. (Yes, the nastiest conclusion did occur to me briefly, but I decided to spare myself the therapy sessions and not dwell on that possibility; Dad had always been too shrewd to fall for that kind of thing and scoffed at his peers' child brides.) Winning him over was a manipulation of reality much greater than her cross-country teleportation, and I was totally confounded.

At my father's request, Brad and the zebra man gave us another ballad (*Take me down to the Paradise City / Where the grass is green and the girls are pretty*) and Dad poured us each a glass from some actually drinkable vintage. He was the happiest I'd seen him, ever. We put away another two bottles—my family from mirth, me filling up the vacuum of dread that had opened up. My mind was two feet below my ass, plopped on top of Tim's documents. We drank until all our mouths were red, our teeth as purple as salami.

It was late, and soon my parents and our musical entertainment stumbled off to bed. I tried to hang back and grab the packet from under the sofa, but Olivia and Peter had begun chatting about Grossheart Unity and didn't look like they'd call it a night anytime soon. There was no reason to think she'd seen the incriminating documents, so I figured I'd wait an hour or so and creep back downstairs.

"Charles," Olivia said as I tried to slip away. "Peter's just going to bed. Let's catch up."

"Night, guys." Peter looked a little starstruck. I hadn't seen him like that since Fred Durst played his fourteenth birthday party.

"Charles, what I'm about to tell you is very important. Let's go to the cellar."

I followed her to the cellar door. I felt like a child about to be punished. But something in her voice took the edge off my panic. It was like I'd done an emotional speedball, pushed and pulled between peace and fear.

"Your dad typed in the code pretty slowly. I don't think he'll mind if we talk down here."

We went down the stairs. Like I've said, I hadn't been down there in a decade, and since then, Dad had expanded it considerably. The racks, indexed like the shelves in a library, stretched so far that, in the low light, they seemed to go on forever. I prepared for Olivia to Cask of Amontillado me.

"Charles, I know this all must look very strange. And I know you've caught wind of things that might have unsettled you. I owe you some explanations. More than that, it's time I brought you into the inner circle. This is going to be hard to frame in a way that makes sense. Some of what I'm about to say is going to sound very weird. I need you to bear with me, and to trust me. I'm going to start at the beginning, and what I want is for you to hear me out without judgment until I've finished. Are you in a headspace where you can do that?"

"Olivia, yes. Just tell me what is going on. You know you can trust me, too. It goes both ways."

"Okay." She turned a nearby bottle over on its rack, took a look at the label, and began her story.

In January of sophomore year, a couple months before the trip to Greece, she got a call from her doctor. Her numbers were bad. Her years of remission had ended.

Olivia had already been through all this, and she knew things were about to get much worse. She made arrangements for treatment in Cambridge and decided she'd keep it secret for as long as she could to enjoy this last taste of freedom without our pity. She did her best not to mope around us, but it was hard to rein in her despair. Her life, as far as she could see it, was over, and it amounted to nothing. All the work she'd put in was a waste, and she'd barely enjoyed her youth. Years that should have been spent living, dancing, reading, doing nothing, were whiled away on a computer or under the fluorescent lights of a lab. She'd only just begun enjoying life with me, James, and Eugen, partying, reading poetry, going on our road trip, and she was deeply grateful for that, but even this was getting cut short before she could learn how to let go of the pain and fear she carried everywhere.

"A few times, in those weeks after my doctor called, I thought about finding a peaceful spot outside of Boston—Cape Ann, maybe, or Provincetown—to swim out into the sea and just let it swallow me."

There was only a trace of the rhythm from her Kenosis speeches. Her smart voice, the audible italics, the long, Chekhovian pauses, all of this was gone. She wasn't even bothering to give me her usual significant eye contact. I was getting the real Olivia.

One night, when she was feeling especially low, she texted Eugen to meet her at the library. The two of them liked to wander around the lower stacks (the book bunkers of C and D) or take the tunnel even deeper to Pusey to look at the old maps. "It's a very similar vibe down here, actually." They'd grab random books, sharing whatever lines their eyes fell on as they mazed their way between the shelves. It was like being disembodied, living in a world made entirely of paper and knowledge, and she especially needed that right then.

"You're sick again," Eugen told her as they sat down among some South American novels (she remembered the green, rebound spines that supported his, a detail the shock of the coming discovery would petrify, like the volcanic eruption that preserved Pompeii). "What's going on? You can tell me."

Olivia slid a bottle back, looked at me for a moment, then pulled out another.

"How did he know? Now I understand it had something to do with the awareness that comes with the Gift, which is what I'm getting to, but at the time I chalked it up to our closeness. That was probably part of it, too."

We were veering into the weird shit. I tried to lock all the muscles in my face and keep my skepticism from seeping out.

"The other day I froze up when you asked about him. The truth is, his role in my life has been enormous. He listened patiently as I laid it all out for him, the bleakness of my future, the morbidity of my thoughts."

When she was done, Eugen said he wanted to show her something. "Look, I can help you. What I'm about to tell you is going to make you think I've lost my mind—I know because I've been there—so I need to show you something first. Don't scream."

He pulled out his hunting knife and ran it across his wrist. She managed to obey him and keep quiet as he moved his arm closer to her. The wound was a good four inches long, and the tissue underneath was purple-black.

"It took a second for me to realize there was no blood. But before I could remark on this came the truly bizarre part: the wound closed, like a tent zipped from the inside."

The cellar lights casting us in gentle orange from udon-thick tungsten—shut off now that we'd been holding still too long for the motion sensor to pick us up. We were left in the faint red of the security system's LEDs. Everything but Olivia's face, which was closer to the keypad, was just barely perceptible, but she continued her story as if nothing had happened and kept on pulling out bottles and examining their labels in the dark. I'd lost control of my face and hoped I at least had enough cover to hide my dropping jaw.

"He explained the Gift to me then in rather vague terms. Had he not just shown me his arm, I wouldn't have believed him at all. He was being oddly circumspect, but I learned later that he was simply putting things the best way I could understand them, what I'm try-ing to do with you now. I came away with this impression, which was ultimately correct: The Gifted are an ancient society of the world's most intelligent and talented individuals, all working to bring about the evolution of humanity to something better, stronger. With tech-nology developed over millennia, they had unlocked the full potential of their bodies and minds, allowing them to do seemingly impossible things. He saw my promise, and he was willing to give it to me, if I wanted it. He told me that there were risks: Some didn't have the right constitution for it and didn't survive. And even if it worked, there were side effects, prohibitions, and a strict diet. Should I want to proceed, he'd still need approval, which is why we planned our trip to Greece."

So it was some kind of self-improvement tech cult, I thought. Eugen had never seemed particularly spiritual, but his fierce privacy meant anything was possible.

They told everyone Eugen was attending a poetry workshop. Their rationale was that this would be sufficiently boring so James and I wouldn't assume it was a mini-Mykonos and try to tag along. When this failed to deter me, Eugen and Olivia figured they could manage anyway. Their story would still provide cover, and it might actually be good for her to have a friend there, since there wouldn't be much for Olivia to do anyway, as she would soon discover.

"I was honestly so grateful that you flew us. I'd never experienced that kind of luxury before." As we took off and Boston shrank below her, she said she could feel her sadness shrinking, too.

"This particular island was one of just seven sites of considerable importance to the Gifted. It was home to a sacred temple said to be built by one of the first of their kind, though I would learn that later. Eugen's home was another, making him a kind of prince among an already elite group. When time means nothing, place becomes more important, as a repository for memory, to ground the Gifted so we don't feel adrift as the vestiges of our old lives fade away."

For a couple days Eugen made his case before the other Gifted who, she was told, were quietly observing her. She wouldn't be allowed to see them until it was time for her to join their ranks, should they consent.

"But I did glimpse them here and there—you did, too—a few times on the beach, and once when you and I stumbled across their meeting in that crumbling temple. I remember you joking about their clothes."

I tried to get a better read of her face in the dim red light, looking for mania in her eyes, some expression to match the crazy shit coming out of her mouth. But she had the perfectly calm expression of a stoned yoga instructor. This serenity was more frightening than any lunatic tell. I was growing more and more afraid of her.

"The little I saw of Eugen came in our early-morning dispatches, where he'd update me on the status of my case. From what I gathered from these rather vague reports, things were moving along, and I simply had to be patient, since the Gifted, like trees and Buddhist monks, have a different relationship with time. But then, by the end of the week, it became clear why he'd been so dodgy."

"'I'm facing some resistance,'" he told her. "'It's your illness. Some think that if you're not strong enough, giving you the Gift runs the risk of creating an abomination, should your sickness take on its power. I'm prepared to move ahead without their blessing, but I need to know that you absolutely want to go through with this. It's not without risk. But if you want to move forward, we'll do it where we're safe, at my home.'"

Olivia had to make a choice, and he said he wanted to know by the following night. She asked if she could hold on to the knife until then, the knife he'd used to demonstrate the Gift's power that night in the library, just to remind herself that it wasn't a dream.

"You've seen the knife, the hunting knife. I handed it over to Eugen once I'd made my choice, but it would eventually find its way back to me for good."

She pulled it out and showed it to me. I'm ashamed to admit it, but the sight of the blade, down there in the dim cellar, frightened me.

"But I'm getting ahead of myself. Eugen had given me one last chance to back out, and I struggled with the weight of the decision. That's when I approached you, that morning on the beach, and you gave me the push I needed to commit."

She put the knife away. I didn't feel any better.

From Athens they flew to Bucharest. Eugen's ancestral home was about three hours north of the capital, and at the airport a car was waiting to take them there.

"The Carpathians are perhaps the most beautiful mountains in the world. The forests are so old some call them 'primeval,' and you really get that sense. Trees thick enough to live inside, every surface teeming with mossy life. Just as we were getting close to his house, I had to get out to vomit, and when I looked up, there was a lynx looking back at me. It had white mutton chops and paws large enough to have been transplanted from a lion."

It was evening when they reached the house. A fortress, really, and she gave him grief for that. He and the driver led Olivia up the walk, and while they chatted in their mother tongue, she admired the maze of finely manicured shrubs and lichen-coated statuary.

The entryway was covered in tapestries so old their designs were mere suggestions of form: ghosts of maidens, phantom harps, a foggy stag. His castle, and that's what it was, was beautiful beyond belief. He was beautiful, too, and had a pregnant glow to him now that he was there.

Over the course of those first three days, he led her on regular nocturnal expeditions through the forests that were his birthright, explaining exactly what it was she'd be taking on and demonstrating just what the Gift would allow her to do. His display in Boston had been a violation of the Gifted's strict secrecy, but now they were safe. He caught a penny she threw at him in the dark. He scaled the steep wall surrounding the fortress like a squirrel. Most astonishingly, he told her, with a subtle change in his voice, a light, barely perceptible hiss, to hold her breath and put her shoes on her hands. She refused, only to find her face getting red as she stood barefoot with her hands booted.

Eugen vanished for hours at a time, leaving her to her own devices. When they first met, she'd thought he struggled with addiction. He'd be magnanimous and expansive, slide into irritability, and then disappear for a while and return flushed with charm. Now she knew it had to do with the Gift. When he'd come back, she furtively studied him, amazed and jealous of his vitality, eager to have it for herself.

"Here and there in his house I spotted the same mark. An infinity sign with teeth. The same glyph was on his knife." She pulled the knife back out and showed me. I could just make it out in the low light. "And I thought I remembered it from my glimpse of the temple in Greece."

She asked him about it.

"It's our sacred symbol," he said. "The sigil of the Gifted, to remind us that we're tasked to protect the Gift's infinite bounty, but I have a soft spot for it."

Eugen had one last thing to show her. On her fourth day there, he told Olivia he was going to fast. He wouldn't be able to see her until the end of her visit, and she should use the time to savor what she'd be giving up.

While he fasted, she followed his instructions and savored the last of what she could never have again. She gorged herself on a boar a local woman roasted for her. She went on morning walks in the woods and saw the red deer with their shaggy necks, so much bigger than the whitetails around the neighborhood where she grew up. One of these stags had to weigh a good eight hundred pounds. A forest god, he seemed like.

"After three days his driver escorted me to the room where Eugen had confined himself. It was a terrifying sight. He'd aged considerably. His neck was so stringy you could have played it like a sitar, and his skin was translucent, revealing a web of veins the same purple-black as his flesh that night in the stacks."

Eugen started drooling like a Saint Bernard when he saw her. He stood there for a moment, making sure she took in his sickly, emaciated state. Then, like a spider freed from a jar, he climbed out the window and vanished.

She didn't see him until the next evening. He looked amazing. His glow had returned.

"Are you sure you want to do this, now that you've seen everything?"

She was. His starved form didn't scare her. She'd seen herself in worse shape.

Finally, it was time. He took her to a dark addendum to the entry hall, a chapel lined with statues of saints made, Eugen told her, in the thinly veiled likenesses of his ancestors. All his forefathers were interred here, and the space held special power for him.

Past the statues and pews hung a huge rendering of their symbol cast in gold and studded with rubies. On an altar beneath it sat some odd implements she assumed had some role in the transference of the Gift, until Eugen rushed over to tidy things up. She got closer and could see what they really were: a tarnished hookah, an aging boom box, one of those club lights from the nineties—a cousin of the disco ball—resembling an alien egg.

"I had this place deconsecrated a long time ago." He cleared the altar. "I've thrown some amazing parties in here." He patted the altar cloth like he was a doctor and it was the wax paper of his examination table.

"He told me to lie down, and I obeyed. He stepped closer, and looking up into his eyes, I felt as helpless and tender as a child gazing up at her father from her crib. And that was when he gave me the Gift."

She stared down the dark aisle for a moment, then aimed her face back at me. Her eyes seemed to take up more of her face than usual, which I attributed to the cellar's uneasy light.

"The Gift is hard to language. Despite its age, it's a self-actualization technology so advanced that talking about it to the uninitiated is like describing a satellite to a caveman. I know you're not yet ready for it. I'm laying the groundwork. Soon I will give it to you, and you'll see just what it allows you to do. I know you've heard some grumblings, but you've been loyal. Today, coming down here to talk to your family on my behalf, all this was a test. And you remained true to us. Still, I understand any doubts or concern you might be feeling now, between what you've seen and now heard from me. You'd be a fool not to, with the limited information you have. You must think I'm fucking insane."

"No, I hear you. It's just a lot, but I don't think you're crazy. So it's a religious movement." I caught a flash of frustration on her face. "But obviously so much more than that."

She was right about my take on things. She'd gone full Zappos. The isolation, stress, and power of her new position had broken her brain. This was why the tech was so fucked-up—the company was run by a religious nut who believed she was the high priestess of some goth cult.

"You're going to need some time to process. Here's what I want. Let the words soak into your mind. The Gift will make itself known to you very soon. Now go to bed. You know my opinion on sleep, but you look like you could use some."

We went back upstairs. I was afraid to touch her, but I forced myself to give her a hug. Her arms were like frozen pipes. I led her to a guest room and slipped off to bed.

I felt a fitting childlike panic there in my boyhood bedroom. I lay in bed for an hour, staring at the ceiling's topography and the dim rectangles of my old Paranoids posters, trying to get my heart rate down to a reasonable bpm. I reviewed what she'd told me. She didn't let on how much she really knew—things were bad enough that I might've heard the rumors anywhere. Before I did anything else, I needed to grab Tim's packet from under the couch. I waited a little longer, and when I was absolutely sure no one else was awake, I went back downstairs.

The house was quiet, save for the occasional floorboard gripe or pipe mumble. I wondered if the birds had escaped, or if they'd found a nice, cozy spot to spend the night. I was rooting for them, partly out of genuine sympathy for the delicate creatures, but also with the hope that they might empty their cloacae on my father or brother.

I stuck my hand under the sofa and swiped at where I thought the packet would be but pawed only rug. Shoving my whole arm down there got the same result. I swept back the sofa's skirt and shone the light on my phone around.

It was gone.

I ran back up to my room and called Tim. It went straight to voice mail.

I hung up and lay there until dawn fingered my window.

## 21

Olivia had already left for San Narciso by the time I came downstairs. She texted me an apology for her abrupt arrival and departure, with no mention of the dossier or her tale in the cellar. I texted back that I was going to stick around my folks' place for another week. This lie would buy me some time without her or her goons intercepting me. As for her corporate *Twilight* fanfic, I had no clue what to make of it. At the very least, it was proof that she was more disturbed than evil, which was some relief.

I tried to corner Dad before I left. I found him in his office, standing at his desk. This was unusual—he tended to ration his standing and walking.

"Dad, are you okay?"

"What? Oh, I'm having a great day. I feel amazing. Your friend, she reminded me of when I was young, starting out. I think I picked up some of her youthful passion. The entrepreneurial spirit. I'm on new meds, too. Can't be hurting."

He sat down, to take the attention off his vigor. Still, I couldn't get past it. His eyes had more light. His skin fit better. The old veins had tunneled back under the surface, leaving him shiny and smooth.

"Dad, you can't listen to Olivia. She's scamming you. She's scamming a lot of people. I don't know why, exactly, but there's nothing there, no technology."

He wouldn't look at me. "Charlie, there's a lot more to this than you can understand. You don't know shit about anything, except maybe shitty paintings and your unlistenable music. You've somehow stumbled onto something here, so just stay quiet and don't fuck it up." He returned the whole of his attention to his phone.

There was no persuading Dad without the bundle of the documents. Once I got back, I'd scan my backup copy, send it to Renata, and hope she might help the old man see what was going on before any more money changed hands.

On the plane, looking down at the varicose rivers and grafted squares that make up our vast nation's dermis, I returned to the questions that had plagued me as I lay awake the night before. What the fuck had happened to Olivia? And what the fuck was the bizarre cult that I'd inadvertently introduced her to? What did she mean when she said she'd been observing me? She had some God delusion, I was convinced. I even thought about looking up Eugen on GetTogether to see if his story matched up. Whether you were dealing in shoes, cars, or crowded office space, with enough money to your name, at some point you were bound to think you were the Light of Light, begotten, not made, consubstantial with the Father, etc. Even then, I was sure she knew what I'd been up to. Olivia must have seen the text in the cave and sicced Clif and his lackeys on Tim.

As I walked through the Obnoxious store on my way to the office, the kids were playing something interesting over the speaker. It had all the modulations of the great Beach Boys songs, but with crunchy guitars and weird lo-fi drum machines.

"What is this?"

"It's Louise."

"Damn, this is really good."

I found Louise asleep in front of her computer. I hadn't seen her so drained since her dad died. She needed some care and attention. If she burned out, the best parts of my life would be cremated.

I went back out and visited a witchy shop in Wormwood. After consulting its resident eyelinered sorceress, I bought Louise a tarot deck, a retooled version of the classic Rider Waite with gold edges and some real heft. I picked up a Bulgari scarf on the gaudy strip, spending more than I did on the deck by a few orders of magnitude. By the time I got back, Louise had left the office. I laid my haul on a card table by her desk and texted her to come see me. While I waited, I draped a spare blanket over my head biblically. When she came in, I did a little Stevie Nicks / Kate Bush dance and handed her the deck.

"Holy shit, these are really nice."

"The scarf is for you, too. I did some research and they say you should wrap them in silk."

"Thank you. Jesus, these are thick."

"Would you do me the honors? Maybe just like a past-present-future spread?"

"You have done your homework. Sure."

She made me cut the deck and draw the cards.

The first card she turned over was a red Valentine heart pierced by a set of long swords, all surrounded by rain clouds.

"The three of swords. It's associated with separation and sorrow. It can also be a relationship that has outlived its usefulness. But the takeaway is that what has died must be let go."

This must've been about my family, my pulling away.

"I mean, the elephant in the room is Thane, right?"

"Yeah, I've been thinking about that. Thane has left us such a fucking mess. I want to honor him, but I'd really like to mobilize our shit around your record next."

"Really? Holy fuck, that's so good to hear. I feel like I've been dancing in the dark with this thing. Frankie and the twinterns say they like it, but they are huge suck-ups. I know you're incapable of flattery when it comes to art shit. Wow."

"I think it's amazing, so far. It's the right thing to bet on and keep up the momentum with *Sucker*. Okay, do my present."

The next one showed a king on a gray throne, a chair framed with the sinister skulls of half a dozen rams. He held a long ankh as a scepter. The Emperor.

"This is major arcana. It stands for male authority. Dads. Royalty."

Now was a good time to tell her. She deserved honesty. Plus, it'd be good to preempt Olivia if she tried to dox me later. If Louise didn't end things, she could help talk our Marxist artists down. And I had faith she wouldn't.

"So . . . there's something I've downplayed. For a long time. It's been destroying me, keeping it from you, but I've been terrified that once you knew, we'd be over." As she tensed up, I pulled an Olivia and made my voice break, hoping the vulnerability would disarm her. "My family is very wealthy. I wasn't lying—they technically do own a ranch, but it's mostly decorative."

"That's really not a big deal. I got the sense you might've come from a little money. You know I grew up with a lot of privilege, too."

"No, you don't get it. They're name-checked in the Panama Papers. And proud of it. They could buy your family, enslave them, and pay off everyone who ever knew them to keep quiet about it two generations down the line. We're talking the one percent of the one percent."

I uttered my lucrative surname. She started cackling.

"No. Really?"

"I'm dead serious."

Louise went quiet, then reached over and started touching my face. She worked her hands up to my forehead and softly rubbed my temples.

"No horns. Not even nubs. You have a tail back there you're going to untuck for me?"

"You can see why I'd want to keep it secret. If it's any consolation, they've cut me off." Mostly true.

"All the secrecy bothers me more than the truth. I don't really care who your family is. I care about you. With everything that's happened to Thane and Sydney, I just think it's important to be there for each other. It's put some things into focus. I'm so glad you've finally been honest with me." She smiled, showing her crooked teeth. I felt a cringe of love. "I'll make a list of my demands later. A trip to Tokyo might be a nice start. I'd go for an SG, maybe a Vespa."

"I think I can make that happen."

"We still need to do your future."

The last card was the ten of cups. A rainbow of chalices stretched across a blue sky, framing a little nuclear family in front of a cottage and mellow stream.

"Okay, I don't know this one too well. Give me a second." She consulted the tarot sages on her phone. "This is great! This one is associated with domestic happiness, spiritual fulfillment, satisfaction. Your thirst will be quenched. It can in some cases represent too much of a good thing, an overflow, but for the most part this is a very positive card."

"Fuck yeah."

I reached over to grab the card and study it more closely, but as I did, I knocked a few more cards off the deck. The Moon and the Queen of Swords flipped over. I stuck them back in along with my past, present, and future.

We were both high on all the intimacy, honesty, and raw eye contact. There, among our computers and copies of *Sucker*, we embraced again, we wept (I'm man enough to admit it), we speculated, we planned, we cried again (well, only Louise this time, but I sniffled and shook), we kissed, we fucked on the couch where Sydney first told us about Thane's disappearance, our lovemaking interrupted by an employee wandering in, which gave us a good laugh. And then, when we were done, I retreated to the upper floors of the warehouse and studied Tim's book.

Like a tiger shark hiding in this wave of tenderness, I felt a little disgust at Louise's acceptance. She had been a pristine, uncompromised punk, and now her love for me had ruined that. Her unconditional love, I have to admit, was a slight turnoff. But mostly I felt like the man in the last card, ready for domestic bliss and fulfillment. I was going to redeem myself in my father's eyes, bring Obnoxious to new artistic and commercial heights, and come out vindicated. Everything was going to go my way.

## 22

That night, while Louise was at one of our other bands' shows, I brought the backup packet down to the office and scanned it. Before I dispatched this horse pill of Truth in pdf form, I composed my own preface, emphasizing my concern for the old man and my confidence in the legitimacy of my source. Then, with an inverted gut, I hit send.

Renata didn't usually fuck around. I expected a response first thing in the morning, but the sun came up and there was nothing new but mildly tempting spam from the food-delivery apps. I dedicated the next hour or so to reaching Tim. I tried the personal email he'd passed along, two or three old university addresses I'd dug up, even sent a message on GetTogether (I used one of my stale, fake accounts for stalking exes and, in my younger days, catfishing foes). No response. My guess was that Tim had been threatened by Clif or Joop and had hung up the old whistle by now. Still, I'd keep trying.

Art has always given me succor in times of distress. I resolved to stop constantly checking my inbox and passed the anxious hours scooping up records on eBay. I swooped up a M.O.T.O. EP from Germany, a Fascist Toejam cassette, and a Sham 69 seven-inch. Rich Kids' "Ghosts of Princes in Towers / Only Arsenic." The Crass *Bullshit Detector* compilations. A first pressing of Sick Dick and the Volkswagens' debut LP, *I Want to Kiss Your Feet*, a steal for just over a thousand. I bought two crates from a former Chiswick employee in Vineland who'd apparently discovered Marie Kondo. (Believe it or not, I've reined in my record-collecting habit. I might have been the anonymous buyer of the only copy of a CD by a certain deep house pioneer sold at auction years ago.)

By the time I finished with my spree, it was already night again, and there was still no word from Renata or Tim.

Bored and aimless, I returned to Tim's dull, sprawling masterpiece to see if there was any mention of Olivia's so-called Gift or any other pieces I could put together on my own.

The following diagrams unequivocally prove the production of a small run of nanotome devices designed to host living tissue, referred to here as "FYO" (still not sure what this acronym stands for). These are the same devices used in the tests on rhesus monkeys (115). My strong hunch is that this is linked to the tazzy cancer research and accounts for the animals' deaths in the illegal tests. But as to why K. is wasting money and risking its reputation on this remains unclear. Why would we give them cancer? And why develop this for human subjects? Is it for military contracts? A bioweapon? That's my best/only guess.

One more note on the attached diagrams: it looks like there's some gesture toward a semipermeable membrane to contain the FYO cells. Never seen anything quite like this before. Thinking it might be to keep FYO cells alive, but for what purpose it can't be said for certain.

Was Kenosis a front for military weapons research? Some kind of cancer pill? Something this fucked-up surely couldn't be legal, though I knew my government, with its bad habit of deposing democratically elected presidents and murdering civilians in bulk, was capable of anything. But it seemed unlikely to me that any company would willingly develop something so unpalatable, and this strongly contradicted Olivia's world-bettering message, even by tech standards. And as for Olivia's insane goth cult, there was nothing. Tim had focused on the more intelligible malfeasance, and this demented thread evaded him.

I flipped through the diagrams and reports until I passed out. The next morning, Dad's consigliere finally got back to me.

She and Dad were taking this very seriously, Renata told me, and they'd be flying out to San Narciso the next day. My parents had an apartment downtown, and we arranged to meet there to discuss how we'd proceed. The email was weirdly formal, but Renata could be like that sometimes.

Not long after I heard from Renata, I went to Kenosis to find Tim. I searched the clinical lab—the messy, functional one—but didn't see him anywhere. I found a lab tech with a wide, honest face pipetting blood into tiny tubes as she listened to an ASMR video on her computer.

"Have you seen Tim?" I asked once she took out her earbuds. "Tim Murnane?"

"No. He's totally disappeared. Yesterday Olivia met with all of us here at the lab and told us she thinks maybe he's a danger to himself, and that she's worried he might have taken his own life. It was a weird meeting, to say the least."

"Oh my God. I had no idea."

Had he killed himself once Olivia, Clif, and Joop caught on? Surely word would spread if that happened. This was just a tactic on their end, to discredit him in case he did wind up coming forward. I hoped he was in hiding in some cabin somewhere, cultivating a lush, paranoid beard like Ted Kaczynski.

I checked my messages on my phone as I drove home. Still nothing from Tim. Wherever he was, I couldn't count on him now. I was on my own.

## 23

My parents' apartment was in the heart of downtown San Narciso. When I first moved out here, I used it as a hermitage whenever I needed a change of scenery. But after a couple parties resulting in some broken furniture and baffling stains, they changed the locks on me. And just as DTSN was getting cool again.

Renata greeted me at the door. Our wealth manager was one of those healthy, clear-skinned people you suspect spent their formative years in an un-American privation of high-fructose corn syrup and white bread. With her stentorian voice and crisp edges, it was easy to envision her standing before the UN, though now, after more than twenty years on Dad's payroll, the only reason she'd do that would be to account for crimes against humanity. Dad had picked her up in the nineties, and since then, she'd shed her other clients and turned her operation into a family office dedicated to the Grosshearts alone. I didn't like our little social worker for the rich—I could feel her judgment—but I had to be nice to her. She was the only one who knew where all the money was.

Renata led me to the dining room, where Dad was waiting. He still had that peculiar glow I'd noticed the morning I left home.

"Have you spoken to any reporters about Kenosis?" Dad asked.

"Hi, Dad. No. That hasn't even crossed my mind. I'm really just looking out for the family here."

"There's a journalist who's been snooping around this, and one of Olivia's employees, this Tim guy, had been talking to him before he ran off." Dad's voice had lost some of its senescent waver.

"I don't know anything about that."

"Olivia says Tim is some kind of radical nut. Not stable. He recanted everything, said he doctored the documents, and then just left. None of us want you to let this wack job hurt your career."

That didn't sound like Tim. Either someone was lying, or he'd been coerced.

I told this to my father and went over everything else I knew. That there was no real product, that the company was looking into deliberately giving people cancer, that the island testing could be disastrous for the Grossheart name, that Kenosis had capital hemophilia. That Olivia and her lieutenant were hiding their relationship from investors. That Olivia believed she was part of some elite, goth secret society. But his face stayed blank. I looked to Renata, but she, too, seemed unconvinced.

"Look," she said, "Olivia and her people have prepared a one-page document for you to sign affirming that you'll abide by your confidentiality obligations going forward."

"Son, I really think you should sign." Dad put his hand on my arm. Physical contact between us had, historically, been reserved for what he called "course correction," and this nonviolent touch caught me off guard. His hand looked as smooth as mine, as if botoxed and de-veined. I saw it had cast off most of its liver spots.

Renata: "There are a couple Kenosis lawyers in the other room. And Joop's here. I'll go get them."

Fuck that. It was an ambush. In seconds Joop, two other lawyers, and Clif had encircled me, shoving a pen into my hand and their paper in my face.

"I'm going to do this," I said. "I know how much stress I've caused, and I'm so sorry. It really looks like I've been misled. Just let me use the bathroom and I'll sign when I come back."

"Sign first," Olivia's revolting fuck buddy said, perhaps aware I was about to deploy the book's most ancient trick.

But Joop's face took on a panthery expression. "Take your time. We'll be here."

I went to the bathroom at the other end of the apartment and locked the door behind me.

Man, they could have had me if they'd understood anything about oppositional defiant disorder. Something else bugged me, too. Dad's rejuvenation freaked me out.

I was well acquainted with the fire escape outside the bathroom, having smoked plenty of surreptitious joints out there to head off Dad-induced anxiety attacks. I opened the window, and with some creaky contortion, soon I was rattling the grate.

I didn't stick the dismount from ladder to sidewalk. I tumbled ungracefully, rolling over a pile of gray chicken bones before colliding with an orphaned ottoman.

I needed a new plan.

## 24

Shortly after our aborted meeting, I received another email from Renata. Now that I'd decided to ignore my responsibilities to Kenosis, she told me coolly, not only would they cut me off, but I had to give up the label. If I didn't sign Olivia's paper, they'd liquidate the warehouse, the equipment, the records—all of which, owing to some crafty maneuvering on Dad's and Renata's part long ago—they were legally entitled to do.

I was getting paranoid. I retreated upstairs, where I know no one would find me.

When I first bought the building four years ago (a gift to myself on my twenty-sixth birthday), the upper floors were the showpiece, my own private Tate Modern. Oh, how I swung my dick around, showing the place off, pretending to have purchased it years earlier, during more deflated times. Many were the nights when I led a slender art heaux up the stairs to impress and eventually lay among the iron titans left over from the munitions plant. I count these (which include my first fucks with Louise) among my most satisfying orgasms. I mean, how can you resist the sexual fields emitted by the machines that made the machines that murdered people? It's ballistic Viagra no penis can deny.

But my work with the label gradually confined me to the lower floors, and aside from the occasional tour of our built-in industrial-sculpture garden to wow prospective bands, I rarely went up there. Now I had time to appreciate my rusty kingdom. There was too much square footage—the second floor alone had more than enough room to house me, Louise, our employees, plus the studio/practice space. To make sure no one would find me, I avoided my own cell, on the far side of the floor past the studio, the rare room in the warehouse with a functioning sink and toilet. When I colonized it, I plugged the window with the most expensive air-conditioning unit I could find, and with a weekly massage, it wasn't so bad. I couldn't hide there, though, so I set to gathering supplies to make my hideout more comfortable. I raided the side where Louise and the others slept, a maze of shelves and old file cabinets littered with sleeping bags, rumpled pillows, and jugs of water. There was a black rubber air mattress lying around, which I looted and carried like a surfboard, knocking over the cardboard boxes functioning as my employees' nightstands as I crossed the floor.

I needed to go higher, where it'd be harder for any Kenosians to harass me, where no Obnoxians would interrupt my thinking. I took the stairs up to the elephant graveyard. I was going to hide in Moloch.

On the nose, I know. The three-story iron furnace was christened years ago by some Ginsberg-obsessed art-school waif I was trying to seduce. Before we fucked in his shadow, she took a pink oil pastel from her fanny pack and scrawled his new name upon its bulging belly, drawn in boxy, imitation-Hebrew script. The punk and hardcore kids, brought up on *Pretty Hate Machine* and Wax Trax! reissues, loved it. Moloch he remained.

I approached the iron behemoth, stepping around chunks of cinder block and the odd dead cockroach. You'd think my employees, like me, would have been drawn to the feet of this cool beast, and that at least one of them would have staked out some turf in his vicinity, but no. The furnace frightened them. They said it was haunted by ghosts of young men mutilated in Normandy or Sicily. This, added to the inconvenience of the extra flight of stairs and the lack of electricity, had been enough to keep my hot little dummies away.

Moloch had a small maintenance door around back, like a butt flap on old pajamas. I tacoed the air mattress through and followed it into the rusty darkness.

I was a mosquito stuck in a percolator. High above me I could see an oval of light hatched by the crossbeams, a James Turrell for the workingman. Sure, it was dark and somewhat creepy, but peaceful, too. I could finally think.

I still had no idea what I was going to do now that there was no talking Dad out of dumping his money into the company. I should have just given up, but my father's faith in Olivia had triggered two strong, complementary reactions in me. The first was an Absalomic drive to best my father and prove him wrong. The second was something like a sense of sibling rivalry with Olivia. We were a couple of baby birds, and now that she'd intercepted the worm of Dad's favor, I was ready to ram my pink sister out of the nest, knocking Dad out of the air on her way down.

My newfound willingness to fuck over Chuck Sr., along with my twitchy animal varieties of fear and the surprising acceptance from Louise, shifted my perspective. Finally, I saw that all the work I'd done to keep my identity from Louise and the rest of Obnoxious was idiotic, an impossible game I couldn't win because I wasn't a player—I was the ball, and I could be whacked by anyone aware of whose pink loins I'd trickled out of. I needed to own my life story, not be owned by it.

With the anxiety of exposure gone, a new, previously unavailable path appeared to me, one that would allow me to use Olivia to come out of this better than when I started. I'd use the press to force the hand that fed me, spinning my betrayal of Olivia and my father as a tale of heroism that could absolve me of all the sins of the Grossheart name but without doing enough damage to make Dad actually disown me. If I went public with the files and my story, Dad would have to come around, though whether it was before or after Kenosis's inevitable collapse would be up to him.

I'd tested the waters of abandonment many times before, and the truth was, Dad couldn't stand losing control of one of his issue. Our eventual reconciliation would be more valuable than his investment in the company anyway, rehabbing his rotting public image. It might be rough for a while, but I knew that Dad, Hobbesian bastard that he was, would respect the gamesmanship, allowing me to crawl up from the insect status of his current estimation. I'd finally be able to step out into the light as the good Grossheart, the arty black sheep who just wants to run his humble record label in peace (a label made even more visible by all the free publicity). Kenosis would give me cover—it wouldn't look like I was simply trying to get in front of the story to keep my label. That way, I could defuse at least one of the bombs they'd drop on me. I could see the shot for the cover story, a gray portrait by Platon rendering the wear and tear of my aging face into a handsome texture, my serious eyes steered right toward the camera by the certainty of my convictions. This was much better than my dueling lives.

I searched the major news sites for the rare journalists willing to rake tech's slippery muck. If Tim had reached out to reporters, like Dad had said, it seemed likely he'd found his this way, and maybe I could get ahold of the same one.

I aimed high, messaging a Pulitzer winner who'd written one of the first clear-eyed negative profiles of Steve Jobs after the release of the iPhone, then a tech reporter a few tiers down who'd lately been chronicling the Caverns' minor sex scandals. I sent both some of the more incriminating excerpts from Tim's findings, letting them know I was a Kenosis employee of some status but keeping my Grossheart blood to myself.

For reasons you can easily guess, patience is not my strong suit. I expected to hear back from them as soon as the juicy emails hit their inboxes, but of course this wasn't the case. I hit refresh every fifteen seconds until the light filtering through Moloch began to dim.

The next morning there was still no word from either reporter.

I thought I would make their jobs easier. I remembered Tyler, the ethical, bearded bro from Tamyen I'd overheard at Olivia's party. After tracking down his number through some exchanges on my Kenosis email account, I called him.

He interrupted before I could finish explaining things.

"I told you guys I'm done. I haven't talked. I haven't said shit. I know what an NDA is. I'm in fucking Ohio. Dayton, Ohio."

"Home of Guided by Voices. And the Breeders. And Brainiac, I think? Just hear me out. I'm not trying to fuck with you. I'm on your side. I've uncovered some scary shit at Kenosis, and I want to see if you'd be willing to go on the record, when we get a journalist to cover this."

"I'm not going to take that bait, man. Tell Clif I'm not going to fall for this shit. Please stop with these fucking *Sopranos* intimidation tactics. Between this and the fucking NDAs you've got nothing to worry about. I just want to be left alone and keep this all behind me."

He hung up.

I went through my wallet and found my predecessor's business card. I hunted her down on GetTogether.

Her profile had been turned into an in memoriam page. People had posted pictures of her meditating with ferns and various bodies of water behind her, as well as crisp shots of her in business mode, offering moral guidance to fit and attentive executives.

Scrolling down, I found a link to her obituary.

She'd died of cancer.

That afternoon one of the journalists finally got back to me. The junior tech reporter, not the Pulitzer winner, but I would have taken a contributor to *The Huffington Post* at that point.

She made me download Cryptid, which was the first I'd heard about it, and messaged me there. She told me it was going to take time to put a story together, and seeing her urgency didn't match mine, I told her who I was. Which is to say, who my dad was.

"Holy shit. Okay."

She wanted to talk in person, to make sure I wasn't fucking with her. We arranged to meet at the park in Inverarity Heights, a shaggy patch of green space named for the same city father who'd built the old bath complex where I met Tim, and only half a mile away.

The next day I was there, sitting at a rotting picnic table on a hill, next to a ginkgo tree housing the celebrity flock of invasive cockatiels. They squabbled and jostled one another like investment bankers in the nineties. I needed to get out in nature more, I thought to myself as I watched two of these fair members of the avian tribe duel over a Funyun.

My savior was right on time. She was even younger than I imagined, just about five feet tall, with hair dyed green. She could have easily played a teenager on TV. A burly friend in a leather vest tagged along beside her.

"Holy shit. Okay." To her friend: "Eric, it's him. Looks like I'm not being trolled by one of those reply guys. I'll meet you down at the

Alchemist in an hour—I'll get your tab. Or maybe we can get Richie Rich to do it."

Her friend took off the vest, slung it over his arm, and lumbered off.

"This"—she waved her hand over my person—"definitely affects things, and you should know that I'm making this a priority." She had a capable manner that, along with her resonant voice, erased the impression I was dealing with a teen.

"I've looked over what you sent. It's a bit dry, to be honest. Send me the documents, everything you have. Can you put me in touch with the person who brought these to you?"

"I'm having trouble getting ahold of him. He's either hiding or they got to him. I'm not sure."

"Well, send me whatever you can."

"How long do you think it will take to get all of this out in the open?"

"I can't say. I'm going to get to work right away, but it takes time to do things right."

This was the price I had to pay for dealing with an actually ethical person. I didn't want to wait. I didn't think I'd be able to.

"I'm worried they're going to keep fucking with me." I pictured Clif swinging his katana as Joop knocked out a set of ripped reps on his pull-up bar. "They're tough as shit."

"I'm going to move on this as fast as I can. But if you want this to be more than gossip about the superrich, and if you want to avoid getting your ass sued off, we're going to need to build the story. I'm going to have to confirm all of this stuff. If things are as bad as you say, there are going to be a lot of people who will want to talk, so we've at least got that going for us."

"There's something else I didn't put in the email. Olivia says she's in some kind of New Age, Anne Rice, secret-society thing."

"You have proof of that? A recording or something?"

"She told me everything, but I don't have a record of it."

"We're going to need to back that up with something hard."

It didn't seem like the Gifted stuff was persuading anybody. Moving forward, I'd have to lean more on the Tim dossier, then break the cult shit later. It was too crazy to win anyone over.

"I'll reach out by the end of the week to let you know how things are going. Until then, I'd keep a low profile. Use Cryptid, don't do anything that will get them to sic their lawyers on you."

She left, but I stuck around a while and set to forwarding her everything on my phone, including the information for the former ethics adviser (I thought maybe her husband might know something), and the number of Tyler, the former Kenosian, just in case she could convince him to talk.

Once everything had been sent, I sat there and admired the view of the city. The last time I came up here had been with Olivia, during our college road trip. We smoked our grade-D weed and she talked about the dreams she'd ultimately pervert with her hunger for power, the dreams I was presently trying to destroy.

The cockatiels were still at it. One landed right on the table. After I admired his Mohawk and the red spots on his cheeks for a while, he began pecking the bleached wood a few inches from my hands, then looked up at me. He did this three or four times. He clearly wanted me to feed him, but I had nothing for the little guy. He flew off, and I lost sight of him among the flock.

The fourth estate was going to take a while. I needed to try something else while I waited, for my mental health alone. I was turning over my limited options when the solution came to me in the form of a calendar notification for an event the next night: *Grapefruit Solution at the Narceum.* It took me a second to figure out how the event got on my phone. One of Olivia's assistants had sent the invitation along after Olivia told me about it in the Caverns. Langenburger, Olivia's mentor, played guitar or sang in the band, and during my first weeks at Kenosis (before Olivia lost interest in me), she'd kept trying to arrange for us to meet up for a little elbow frottage. She hoped I might take advantage of the musical connection and court him as a mentor.

Langenburger sat on the board of directors. If I could convince him, I thought, I might be able to get the rest of the board to act. Then Dad would see I was right.

The day of the concert, I pored through the briefings linked in Olivia's assistant's email. From these profiles a clear portrait emerged, that of a wealthy, eccentric uncle in tech's dysfunctional family, a cantankerous prophet whose pre-public-offering investment in now-billion-dollar companies (collecting data on you as you read this) had given him enough wealth to publicly condemn them without getting sued into submission or mysteriously mercked. Ralph Langenburger. The same timeline appeared again and again. There was his acidic youth in the city's golden age, his rise as an investor at the prestigious VC firm Emory Oak, his GetTogether bonanza, and his more recent roles as the head of his woke Elevision Fund and, more generally, the voice of reason among the ruthless technocrats.

The journalists were uniformly wary of his hubris, but I saw something else through *The New Yorker*'s subtle negs. A luminary. A man with no fucks to give. It was as if you took everything nice about Pops (that is to say, his money) and retooled the rest with, I don't know, moral GPS, vision, and, crucially, a personality. I'm not dumb—I know how susceptible men my age are to substitute daddies. But those days in Moloch had primed me for insight and mentorship. I wanted to go meet the man and see what pearls of wisdom he might toss this hog.

Half an hour before the show, I snuck out of my furnace with Tim's dossier under my arm and, once I was a safe distance from HQ and any employee who might wander outside with their American Spirits, summoned a car to the Narceum.

In its heyday, the Narceum had been *the* venue for bands on the verge of mainstream commercial glory, a decisive step on the path to immortality in the dorm-room-poster canon. But where once it had been a trampoline bouncing talent upward to stadia, world tours, and second or third wives, now it was more of a safety net, cushioning the falls of legacy acts before they plummeted into their rectangular grave holes.

In the lobby, I could already hear the uninhibited guitar noodlings that are the dead giveaways of all jam bands and followed these squiggly licks into the theater proper.

The Narceum's interior is perhaps best described as three-dimensional paisley. Schools of curly commas populated the arches and pilasters. The small crowd was consolidated into a douchey rhombus in front of the stage. Despite a ticket price that would permit you to behold a lesser Beatle or solo Stone, the turnout was meager and couldn't possibly have made much of a dent in the cost of booking the place. This was a subsidized affair.

I was wearing a giant bucket hat I stole from the employee clothes pile, along with a pair of Louise's old glasses, some dark green bubble shades. I was worried a Kenotic agent might be hidden among the ranks of these jam band dweebs, waiting to snatch me. But really I was safer here than at the warehouse. Olivia had said she wouldn't be able to make it, so there was little chance I'd bump into her. And this was the last place she'd expect to find me, at an event she'd invited me to.

The earnest jam band was finishing up their set. The singer confessed his unironic desire to "pull a Chris McCandless," and I stopped paying attention after that. I wormed through the crowd, claiming a spot behind a group of small-headed Buddhistocrats clutching bright orange beers.

People started clapping. The set wasn't eternal after all. Soon Langenburger's band was testing levels, though their leader remained to be seen.

As the drummer thumped his toms, I thought he looked eerily familiar, but I couldn't quite place him. The investor tours? Had he gone to Dewey Willson? I didn't have long to speculate where I knew him from, though, because then Langenburger stepped onstage.

Everyone cheered, and he played cheesy (knowingly or not, I couldn't be sure) riffs on a Gibson archtop that I knew from my research had once belonged to Junior Fats and cost roughly ten grand. He wore a purple-and-green paisley oxford (more paisley!), the kind of thing Jimi Hendrix might wear if he worked at Salesforce. I'd have to ask the man about his skin-care routine. He somehow looked younger than when I saw him at Kenosis. If his taste in music and clothes didn't precisely date him to the first third of the baby boom, he could have passed for an older Gen Xer. I thought back to my father's new-found vitality, but both men were among the wealthiest of all time. There were any number of exorbitant cutting-edge explanations for their unnatural spunk.

Langenburger gave his band a nod, and together they launched into their opening number, a tune titled "420, 24/7." About halfway through this extended tribute to the milder side of Schedule I, the bros behind me started playing a game of guess the net worth. The bassist was, according to a penis-headed baldie at my four o'clock, a junior partner at Thaddeus Ventures and, as such, easily the most impoverished of the gang. The rhythm player, about Langenburger's age, had started Gnossos Partners and weighed in around a respectable billion. The keyboard player (the oldest of them) had been a founding member of General Gary and His Blind Mice back in the sixties and had, thanks to some key investments at his current bandmates' behest before the last boom, added a couple more commas to his assets. I tried to listen in on the guesses about the drummer, but I missed his name, catching only the mention of his hereditary wealth and gig at Emory Oak. I whipped out my phone to try to google him, but immediately one of the men behind me asked if I could put it away and "try to be present."

I decided to heed this bougie maharishi and found I was enjoying myself. Sure, it wasn't the coolest thing I'd ever witnessed. Langenburger, the bassist, and the rhythm guitarist had dorky wireless set-ups, which allowed them mostly unused mobility onstage, and every song had at least one extended solo that made Jerry Garcia sound like Steve Reich. But still, their chops were good, and while they weren't the most original musicians, it was easily one of the less embarrassing vanity projects I'd seen. And I say this as someone who is, essentially, a living vanity project.

A few minutes into the set and there was no sign of any Kenosis employees. I could relax a little. I kept the hat on but shoved the glasses into my pocket.

After six more songs about getting high, space, and "mystic ladies," followed by a superfluous encore, the show was over. I hung around the stage and tried to look up the drummer again, but it turned out that Grapefruit Solution, like the classic jam bands from which it was derived, had a long roster of former personnel, enlisting anyone in the Caverns who could fret a note. Before I could determine his identity, the band reappeared. They took pictures with wives and fiancées, and I followed them to the merch table in the lobby, where they were greeted by a long line of tech fanboys waiting to touch the hem of Langenburger's paisley and pitch some flaccid apps.

The drummer sat off to the side folding shirts. I finally had a chance to talk to him and see if his voice might jog my memory, but as I approached him, he picked up his phone and stepped outside to take the call.

When the line had died down some, I joined in. The man in front of me tried to win Langenburger over with his idea for "VR concert-going experiences" that inexplicably involved some form of rock 'n' roll time travel. Langenburger graciously placated him and signed one of the copies of his book (these took up about half the table), and then it was my turn.

"I love your guitar," I told him. "Is that an ES-125?" I already knew it was, from my research, but I wanted him to think I possessed the deep luthier, guitar-wizard knowledge that is the coin of the realm among musical boomers.

"Good eye. It used to belong to Junior Fats. I like to think I'm its second wife. Not as passionate, but comfortable." His voice landed somewhere between the hippie fry of Tommy Chong and the nasal bleat common among boarding-school English teachers who abruptly quit the gig after a series of vicious pranks spearheaded by a boy whose dad and uncle have for decades been sandwiched by Waltons on the Forbes 400.

"I'm a friend of Olivia Watts. Actually, I work for her, too. I'm a creative consultant over at Kenosis. We met a while back at the sylvarium." Usually I was the one who had to be reminded of these things.

"Oh, awesome. I heard you might be here. You're the one with the punk-rock label, right?"

"That's me." I wasn't exactly tickled Olivia was telling people about my other life, but there couldn't be much harm in Langenburger knowing if it endeared me to him.

"So you're right on the bridge with the captain. You're a real Will Riker. Or Data, maybe, skin-tone-wise. That must be really exciting. I'd love to hear your thoughts on how things are going. Some of us are headed back up to the greenroom. Want to come?"

I told him I'd love to.

"I think we held it down pretty well tonight. I could've done better, though, with some of those solos. Too much pentatonic bullshit when I should've been thinking about chord tones. Nice hat by the way."

I liked and respected the guy, despite my interior jabs at his boomer project of making one last, uninhibited grab at youth before his knees gave out. At some point, all of us, if we don't drive our Audis into oncoming semis, if the fentanyl doesn't get us, will look ridiculous, no matter what we do. I could easily see myself in Langenburger's shoes, if not actually playing in a band, then at least being that gray-haired (or, the way things are going, no-haired) geezer at the punk show. His lack of embarrassment was enviable and inspiring.

As I followed Langenburger up a tight helix of stairs to the green-room, I still awkwardly held Tim's documents like a nervous evangelist clutching his Bible, not quite ready to go full fire-and-brimstone. I'd been to plenty of greenrooms with various bands, mostly cheerless closets with microbial sofas, some approaching the comfort of decent hotel rooms. None quite so plush as this. With its full bar, door-size TV, and ample spread of snacks, it looked a lot like the Kenosis executive lounge, though instead of photos of Einstein and Olivia, we were surrounded by the pictures of 27 Club members whose epic trajectories had brought them through here before fatal vomit clogged their golden windpipes. There was even a waiter, making rounds to ensure we had the PBRs, Heinekens, and Diet Cokes we required as we slouched into the sofas and beanbag chairs that populated the loft. Only when the waiter started rolling a joint for our techno-utopian sage did I understand he wasn't Narceum staff, but Langenburger's personal assistant. His rolling skills were enviable. His thumbs were nimble as ferrets.

As I took my polite toke, I saw the drummer make his way up the stairs and into the room. His hair was long, like Langenburger's, and he wore an oversize tie-dye shirt, a swirl of purple and green that conspicuously complemented Langenburger's getup. This covered a paunch of solidarity with his older bandmates. I wanted to ask Langenburger about him, but he was already deep in a monologue about the state of present-and-future tech.

Lang, as they called him, went on about the surveillance and use of our data, the foreign interference in the last few elections, all the ills that the current models in the industry hath wrought. He reserved special scorn for Nate Zuckerman, that son of a middleweight novelist who "got us in this fucking fascist mess."

"And how much GetTogether stock do you own?" the bassist impishly asked.

"Oh, shut the fuck up. These assholes only listen if you own a piece of them." Then to me: "He knows that. He just likes to rib me. They all want me to shut up, but I won't. I can't. I have a hippie value system. I'm always going to speak truth to power."

He sipped the same wine-colored kombucha I'd seen in Olivia's refrigerator—some hippie had clearly struck gold peddling this stuff among the technobility—and took another hit off his joint, still shaking his head at his bassist.

"Anyway," Langenburger continued, "that's why I've turned most of my attention to the Elevision Fund projects, like Kenosis. That's really my purpose, my calling. Everything else, this siren-server dystopia, all of it will be blown away by benevolent tech. Brought about by truly gifted visionary minds, like Olivia." (There was that word, *gifted*. Surely just a coincidence.) "Don't get me wrong. There has to be a balance. You have to balance out the evil with the good. Back when we were punching holes into cards and waiting for our balls to drop, I used to hang with Miles Paranoid, and everyone used to give him so much crap about letting bikers hang around the band all the time. It was mostly the Playboys, back in the sixties. Everyone was always saying, 'Why keep these guys around? They're rapists, murderers, I-don't-know-whats.' And Miles would always say, calmly, 'You can't have the good without evil. You can't have the good without evil.' You need a balance, that's what I'm saying. And right now we've swung too far. No balance."

He knew Miles Paranoid! Holy shit! It was a sign. I was ready to tell him everything.

"I'm a huge Paranoids fan."

"Miles was interested in computers. That's why he let me follow him around. I was there when he got his hands on the custom Minimoog he made so famous on *Counterfeit*. He said they were evil, demonic, apocalyptic even—but I think he loved them. One thing that people don't understand about the roots of San Narciso culture is our capacity for paradox. Even now, I still think you can save the world and make truckloads of money doing it. I know that's not exactly a popular thing to say."

Paradox—I could use that. I liked it better than hypocrisy.

Langenburger turned to his assistant. "Hey, put some Paranoids on the playlist. In the queue. To my original point. What I'm trying to do is bring ethics back into the conversation. That's my mission, for this chapter of my life."

"Well," I said, "that's kind of what I wanted to talk to you about."

It's not like I'm in the Monkey Wrench Gang or anything like that. I'm closer to Jaron Lanier, though I will say I've had these ideas years before any of his books came out. He does look good with the dreads though. I think I could pull them off, too, though I'm told there's an element of racial appropriation people find distasteful. What do you think?"

"White people with dreads should be shot in the street," the bassist said. "And I don't believe cultural appropriation is even a thing!"

A river of language rushed forth from Langenburger's lipless mouth. It was hard to get a word—even a syllable—in edgewise. It was becoming pretty clear that he was incapable of making normal conversation and, like his protégé, could only talk in TED.

Somewhere in one of these long verbal guitar solos, the drummer came over and sat down on the nearest beanbag.

"Chuck? Holy shit! It's me—Jimmy."

It took me a second, but then it all came together. James, my old rival.

"I thought you OD'd," I said.

"I did! I've been in recovery for a bit. This guy's really taken me under his wing." James gave the tech seer a funny little bow. "I had to lay low for a while. Spent a lot of time at Mom's place in New Hampshire, just trying to figure out what all this is supposed to mean. It's where I picked up the drums, if you're wondering. But things are good. I've married, even reproduced, if you can believe that. I've got a baby girl, cute as fuck, with a perfectly round head, ninety-eighth percentile for dome size. I hear you're doing great things over at Kenosis. And you've still got the label—really proud of you, buddy. I've been meaning to reach out to congratulate. I checked out that record everyone's been talking about. It's fucking great. Sorry to hear about the singer and everything, though, that's just terrible."

James! Where had my perfect, rude asshole gone? Who was this bland, thoughtful, evolved, shitty replacement?

Then I remembered what Olivia had said in the cave, about how I'd outpunked my peers. Olivia works in mysterious ways, yes, but my father's house was built on stunting and manipulation. Even in the greenroom, stoned as fuck with my ass sinking into a bag of beans, I could see what she'd done when she planned this weeks ago. Sure, maybe she wanted me to buddy up to Langenburger, but she already had his money and faith. She wanted me to see James. Where he had Grapefruit Solution, I had Obnoxious. Where he had Emory Oak, I had Kenosis, a company much sexier, much more beneficial to the species than his VC firm. I was winning, as far as our old game was concerned. And I owed it to her.

Langenburger, for his part, was impressed by our shared history.

"Someday there'll be a documentary about you guys. I'll get to reprise my role as talking head, if I'm still alive. Just kidding—of course I'll be alive, because Kenosis will have cured death by then."

The guru, catching some mention of the blues in a neighboring conversation, started lecturing his bassist on open tunings, giving James and me an opportunity to talk one-on-one.

"I was sure Olivia would wind up at Goldman Sachs or McKinsey. Credit Suisse, maybe. One of those evil places. It's amazing she's become so good."

"I know." I didn't know, but he was so assured I figured I'd go with it.

"One time I was with her as she pulled papers out of a professor's mailbox and slid them into the paper shredder. She'd skim one, then laugh as the machine ripped it up. A professor even came in, but she was so self-possessed she just told him we were TAs and kept on shredding! I thought to myself, 'That bitch is fucking hard-core!' She always scared me, and no one scared me back then. Except maybe Eugen, too. Not you though. But I misjudged her, obviously. I wasn't exactly Ruth Bader Ginsburg, judgment-wise. I wasn't even Scalia."

"I don't know if you did. I actually came here to talk to Ralph about her. She's running some kind of scam. There's no science. There's no product. I mean, that's not normal, right?"

"That hasn't stopped anyone around here before. You have proof?"

"I do. I brought it."

"What does this say is happening?"

I explained everything to him as best I could. "God, I sound like a conspiracy wacko, I know. She's also been talking about some kind of cult thing, some woo-woo shit. 'The Gifted.'"

"That sounds pretty extreme, but I think everyone at that level gets a Christ complex. Ralph has used that word a lot lately. 'Gifted.' You know how much these disruptors love to conform."

"She's hoovering money out of Dad. I'm worried. But that's silly, right? That's like worrying about the sea, or the air."

"I mean, you should worry about those things, and probably because of him. But even if he loses his entire investment, he'll probably be able to claim a tax write-off on his other earnings. I don't know what to tell you about Olivia, without the whole picture. It does sound fucked."

I could tell James didn't entirely believe me. He didn't think I was lying. He'd just seen enough of me to know I was too stupid to be right.

"Still, can't say I'm surprised about Olivia. She's the one who introduced me to Lang, when I came back into the world. I think just to show off. She offered me a gig at Kenosis, too, but while I'm cool with EO tossing some money her way in the Elevision Fund, I don't think I could work for her. I've tried to keep my distance, no offense. It is actually good to see you, though."

"Do you think I can get Ralph on my side?"

"There's no way you could convince him Olivia's done anything wrong. She's his redemption arc, man, and he loves the immortality play. He's dedicated a whole fund just to Kenosis, on top of Elevision. She could be running a toddler gulag and he'd still give her the benefit of the doubt. The rumor is she's given him one of her implants, one of the prototypes."

"I think she gave one of those to my dad somehow. He seems healthier. I don't know. God. I have to try."

"Look, buddy, I've got to get back home. It did my heart some good to see you. Be in touch."

"I will," I lied.

He stood there for a few seconds. "I forgive you," he said, and walked off before I could ask what my sin was.

Langenburger had installed himself by the bar, where I caught him berating the theater manager. When he finally hit a measure of rest, I cut in.

"Ralph, so, I wanted to talk to you about Kenosis."

"One of my favorite subjects."

"Yeah. Great. So I don't think things are going quite as well as Olivia has led you to believe. The tech is—how can I put this?—still pretty hypothetical. I think you've been misled."

"What?"

"There's a lot of weird shit going on. Animal testing, shifty work-arounds with the FDA, something to do with spreading cancer? And barely any usable tech. It's a lot more than growing pains, I know that. And there's this cult thing I don't know what to make of. Just look at this." I tried to shove Tim's report into his arms, but he wouldn't take it.

"Do you think I would put my reputation on the line for some bullshit like that? Do you think me, of all people, would let myself get duped by fake technology?"

"No."

"Charlie, I'm sure to you this is all very real. I believe that you believe something is a little off. But you have to admit it's possible that you don't perceive the whole picture. Can you admit that's possible?"

"I admit it is possible. But—"

"Think of it this way. When you're driving through a valley—bear with me here—you think you're way down low, in the holler with the hillbillies eyeing you bisexually. But if you zoom out, the world is really just a smooth ball. Even Everest is an imperceptible bump. With what you do at Kenosis, no offense, you're just a car on the road, a Mini Cooper in that dip in the road. Olivia has to keep that whole planet in her head, at all times. That's the thing you can't understand unless you've helmed the ship."

"I get that. But there are numbers, emails. Facts!" I thrust Tim's dossier at him again. "All the monkeys, all except one, died when they put the Gutenbergs in them. I have proof right here."

"I'm told there's just been a huge breakthrough on that front, some-thing to do with enzymes. I texted Olivia when we got up here—how about we wait until she shows and listen to her side of things, before any more vibe is killed. You have to understand, everything she's told you, she's had to put it in terms you'd understand. The Gift especially. Just take a seat and I'll call and see where she is."

I sat. I didn't want to—Olivia was coming, probably Clif and Joop, too—but I had no say in the matter. I don't mean with Lang. I mean with my legs. They'd chosen him over me. As he left the room to place the call, I stared at the back of his head with awe.

I hadn't mentioned the Gift.

My legs ignored my brain entirely. Moving them was like trying to run or throw a punch in a dream. The sensation was familiar. I remembered something like it when I was in the cave with Olivia and felt that flood of illogical trust. A forced feeling. This time it was obedience, and I couldn't resist it like I had underground. It was as if a new brain had slithered into my head and taken over, ignoring the protest of the old one. I focused all my energy on moving my leg, even just wiggling my foot, but the only twitch came from my accelerating pulse.

The Gift was real. Fuck.

A minute passed, and all I managed was to wiggle a toe. And sweat. I tried to speak, to get someone in the band to help me, but my lips and tongue were as numb as my legs.

I was saved by a song—an old cliché, but true for me, in this instance. A long, psychedelic jam ended, and I picked out the next track right away. It was a Paranoids song, "Japonica by Tubelight." The overdriven chug of the guitars, the rudimentary organ chords, the chimpy drums. It was the music of my teenage rebellion, and miraculously, it still possessed the ability to trigger revolt, this time not from my biological father, but from a man who had, until just moments ago, been my dream dad. By the time the vocals came in, I was up, and by the outro (the song is only a minute and twenty seconds long), I managed to coax each leg into movement one at a time. With each defiant step I regained a little more of my regular motor skills, and by the time I made it across the room, I was more or less back to normal.

At the door I felt a hand on my shoulder. My pulse bloomed into my vision.

"You okay?" It was the bass player. "Want me to call you a car? Don't drive fucked-up, man."

"Someone is coming for me. I'll be okay."

"All right, buddy. Just don't want to read about you in the morning paper, blowing your mind out in a car, nobody sure if you're from the House of Lords and all that."

"Thanks, man."

I hurried downstairs, past Langenburger's assistant consoling the weeping theater manager, and soon I was in the alley behind the theater.

Just then I saw a couple men, both Clif-shaped, walk by, probably headed for the main entrance. I ducked behind the dumpster, counted to thirty, then ran a couple blocks and summoned a car.

## 26

As I waited for my ride, an ugly old man passed by. He wore a white fedora, and under its brim was a thoroughly corrugated face. With his socked Birkenstocks, a Gucci hoodie, and a fanny pack, he sat right on the border of a bygone strain of knowing normcore and petroligarch tackiness. He gave me a little nod when he caught me looking at him.

Still unnerved, I turned my attention to my inbox while I waited. Now that it was clear I wasn't going to cooperate, Renata and Dad would take the next steps to strip me of the label. In my despair, I messaged the journalist on Cryptid to see if she'd found anything.

She called me. "I've been busting my ass since we met up. I reached out to the names you passed along. Having trouble getting ahold of anyone willing to talk. Not for lack of trying. No answer from Murnane. Tyler, the engineer, is paranoid, for good reason. Looks like someone got to your predecessor's husband after she died, though I'm going to try him again once we have more momentum. Anyone else who might talk with me? If we had one more hard piece of evidence, another witness, or something more sensational, we could fast-track this thing."

I needed to give her something else. I had an idea, but it wouldn't be easy. I was tired. I felt as old and frail as that geezer on the sidewalk.

I hid in Moloch, working out my plan. When I mustered enough energy, I went to the office, printed some documents, then woke Louise on the residential floor.

"What's going on? Is everything okay?"

A brilliant lie had come to me, one that would ennoble me and help absolve me of my recent sketchiness, unavailability, and less artful deceptions. I'd tell her that I'd recruited some unsavory characters to track down Thane, leaving it all in thuggy euphemism, and explain that now they had turned on me, demanding more money.

"So, after my parents cut me off . . . ," I started, but then something truly unsavory came out. I puked the truth. "I needed money to keep Obnoxious afloat. I started working at a start-up founded by one of my friends at college. It's called Kenosis."

"The fuck. You mean that bald neoliberal bitch who talks like a robot?"

"That's a little harsh, but, yeah."

"No offense, but what did you have to offer them? Did you, like, DJ the parties? I just can't see you being that useful in that context."

"I was a 'creative consultant.' It was a sinecure, I'll admit. I helped her with the original idea back in college. Anyway, it turns out they are up to some terrible, terrible shit. It's too much to go into. But it's very serious. Not serious enough that you should worry about me. But in case anything happens to me, which I know it won't, I want to sign the label over to you. You run it anyway. It should be yours."

It couldn't be taken away from her as easily as it could from me. Dad and Renata would, of course, win out, but it would buy me some time. And some wiggle room with Louise, who, I knew, under her fear and concern for my well-being, would be moved by the gesture.

"There's one other thing. I need you to hang on to this until I come back." I handed her my copy of Tim's dossier, which had, by now, absorbed about a quart of nervous sweat and bore a pair of condensation rings from beers in Langenburger's greenroom. "Just keep it safe."

"Chuck, isn't there another way to do this? Like, with cops or something? I know they're all pigs, but do you need to put yourself in danger? Do you have to be the one to fix it? Not to be a dick here, this isn't my usual mentality, but why start being an activist now? Why go full Brockovich? What if we just went on a long vacation? We could go to Berlin, or Mexico City. I feel like we're finally really on the same page. Don't let this mess it all up."

It was a good point. If I hadn't been a Grossheart, I would have just let it all go and taken Louise to Berlin. But now I needed to fuck up Olivia and Dad's plan. And, sure, there was the possibility of saving thousands of people from fraudulent medical technology.

"I've been such an asshole my whole life. I need to do this."

I filled out the contract I'd printed earlier, signed it, and handed it to Louise.

She took the papers reluctantly. "I'm all for you doing the right thing, but I just want you to promise me you'll be okay."

"I have real clarity for the first time since I met you. I'm going to come out of this fine, even better than before. Don't worry."

Her phone started ringing.

"Fuck, it's Sydney. The two of you are fucking killing me."

She picked up and began a series of affirmative mumbles.

"Okay, Sydney needs me. Stay right here. I'm going to go pick her up out in Wormwood and be right back."

Louise left. I filed away the contract, grabbed a piece of recording equipment from the studio, then summoned an Uber.

Thirty minutes later I was at REI. I bought a tent, a flashlight, a thirty-degree sleeping bag, a portable phone charger, a box of Clif Bars (a fuck you to the asshole who shared their name), a canteen, and an irresistible black knife used by the French Foreign Legion. Out in the parking lot, I opened my boxes and arranged my supplies so they'd be ready for my next expedition. With everything stuffed into my duffel, I kicked the boxes out of my way, stepped back into the car (my driver had been more than happy to wait), and gave the address to my next destination. I was headed to the Caverns.

## 27

It turns out I didn't need the key Olivia had given me. At night the Caverns were half-assedly blocked by one of those metal grates used to secure bodegas and Hot Topics. Whichever park employee had shut the place down only secured one of the two locks holding the grate to the rock face. Anyone could've peeled the mesh back and slipped through.

I'd have Olivia meet me here. The caves meant a lot to her, and I was hoping her sentimentality might work to my advantage. More important, I knew Clif refused to set foot in here, and I trusted her bodyguard's assessment of the place as a security nightmare, which was why it'd worked for old Hippolyte Bouchard two centuries ago. The space in the crypt would let me see her before she saw me, so I could always jump ship if she brought any lawyers or other sidekicks. I just had to settle in before I reached out, lest she try to beat me here and ambush me again.

The red footlights were still on, there to guide me as I lugged my gear down the tunnel.

Halfway to Hippolyte's Crypt, I heard something down the hall. I froze. Listening more closely, my best guess was that it was the sizzle of a downed electrical wire. I flashed my light toward the sizzle to make sure I wouldn't off myself on a dangling line. But I didn't see anything. The sound stopped.

Was someone else in here? Some vandal teens, or assholes getting high like I had? I turned my flashlight off. Best to treat them like animals, to give them plenty of warning and keep from cornering them.

Only when I reached Hippolyte's Crypt did I discover the source of this weird sound. As I shone my light along the walls of the stone chamber, I heard the same volty crackle and felt the air change.

Something sailed toward my head. The sizzling became painfully loud. I ducked down, then turned to see what it was.

A dozen or so bats rushed out into the hall. Illuminated from below, they looked like umbrellas made of skin. In my bucolic youth I'd encountered bats plenty of times (the groundskeepers flushed them from the outbuildings every summer), yet I'd never heard any that loud before. But of course it was bats making that weird sound. I calmed down some.

Once they'd passed, I hoisted myself over the rail and set up camp in a gap in the crypt's dentition, carefully dodging the pungent mounds of guano. The smell of my freshly opened consumer goods masked that of the bat feces, and snug in this plasticky aroma, I fell asleep right away.

The next morning I texted Olivia.

I apologized, told her I was ready to end all this, and asked if she could meet me in the crypt at noon. She was leaving DC right now, she told me, but would be back in the evening. We agreed to meet at 9:00 p.m. She promised to come alone.

I took a good nap in my tent, then streamed the latest episode of *Bad Company* (the writing is clichéd, but it's very watchable). An hour later I took a shit behind a thick column of rock and felt the primitive wind against my ass cheeks.

Around seven I tested the recorder I'd picked up on the way out of the warehouse. With its pair of pincered mics on one end, the thing looked something like a Taser. We used it for field recordings and dem-oing, as well as for taping live shows. Even under my shirt the quality was more than adequate for my purposes, way better than a phone. I secured it right above my gut with some tape.

I staked out my position in an alcove housing an ugly statue of Hippolyte. It was just deep enough to conceal me, and with the extra feet of elevation it offered, I could see the entire path back to the entrance.

I still had the purloined eye patch from my reunion with Olivia and meeting with Tim. I stretched it around Hippolyte's bronze, curly mop and pulled it down so that it formed a Hitler mustache above his lip.

At last the red lights went out in the cavern, and I could hear the bats getting ready for their commute.

Nine came and went. I'd thought she might flake, as a power play, but I could wait another day. I'd let her reach out and see if I could try again tomorrow.

I retreated into my tent, which the bats had drizzled with guano. The darkness around it had an insulatory quality. I felt as safe as a red-state fetus in my nylon womb. I put away my phone, killed my lantern, and stepped out of the tent to appreciate the quality of the darkness.

I was hit with the gentle heartburn of nostalgia for those wholesome days back when my brain still manufactured its own serotonin. A time before I first logged on the old Acer and learned how bad my dad was. Where I grew up, the nights were clean. You could see every star like it was a house in some flipped city high above us. Thanks to a telescope the size of a circus cannon my uncle had gifted us, Peter and I could even gaze upon the fuzzy green star nurseries several light centuries away. We stared at it about three times before the stellar NICU lost its sheen, but I've carried the awe with me over the less innocent intervening years. In my bedroom, on those rare nights when the lights of the guardhouse were off, the dark was about as complete as that of the crypt, with hardly any difference between what I saw with my eyes open or closed. I could've vanished into it, I felt, and reemerged as some other non-me, non-Grossheart, and hopefully non-zebra creature.

So I played that old game there in the crypt. I opened my eyes, closed them, repeated, relishing the futility of my blinks with eyelids flapping like clipped wings.

But with my eyes out of commission, my ears—trained as they are by stereo mixing and years of audiophilia—clocked into their guard-duty shift.

I heard something move outside the tent. I climbed through the flap and it panned hard right. I turned around and it panned left. I tried to face it, them, what- or whoever, and suddenly their rustling came in like drum overheads. They were above me.

I turned on my phone's light and flashed it around. The weak light was all but swallowed by the cavern. I fell onto my shit-covered tent, reached inside the collapsed lung of it, and pulled out my flashlight, but its thousand lumens weren't much better, revealing only the ring of chalky horns around me.

My ears were still working, though. But what they told me made no sense. This thing was above me, behind me, to my left and right, squarely fixed in the pocket of my periphery. The sound itself was getting louder, and now, in addition to the rustling, there was something else: the electric crackle I'd heard when I first arrived.

I left the tent behind and ran. The bases of the spikes, which I'd playfully skipped over on my way in, now formed a brutal maze of booby traps. Twice I fell flat on my face, but such was my adrenal rush that I was able to get up and carry on until I finally reached the guardrail.

It was there that I first beheld, if only partially, my shadowy pursuer. As I yanked my leg over the steel beam, I saw something fall from the hanging spikes down to the cave floor. It was like someone dropped a big black T-shirt. My mind conjured up images of the sabertooths that had become our local mascots. Then I imagined, more plausibly, one of their ferocious heirs, the celebrity Clemans Park mountain lion. What else could move through the dark cave like that? I cursed my long-held disdain for CrossFit and rock-climbing gyms and booked it for the red light of the tunnel.

The rest was a sad episode of *American Ninja Warrior*. I sprinted down the hall, tumbling again when my foot nicked what I saw (too late) to be a full two-liter bottle of Mountain Dew. I hit my head on the back of a NO TRESPASSING sign I hadn't registered on my way in. Finally, I jammed my shoulder into the grate while praying my pursuer was too bulky to fit through.

Outside, the San Narciso night was gloriously aglow with light pollution. For a second I thought I saw the celebrity mountain lion skulking in front of me, until I realized it was just one of the concrete Rancho sabertooth statues.

Right then a bag was pulled over my head, and my assailant forced my flailing arms together and bound my wrists. As I twisted like a roped crocodile, I put it together: I hadn't been chased, I'd been herded and worn down. Then I felt a prick on my right arm, and though I'd never administered it this way, soon I recognized the full-body buzz as the calling card of my old friend ketamine. My apparently jacked foe (Clif?) hoisted me over his shoulder, and it was then, I thought, that the ketamine really kicked in, because I felt like I was flying.

# 28

When I came back to my body, my wrists were still tied, but someone had kindly removed the bag from my head. The lights were off, and the room I found myself in was visible only in a dim grayscale. I made out a coatrack in the corner and the bookshelves along the wall. Behind a desk was my Remedios Varo print in low contrast. I was in my office at Kenosis, doped and roped by Olivia and Clif.

They hadn't accounted for my tolerance for ketamine, and it bought me some time. With an awkward break dance, I was able to stand. The recorder was still attached to my chest. I tried playing it back to see if it could tell me anything, but all I could hear were pops, hisses, some wind, and my own panting. I resecured it and made sure the thing was on, if only to record my death.

Moving around, I could feel my crotch was wet. I'd like to think it was the ketamine, but I had a strong hunch I'd done that before I'd been bagged. I backed up toward the light switch, but nothing happened when I toggled it with my shoulder. Then I remembered something. I went over to my desk and, after much fumbling, grabbed the plug to my SAD lamp and stuck it in an outlet.

Now that my office was antidepressively illuminated, I contorted myself until, using the edge of the desk, I was able to push the REI knife out of my pocket. It took a while, and I dropped the blade more than once, but eventually I was able to free my hands of the zip tie that bound them.

Just then, I heard someone behind the door. Before I could kill the light and hide, it began to open.

I saw Olivia's face for less than a second. Then came a loud, fajita-like hiss, and she retreated immediately. I caught the door before it shut and looked down the hall for any sign of her, but there was nothing but a twitch of shadow on the opposite wall. (I was too stupid and afraid to understand what had just happened—the logic of it would occur to me later.)

I grabbed my camping knife and ran.

I went the opposite direction from Olivia and snuck down the stairwell to the floor below, where I hoped to take the elevator to the lobby. I was careful to avoid Kenosis security. Kenosis was defended by a rotation of ex-military guards (knockoffs of my father's SEALs and Green Berets), reducing our risk of infiltration—from our competitors, from hostile foreign powers, from America's ever-growing list of terrorist haters—to zero.

But as I ran the maze of hallways to the elevator, there wasn't a single guard anywhere. In fact, there was no sign of anyone. Not one engineer, programmer, or scientist from the vigilant team "working round the clock" as Olivia liked to brag. My only company was Biggie, shouting, "Gimme the loot! Gimme the loot!" as I passed one of Olivia's muralized Precepts reading, *Who needs sleep?* A question answered by the marooned offices and empty Google-rip-off collaboration zones. I ran (by another Precept, the taunting, unhelpful *Speed matters*) to the elevator, and thankfully, it still worked. They'd taken my phone, but I still had my wallet, with my key card tucked behind my Visa. I hit the starred button for the lobby.

My attempt to leave through the front door was an idiotic move I now attribute to the volume of ketamine and adrenaline looping through my mortal coil. As the elevator doors parted, I spotted Clif far across the lobby, standing by the entrance.

I made a quick, less stupid calculation before he saw me. I'd go to the sylvarium and hide there till morning, when I'd beseech whatever reasonable employee I could find and use their phone to call the cops. But in my panic I mashed the buttons for several upper floors in one desperate swipe.

Now Clif was running toward me, but despite all his tactical training, the galoot was too slow. But just before the doors came back together, I saw a blur come between us and move toward me. There was a sound on the other side once the doors shut, like someone kicking a bag of cicadas. Then a babble of tinny scratches on the steel that quickly went quiet.

The climb, which probably took ten seconds at most, seemed to last about as long as a Tarkovsky movie. (The secret organ that measures time had begun to dilate, just before its final prolapse.) At last, though, the doors opened, and I prepared to sprint.

But it wasn't the sylvarium. It was the same scabby sample storage floor I'd wandered onto weeks ago. The smell was unbearable. There was even more spilled blood than before. Up ahead, down the aisles of bags, I could see a faint red light.

The rows of racks offered plenty of places to hide. I grabbed a dolly and used it to prop open the door, so my stalker wouldn't be able to use the elevator. Then I ran toward the source of the light.

It took a while, but eventually I came upon an open space in the middle of the chamber. A henge of black server towers surrounded a spiral of channels embedded in the floor, a shallow maze like a medieval labyrinth. Tangled tendrils hung from the ceiling—roots from the trees reaching down from the sylvarium. A faint light came from deep inside the servers, casting everything in red.

A rack behind one of the servers would be the best hiding place. If the thing appeared, I could lose it down one of the many aisles that fed into this hub. I shoved some blood bags aside and lay on one of the bottom shelves, hopefully outside of the thing's line of sight.

It wasn't comfortable. After a few minutes without any sign of my stalker, I rearranged some of the plump blood bags to support my neck. Just as I finished moving them around, I heard something in the hub and froze.

An old man stepped out from between the servers. He was completely naked, though for a moment I mistook the loose skin hanging from his arms and legs for an oversize T-shirt. With his back hunched over and his arms curled tight against his chest, he looked like a cocktail shrimp. I recognized him. I'd seen him outside the Narceum in his wacky outfit the day before. Judging by his pace as he made his way toward the center of the circle, I knew he couldn't have been the one who was chasing me.

Once he reached the middle of the ring, the servers started humming, and I could hear running water deep inside the one next to me, like the first cycle in a washing machine. Seconds later, the hum dropped an octave, the machines made a loud snapping sound, and the channels began to fill up. The liquid looked like ink, but it didn't take long for me to put it together. It was blood.

As the maze filled, the old man was lowered on some unseen platform. His withered body slowly disappeared, a cocktail shrimp dipped in sauce, until all I could see was his gnarled, bald head. I thought I heard him sigh, and then, after splashing some of the blood onto his face, he went under.

While he was submerged, I saw that the channels in the floor were made in the shape of the barbed infinity sign I'd spotted under the desk and on the blade of Eugen's knife, the emblem of the Gift.

The machines fell silent. I could hear the blood draining from the channels. The old man's head poked out of the slick labyrinth as the platform began to raise him up again.

Through the fresh coat of blood I could see his body had changed. His skin was taut. The flying squirrel folds that had sagged off his arms and belly had been inflated. He now stood straight and looked to be about half a foot taller. He licked his lips, squeegeed the blood out of his eyes with his fingers, and licked those, too. Aside from the baldness, he looked like a teenager. Then I realized I knew him. It was Eugen, my old college buddy.

Something was wrong with his eyes. They were full of blood and looked like a pair of misplaced clown noses. As he let out a satisfied burp, his irises slowly emerged from these red bulbs, each glowing orange.

I was terrified these orbs would find me lying helplessly on the shelf. I shifted back so I'd be less exposed, but my movement knocked over one of the bags I'd used to support my neck. It hit the floor, bouncing into the middle of the aisle.

I peeked over. It didn't look like Eugen had noticed. But something else had. When I turned back, there was the monkey, the same vile creature I'd met weeks ago, with his clumpy skin beard, his twisted antlers, and those mustard-colored eyes. He smiled at me before turning his head toward Eugen and letting out a loud, sinister chirp.

Eugen opened his mouth wide, revealing a row of teeth as long and yellow as cigarette butts. He let out a faint hiss, and my ears popped. Immediately the dark, blurry form of my stalker appeared behind the servers.

The monkey vanished. I rolled out onto the next aisle and sprinted toward the elevator.

I was about halfway there when I saw two hulking men block my path. It was the oafish pair I'd stumbled across playing video games in the lounge. They moved slowly but erratically, like drunks or toddlers.

I took a detour and ran until I came upon another hub with a long silver structure in the middle of it, something like a horse trailer. The door was unlocked, and I hid inside. It turned out to be a walk-in freezer.

There was a light switch by the door, but I felt safer in the dark. All I had was the drop of light from the thermostat. I drew to the back of the cold room until I bumped into something. I caught a glimpse of a face in the thermostat light. Someone was in there with me. I lurched for the light switch.

Strapped to the wall in the back of the freezer was Tim. His body, at least. His soul was long gone. His glasses just barely hung on to the tip of his nose.

I managed to keep from screaming and ran out of the freezer. I made it most of the way back to the elevators.

"Charles."

Down the dark aisle of blood bags stood Olivia. Her eyes glowed in the light of the elevator behind me. They had the same orange luster as Eugen's, though less bright.

She came toward me, faster than she should have. Something about how she moved, a swift calligraphy as she flew down the aisle, made clear what I should have already put together when I came to in my office: she'd been the one chasing me this whole time.

I ran back into the elevator and kicked the dolly out of the way. The button for the next floor was still lit. I prayed I'd get there faster than Olivia.

## 29

I ran off the elevator and right into a cloud. The sylvarium was thick with mist. I could just barely make out the monumental trees. I remembered they were packed tightest in the center, around the glade where Olivia delivered the opening lines of her Kenosis sermon, so I went that way.

Olivia had killed Tim. Probably Thane, too. I knew too much, and now she was going to kill me.

This was what was going through my head when I rammed it into a tree. Blood started dripping down my teeth.

"Charles!" Olivia shouted through the fog. "Wait! Let's talk! Please!"

My nose throbbed like a guinea pig's heart. I strode deeper into the heart of the forest as I licked the blood off my teeth. I'd made it halfway to the glade when I saw something move in the mist. It looked like a walking tree.

I scrambled for my knife, but I'd dropped it when I hit my head. The walking tree came closer.

Olivia's buck, Fyodor, stepped out of the fog, twitching his elm-leaf ears as he walked toward me. I got close enough to see the sheaves of velvet dangling from his headgear. His eyes, like Eugen's, were full of blood, twin maraschino cherries. A long fang, the size of a golf pencil, hung past his lip. We'd both caught each other by surprise, and for a couple beats each waited to see what the other would do, until at last he turned to sprint into the pines.

Only then did I see he carried a passenger. Squatting on his back and gripping his thick neck hairs was the monkey. A tiny, evil jockey. He gave me another grin as the stag dashed off.

The trees grew closer together here. I looked for one I might climb, or a hollow that might conceal me from my attacker. I caught a dark blur to my left. The deer and the monkey hadn't run off. They were circling me. And to my right, the lumpy outlines of the ogres from the lounge ambled through the mist. I had no hope for escape. Olivia had herded me again, this time to the heart of her stronghold, and now I was helpless.

"Charles, please just listen to me."

Her voice came from everywhere, in Dolby Digital Surround. The recorder was still on. Maybe I could still get something incriminating.

"Charles, everything has been taken care of. You're safe. You're protected. This will all make perfect sense very soon. Just hear me out."

I saw her. She wore her usual uniform, but something was different about her face. Her eyes were much larger, like the monkey's. Her ears moved on their own, just like the deer's. And between her calm entreaties, I heard something else—the same electrical crackles from the cavern. She had located me.

"Charles." Olivia looked right at me. Her voice had lost its omnipresence and now came out of her mouth alone. "You need to trust me one last time. You're my oldest, dearest friend. Why would I hurt you?"

I sputtered some terrified grunts about Tim and Thane as I scanned the ground for a branch to beat her away with. In the pine needles, I saw something glimmer.

A selfie stick, left behind by an investor no doubt wanting to show off the sylvarium to his Instagram followers. My Excalibur. I drew it from the needles and brandished my truncheon, whipping it back and forth in Olivia's direction.

"Charles, please stop. You're leaving me no choice here."

My piques and slashes became more desperate.

"Charles, I'm sorry I have to do this. It'll only hurt for a second, and then it will all be over."

A branch cracked above me. When I looked up, Olivia eclipsed the moon. She descended toward me slower than physics should have allowed. I understood that she would be the last thing I'd ever see, not the fit mistress thirty years my junior on the shimmering stretch of Ibizan beach I'd always imagined.

She fell on me like a blanket thrown on an evil cat, and I was knocked to the ground. Pine needles stuck to my face and went up the back of my shirt. Olivia grabbed my arms and held me down. She hissed, then reached under my shirt and tore away the recorder.

"Shh," she whispered, as if I were a horse she was breaking. "This will all be over soon."

For a second, despite this long hunt, despite Tim's body moldering a floor below me, I trusted her again. I ceased my flailing and looked into my friend's freakishly huge eyes. I relaxed.

And then she opened her mouth. Her teeth had grown even more than her eyes. They looked like long white fingers, I thought, just before they entered my neck and everything went painfully dark.

## 30

The Gift manifests itself differently in each of its users based on her biology, will, and willingness. It follows that the period of change is variable, dependent on these same factors. For some it takes weeks, for others, only an hour, and for some, those most naturally receptive to the Gift, mere minutes.

Eugen told me that, with my illness, it would probably take a couple days, maybe even a week, for my body to acclimate to the Gift, but it didn't take nearly that long. I woke up that same night, only a few hours later. I felt amazing, better than I'd felt before I got sick, better than I'd ever imagined feeling. You'll feel this soon, too. I wanted to use my body and its new strength, its new life, right away, so I got up and went outside, to the woods that took up most of the estate.

Looking around, no detail escaped me. I'd been completely upgraded. The world went from VHS to 8K resolution. An owl shivered in the branches above me. Mice and voles darted through the underbrush. The leaves softly clapped, applauding my new vigor. Up ahead, I sensed a larger creature and soon came upon a stag, the same giant I'd encountered a few days before. I admired him for a while. I knew how he felt, to be so strong and alive.

But then I started coughing. I worried that perhaps I'd been too ambitious and overexerted myself. It was painful and got to the point that I thought everything had failed, that I was back to my old, sick self. For some reason, even as I was hacking away, the deer stayed put. I'd figure out why soon.

The coughing became excruciating, and right when I thought I might pass out, something came out of my mouth. It was yellow, about the size and shape of a baby's hand. It hit the ground, twitched in the dirt, and began to crawl. Quickly, toward the deer. The peculiar creature scuttled over the humus, then right up the animal's leg. This snapped the stag out of it, and now he reared and kicked at the air. But it was too late. The yellow thing crawled into his nose, and after a few final, weak kicks, the deer stood still, fell to the ground, and began to convulse.

"I've never seen that happen before," Eugen said. How he'd managed to sneak up on me, with my new awareness of just about everything, baffled me. "It left your body. That's wonderful."

I asked him what it was.

"It was the last bit of your sickness. It's been transformed, too. It's going to live a long, long time, but not in you."

The deer got up and looked around, as if waking up the morning after a bender. Its eyes had gone entirely red.

"I can feel it," I told Eugen. "I think I can feel the deer."

"There's always a special bond between those that share the Gift, though I've never seen it transferred quite like this. You know, it's perfect. We've always had a connection to these animals. There's a stag on our crest. That's why I had this made."

He pulled his hunting knife out of his pocket and handed it to me. "I think you should have this now. I know how much you like it. Think of it as a graduation present."

I wanted the stag to step closer, then he did. I wanted him to lean his shaggy head forward, and he did that, too. But the most peculiar thing happened when I touched him. It was like putting your palms together, the dual awareness of each hand feeling and being felt. Except in this case, in addition to the coarse fur between the deer's eyes, I could feel the tickle of the fingers stroking that fur. Some channel of will and sensation had formed between us. Being of a scientific disposition, I decided to test my hypothesis about this link and concentrated on two commands: I wanted the deer to rear on his hind legs again, then run toward the castle. He did exactly that. We did. Soon Eugen would teach me to wield the Gift's persuasive power. But this was something much stronger, more immediate. The two of us were on our hind legs, then cruising through the trees. The intensity of this sensation diminished once the deer's body was a good distance from my own, but I could still feel a light tug indicating his location in relation to mine.

This was truly when everything began to come together for me. Not everyone can have the Gift. It just can't work, statistically. Even with the traditional reproductive restrictions the Gift brings about, those of us who possess it require far too much energy for it to be a viable cure for human mortality across the board. It's a resource-intensive mode of being and should be reserved for those wholly committed to furthering humanity. But I soon realized there might be a way to harness this new thing that had been born of my illness. The yellow thing that linked us would become inspiration to shape the tech I'd already partially dreamed up. This was a huge leap from that, however. I had a vision for truly symbiotic technology. The cells that had left me and entered the deer possessed unthinkable longevity and resilience. If properly studied, replicated, and contained, much like with a vaccine, they could extend the lives of millions, perhaps billions of people. And as they came from me, I could centralize the administration of their power, eliminating so much human weakness and inefficiency. It meant that cancer wasn't just this terrible thing that happened to me. It was meant to be, part of my destiny. For me, the Gift is not an end unto itself. It's just a tool, a weapon, one I could use to fight for this new tech and bring it to the world, to help reduce the heavy burden of human suffering and steer the species toward justice, peace, and equality.

It's been quite a task, even with the considerable power the Gift has bestowed on me. I've had to run not one, but two operations.

Something big and palatable to help me raise my funds and profile, to suss out loyal talent, and then one that, due to its revolutionary character, naturally had to remain secret. Fate has helped me some, in the timing, as we were having to resort to fairly sketchy methods even for our facade, but now we've had sufficient breakthroughs and new advocates who can move the cause forward without much need to put on such a big show, save for some marketing to the public.

After our second round of funding, I had Eugen bring the buck here. I needed to study him, but also I wanted to keep him as a reminder of death, the death I could have had, whenever my new life felt bland and endless. It's thanks to him, and what we've been able to learn about transmissible cancer cells among dasyurids, that we'll finally be able to bring a degree of stability to the world, to extend life for all. It took a while to find a way to isolate the cells so they wouldn't integrate with users, but that challenge is safely behind us.

Charles, I know I haven't been perfect. Mistakes were made. There were times when I should have been there for you and I wasn't. I had a rare lapse of judgment in handling Tim and let him spread his toxic shit around, and I know that confused you. But you should know that there's no one more loyal to you than me. I've been watching over you this whole time, trying to bring you to this point. I've had Eugen follow you, looking out for you, making sure you don't ruin things for yourself. I tested you at your parents', and you were loyal. And I respect your tenacity pushing back. I would have done the same thing, had I your limited view of things. Eugen, your father, neither of them think you're ready, that you have the strength to go through with this, but I do. And, frankly, and I say this dispassionately, I've become considerably more powerful than either of them, if you can believe that. My opinion matters much more than theirs.

And so now you must make a choice, as I did. I'm sorry I forced it on you like this, but you left me with no other option. You are right on the line, right on the border between life and death. If you give up now, you can just fall asleep and that's it. Or you can push through, embrace the Gift, and be cured of mortality forever.

Olivia's words washed over me in my near-vegetative state. Her story was so real I could see it, an in-flight movie as my soul floated aimlessly through the dark.

I now had to make my choice. I considered my gloomy options. As I lay there, I realized there was still something I could do to stop Olivia. If I were to give up, my death would surely stress Olivia's relationship with my spiteful dad. And even if their bond held strong (possible, as Dad and I aren't especially tight), the disappearance of a Grossheart would certainly draw unwanted attention. My journalist, too, would register the strange coincidence and would certainly make the connection to Kenosis. It might be enough to draw light onto Olivia's scheme.

I never wanted to live forever. If anything—not to go full emo on you—I wanted to die sooner, to get a fresh start, another spin of the creaky wheel that would free me from the unfortunate circumstances of my birth. I wished I could have said goodbye to Louise but took solace in the idea that maybe my early death, like Thane's, might beatify me. I'd be redeemed for all the sins of my selfish, petty life.

I prepared to surrender. I could feel my brain shutting down like a closing restaurant. Lights out in the dish pit. Lights out behind the bar. Lights out in the kitchen. One more light and this weary waiter, this battered bartender, could walk out into the night.

But then something else worked inside me. With Death suddenly in sight, my mind went to the circumstances of my birth. Who, in all of human history, had ever been as lucky as I? Louis XVI, maybe, thanks to his magnificent grandpa. Octavian? I stood to inherit the GDP of a mediocre African country. I'd won the lottery. The odds of being born to a family like mine were less than the chances of being born with wings or horns or a tail. All that just to die like this, cut down in the subprime of my life, in some flashy terrarium? Not today, Thanatos, you goth-angel asshole. Fuck that.

Back in the diner of my mind I saw movement. I sensed a presence, that of some primordial creature lurking among the stools and tables of memory and ego.

I chased it through my mental restaurant, catching glimpses. A gray flash. A hoof vanishing around a corner. Strands of black hair, a paintbrush tail moving out of frame.

I finally caught up to it and beheld the beast, this slippery Jungian varmint.

A fucking zebra.

With my dream logic, I could see the thing for what it truly was. My soul, my spirit, my essence. Suddenly, at this moment of recognition, we weren't separate. It occurs to me now that maybe this was a loose remake of the story I'd just heard, Olivia's creepy deer-bonding cast with a new, more familiar ungulate from my psychic hellscape. Whether suggestion or spirit was the cause, I now looked out from zebra eyes. I was held up by those stout and deadly legs. I inhaled the cool air of my mind through my nasty nostrils and released a puff of foul zebroid breath.

My diner was gone. I ran across my dream plains, kicking a pride of lions that pursued me. I felt the same fight, the same pure, bestial will that had entered me shortly before Olivia delivered her chomp of destiny in the sylvarium.

I crossed a vast desert, bucking at the lions of death. I came to the edge of a continent, gazed upon a vast green sea, and kept on running into the water.

I swam with the lions still in pursuit. Sharks joined the chase, along with some terrifying, tentacled sea monsters, but I was too belligerent to be swallowed by them, either. Soon I came to the opposite shore, waded through sticky marshland, galloped through ancient forests, mountains, fruited plains, mountains, more desert, and then, shining like a city on a hill, I could see it. Kenosis headquarters. I kicked down the doors, nudged an elevator button with my nose, and rode my way back up into my human body.

Olivia was talking again, or still. I couldn't wake just yet, but something had certainly shifted.

"I know you've read Tim's files, and the idea of giving people cancer, if you can even put what we're doing in those crude, willfully ignorant terms, might seem unsavory. But that's so myopic, the kind of thinking that consistently holds civilization back. Sharing these cells with humanity still accomplishes our goals of centralized medical care. The nanobots were just a way to make this idea palatable. But these cells can do so much more. Our species has become so polarized and fragmented. This can unite us, on a biological level. Humanity must upgrade to a higher consciousness. Eusociality. We'll be able to function with the complex responses of an ant or bee colony, with the Gifted scattered among the population as more specialized beings, shepherding the rest along, helping steer with the wisdom that comes with our extended lifetimes. Surely you see how this differs from the nasty picture you've probably put together from Tim's illegal leak."

This might all sound great, couched in a blend of Obaman hope and Jobsian vision, but you, reader, know what it means by now. I certainly do. While the Gifted cancer cells in the nanotomes don't give her the complete control she has over the deer, you might have noticed a little more docility among your friends or family walking around with a Kenosis device stashed in their torsos. Were they to meet Olivia, you'd see them take on a hard, full-body blush, then fall dull and sluggish until she gave them some task, like the goons who pursued me on the blood floor and sylvarium. I've seen implantees in demonstrations do unspeakable things at Olivia's beckoning, just to prove her power. The nanotomes might add twenty or thirty years to your life, but they also make it a lot easier for any Gifted to track you down and suck you empty like you're a Capri Sun.

As she droned on and on about how Kenosis would change the planet, I could feel myself changing, too. She mapped her plan for the company to grow and spread, and it was as if it was growing and spreading inside me. With every word, I regained a little strength. Not *regained*—no, this was a new strength, as if every cell in my body was being replaced one by one with that of a doped-up gymnast. Later, I'd discover that two weeks had gone by, but it felt like a single night thanks to the Gift's hard reset of my internal clock.

She told me my father had taken to the Gift naturally: it had only taken the time in the cellar for him to recover, and Peter was nearly as quick (Mom didn't fare so well; Olivia wouldn't tell me about her passing until after I'd fully healed). Suddenly I could see the faint outline of the bed, the shelf holding Olivia's awards, her head leaning over my frail frame. She told me that just the day before investigators had broken down the door to Tim's apartment, where they discovered hundreds of computer-printed photographs of Thane, a box of defaced copies of *Sucker*, and traces of Thane's hair and blood in the carpet fibers. As this news filtered into my consciousness, I found I could move my fingers and toes and felt the tube running down my throat, filling me with pure, liquid energy.

She told me about the breakthrough, the same one Langenburger had mentioned. How, in the middle of another sleepless night, her homely twenty-one-year-old prodigy—the one she'd shown off that first tour—had discovered some kind of protein or enzyme to coat the evil Gutenbergs and ran his findings by his colleagues shortly before passing out from exhaustion. My arms and legs were galvanized. I had enough control to lean over the couch and puke out the last of my old, un-Gifted self into a bucket Olivia had set out for me. Thanks to the latest leap forward in R and D, the island testing had been a tremendous success, and it looked like with some light finessing they'd be able to move forward on the regulatory front. I sat up in bed and opened my eyes.

The room was painfully bright. I had to squint to see Olivia, who stood there sparkling like some beautiful saint welcoming me to that gated community in the sky. Only then did I see that all the lights were off. Just a sliver of moon shone through the window.

"You're ready." There, hidden under her voice, was a fuzzy layer of clicks and pops, an electricity I could feel all over my body. It had been there since she'd returned from Eugen's ancestral home, I realized, but now I could apprehend it fully, as if I'd finally pulled the plugs out of my ears.

Olivia walked over to the window and opened it.

"Follow me."

I would. Not long thereafter, I'd follow her to key meetings in DC to secure a beefy military contract. I'd tag along behind her for negotiations on a partnership with the largest chain of pharmacies in the United States, bringing Kenosis to every town from Portland, Oregon, to Portland, Maine. I'd follow her to China, and to Russia, where we'd land more hefty deals, and where we shared the Gift with a batch of select princelings and petroligarchs. We'd take the monkey with us. I'd warm up to him. He's been my sole companion as I write this in the comfy darkness.

And what's the end of a comedy without a wedding? For this one, it's the nocturnal nuptials of Peter and Neve. I was best man; Olivia, maid of honor. This partnership, in addition to producing a pair of curly-haired heiresses (if you're wondering, Neve would hold off on the Gift for nine months and Peter froze his seed), would also bring forth a host of new inventions employed by governments everywhere and—now I'm blabbing because this is top secret—the prototype for the first living house.

I'm rushing things, but I find the time after Olivia's throat nibble, eventful as it is, utterly bland to recount. I used to want to shove my past into the wood chipper and watch the spray of bone chips and pink goo shoot out the other side. But now there's not enough of it, and way too much future. The Gift has made me see the arc of my life as cinematic history in reverse, from Technicolor to black and white, talkies to silent film, now just a mundane reel of rolling wheels and sluggish dancers. I have to live by narration. I feed off my past. Not literally—I'll let you infer my new diet.

Late one night, not long after my transformation, I'd return to the warehouse. I quickly made my way through the store. Our inventory, my world-class collection tucked in the back office, it meant nothing. I thought the Gift would make music better, like weed, but I have no appetite for it. Music, after all, is just flavored time, and nowadays the seasoning of rhythm and melody is like salt on cardboard.

The ugly, snarling faces staring back from the album covers and old posters were too depressing. I went up to the second floor.

Right away I picked out Louise from the rest of the sleeping bodies. She'd been texting and calling me all through the comatose weeks of my transformation. Now that she knew who my parents were, she'd tried getting ahold of them, too, but all anyone would tell her was that I was alive and fine and would be in touch soon—boyfriend customer support, essentially.

Sydney lay right beside her. It seemed inevitable they'd get together, with their shitty partners and trauma-bond. My stomach growled some seeing the sad, successful drummer. Music might have lost its appeal, but musicians (even more than other artists) have a particularly delightful tang.

The Gift let me walk up to Louise in perfect silence and see her

face clearly in the dark. She'd fallen asleep with her giant glasses still
on, clutching her phone. I reached out and touched her hair. Creepy,
I know, but I was feeling sentimental.

It woke her up.

"Chuck? Chuck, is that you?"

By the time she probed the dark with her phone, I was across the
room. I collected the jewels of my wardrobe, grabbed the spare copy
of Tim's dossier from the office, and said goodbye to Obnoxious forever.

From there, I'd keep following Olivia, to conferences and summits,
to the technologist bunkers proliferating up and down the coast, to the
future sites of Kenosis East and our facilities in India and China. She
would be president, or something better than that, I knew.

But none of that had quite happened yet.

I got up from Olivia's couch, amazed at the springiness of my legs.
Olivia stood on the ledge and stretched her arms, which appeared to
turn into a pair of caftans. Then she was gone.

I took her place at the window. I could sense her, sailing out into the
night a couple hundred yards ahead of me.

Still, she hadn't left me alone completely. As soon as she leaped, dozens of tiny creatures took off after her. The sound they made together
was like that of a family of crickets trapped in a window unit. I leaned
over and made out a few dark forms stuck to the side of the building.
I muttered something like "whoa," and they snapped into view, as if
my mouth had spat light upon them. Little bats, each no bigger than a
hand. The sound of my voice had roused the stragglers. They started
chatting back at me in what sounded like a squirrelly Morse code, and
then two or three were hovering by the window. With my new athleti-
cism, I was able to snatch one out of the air.

The tiny creature was mechanical, made of some kind of rubbery
leather. I turned it over and saw that scratched into its belly were the

words GROSSHEART UNITY. We were related. I released it and watched it rejoin the flock.

It was time to go. I should have been scared to leap out after Olivia, but I wasn't. I knew beyond a shadow of a doubt that I couldn't die, the same way I knew I'd never forget to blink or have to work at a McDonald's. I was perfectly calm—my breathing was steady, my heart didn't pick up speed. I put my hand to my chest and realized it wasn't beating at all. My chest was hollow. I had no heart. I didn't need it.

# Acknowledgments

My agent, Chris Clemans, and editor, Anna Kaufman, are so absolutely kind, smart, and talented that sometimes I wonder if they are real. I can't believe I get to work with the two of you, and I'm so grateful you dropped into my life. Jasmine Lake and Roma Panganiban have been absolute dreams to work with, too. To the wonderful team at Anchor—Edward Allen, Steve Boldt, Steven Walker, Perry De La Vega, Julie Ertl, and Annie Locke—I'm truly amazed by how you've pulled off the alchemy of turning a Word document into a tangible book.

I need to thank Andrew Martin, Nat Aiken, Courtney Sender, Alex Higley, Justin Taylor, Jared Bartman, and Alice Bolin, who read the manuscript as it grew from a larval novella into a creepy monster. Without you, *Sucker* would absolutely suck.

Emma Törzs gave me the push I needed to start this one. Another thanks to Jared Bartman, who has been my dear friend and art hotline through it all. Brent Nobles has for years now been my deep-sea diver into the realms of the weird and numinous, and I owe dozens of this book's more interesting details to his research on my behalf.

A special thanks to Morgan Elbot and Dimitri Protopsaltis, two real geniuses, for letting me interview them for this project. Also, thank you to Ryan Manes, Zach Mitchell, and Charlie Davis, the great drummers of my life, for all the support, and for keeping time for me (also to Chris Rubano, not a drummer but great at bass). And to Liz Lane, too! And to Dan Wieken, who helped me sketch out the many branches of punk's phylogenetic tree that night at the CC Club—thanks, man!

Peter Ho Davies has been such a kind and generous mentor since my MFA days. And Chris McCormick and Mairead Small Staid, thank you for a decade of arty friendship.

Thanks to Chuck and Laurel of the Lamplighter, the baristas of Otherlands in Memphis, and the owners and employees of Milkweed coffee shop in Minneapolis for letting me pretty much write and edit all of this book there.

Shout-out to Small Twitter (you know who you are) for all the help along the way. And much love to Caki Wilkinson, Karyna McGlynn, Marcus Wicker, Emily Skaja, Mark Mayer, and Ashley Colley, aka the Memfriends. And to Brett DeFries and Emily Jones, aka the Boneyard Dogz.

Love and eternal gratitude to my family—especially Mom, Dad, Brigid, Michael, Aunt Kate, Uncle Dan, Uncle Pat, Mary, Bob, Charlie, Tom, Gino, and Grandma Rose. They'd have to add dozens of pages to this book for me to thank you all properly. Mom and Dad, I love you so much, and lucky for me you are nothing like the parents in this book.

And finally, to Alice. (It was her idea to scatter the infinity symbol throughout the text.) You're my secret weapon and my whole universe.

# About the Author

Daniel Hornsby is the author of a novel, *Via Negativa*, and his stories and essays have appeared in the *Los Angeles Review of Books, Bookforum, Electric Literature, The Missouri Review,* and *Joyland*. He lives in Minneapolis, Minnesota.